DEAD RINGER

V.P. MORRIS

Black Rose Writing | Texas

ISBN: 978-1-68433-915-0
PUBLISHED BY BLACK ROSE WRITING
www.blackrosewriting.com

Printed in the United States of America
Suggested Retail Price (SRP) $20.95

Dead Ringer is printed in Book Antiqua

*As a planet-friendly publisher, Black Rose Writing does its best to eliminate unnecessary waste to reduce paper usage and energy costs, while never compromising the reading experience. As a result, the final word count vs. page count may not meet common expectations.

DEAD RINGER

PART 1

CHAPTER 1
TAYLOR CALLAHAN

November 1, 2015
29 Days After The Switch
"Today's my birthday," I whispered to myself in the dark bedroom. "I'm twenty-one," I said but no one heard me. It felt good to say the truth out loud.

I wouldn't be celebrating my birthday at a bar. I wouldn't be celebrating at all. Because to everyone around me, I was only sixteen years old.

For the last month, I slept in a twin bed in a suburban house, I went to class at the local high school, and hung out with teenagers who thought I was their friend. I'd write "Jamie MacKenzie" at the top of every homework assignment I turned in. But I wasn't Jamie MacKenzie and no one else knew it.

It was the middle of the night. Jamie's sister, Faith, was asleep in the bed next to mine. She didn't hear me speaking to myself in the dark as I sat awake. My foot was in a boot under the covers. My hands were pink and still sore from the burns. I had to injure myself to keep them from discovering my real identity. But it was worth it.

Anything was worth escaping my old life.

Even though I didn't miss my old life, I still was curious as to what happened to *my body*. I pulled out Jamie's phone and searched for my name on the internet. Several articles came up regarding *my death* but that wasn't what I was interested in. After more scrolling, I found it. My grave:

Taylor Callahan.
November 1,1994 - October 3, 2015.
Buried at the government-owned Green Oak Cemetery.

My heart hurt for a moment. My family didn't even claim my body. I guess it was a good thing I became someone else. Someone with a loving family, countless friends, a decent future—and most importantly—a clean record.

"November first, the Day of the Dead," I almost laughed to myself. It was too perfect. There was a grave with my name on it but I was here and very much alive. I was here and Jamie MacKenzie was the one who was six feet under.

CHAPTER 2
TAYLOR CALLAHAN

October 2, 2015
One Day Before The Switch
It all started when I was sitting there at that lame high school football game. The cold bumpy bleacher seats were pressing into my ass cheeks as I sat hunched over in my hoodie hiding my face. I was still young-looking enough to fit in there, but I didn't want my face to be seen by anyone.

An explosion of cheers erupted, and I peered behind me at a group of face-painted morons shouting as their team scored a touchdown. A few other teen boys around them didn't even notice their team's win as they stared at the cheerleaders who danced around in tiny outfits in the name of school spirit.

To my left, three pale-faced losers were paying more attention to their conversation on World of Warcraft than anything happening on the field. I laughed to myself as I thought of their middle-aged moms threatening to take away their computer if they didn't go out and socialize.

I felt a weight brush against my left side and slide down into the seat next to me. A boy with long blonde bangs that he shook to the side sat down next to me.

"Are you T?" he asked.

I didn't look up. I didn't want him to get a good look at me. It's safer that way.

"I sure am. You Derek?" I replied.

He nodded and slid two crisp hundred-dollar bills from his pocket and leaned over to shake my hand. I shoved a baggie of white pills into his palm and the deal was done.

3

"Thanks," he said and booked it.

I waited for a minute. It would look too obvious if we both darted away at the same time. So, I watched the brain-dead cheerleaders shake their pom poms in various formations, the band geeks pound out their fight song on cumbersome instruments, and teachers laughing with a few of their students, probably the teachers' pets. And for one moment, I was overwhelmed with a weird feeling: It wasn't disgust or annoyance but jealousy. I wished I could go back to high school.

I could see it all so clearly, walking the halls of this pristine high school, fiddling with a combination lock every morning as teachers waved at me on their way to class. I would be their favorite, a good student who made Honor Roll and volunteered to help with some pathetic bake sale for Save The Children or Save The Whales or some shit. I would actually be someone with a real life ahead of me.

I had to shake my head to clear my mind as I walked towards Ivan's old Pontiac with rust patches speckling a decade old paint job. I'm still pissed he let me talk him into using our profits to buy this rust bucket. We should have saved up for something cooler like a BMW.

During the drive home, all I could think about was how I messed up. No, I fucked up. Big time. I was a lowlife drug dealer with no education and a criminal record. There was no future for me: No single-family houses with little gardens outside. No job with a legal paycheck. No family who would ask me how my day was when I came home.

It felt like the rattling plastic doors of the Pontiac were inching closer to me as if my world was caving in around me. I saw my future bright and clear: I'd rot away inside another jail cell, or I'd become the haggard spinster at the end of the lane who dealt little baggies of her prescription drugs to kids.

Ivan stopped the car at a red light. My heart pounded with a painful sensation of dread I don't think I've ever felt before. *Will that be my future? Do I still have time to change?*

If I could just go back in time, back to high school when my life turned to shit and actually do things right. I wanted to be the good girl, the one who goes out for smoothies with her friends after class.

The one who dates the president of the debate team or the captain of the soccer team instead of a twenty-five-year-old manipulative coke dealer. I could have that life and do it right if I could just have one more chance.

•   •   •

We walked down the urine-yellow hallway to our shitty little apartment. I threw myself down on the black futon and decided to bury my regrets in a Tom Hughes marathon.

I was about finished with the *Breakfast Club*, throwing my fist up in the air yelling "Oh. Oh. Oh. Oh. Don't you forget about me," when Ivan came running in the room.

"Holy shit, Taylor, Holy Shit. Holy Shit." He grabbed at his short red hair and ran his hands down his face.

"What is it?" I sat up straight.

"I just got a text from Emilio who found out from Cameron's best friend's cousin on Facebook that Zeke just got out of prison." Ivan's eyes were all buggy with panic.

With a jolt of anxiety, I jumped to my feet. "What the fuck? He's supposed to be in there for another two years." Dread gripped my stomach and I felt nauseous with fear.

"Well, you of all people should know that it's possible to get out early."

I didn't have time to acknowledge his snarky comment. "Shit. What do you think he'll do?"

"Probably forgive and forget. You know violent felons are so kind to those who steal their shit and rat on them," Ivan snapped.

"Fuck," I huffed as I began to pace, walking my nervous energy off as best I could.

"You've got to leave town now," said Ivan.

I put a hand up. "Just let me think."

My phone vibrated on the futon. It was a text from Derek: "Hey. My friends R looking 2 buy. Major Party. Need 420, Blow & E."

I showed the text to Ivan. "I have to take this."

"No, you don't. Get out and run." He snatched the phone from my grip. "He's coming for you and I can't let him—" Ivan blinked back tears.

I put my hand on his shoulder. "I know you're worried about me but if I have to run I need the money and right now most of my cash is tied up in pharmaceuticals."

He grimaced and released my phone.

I replied to Derek: "How much? When & where?"

Derek put in a large order for weed, coke, and ecstasy and told me to meet his friends at the pier tomorrow night.

"You shouldn't go through with it," Ivan protested once again. He ran his hands over his short buzz-cut hair and stuffed them into his oversized trench coat.

"It's one deal for 900 dollars. Then I'll have enough to run. I'll help these rich kids throw a party and they'll help me escape. Plus, I don't think Zeke will find me in a day. He'll do what I did after I got out."

"What? Start begging on the streets with a fake pregnancy belly to bolster sympathy?" he asked with a smirk on his face.

"No, I used some of the forty dollars in my wallet to eat something that wasn't made in a vat. Then, I did whatever I could to get as far away from that place as possible. Trust me, he'll have other things on his mind his first day out," I said, trying to convince myself more than I was trying to convince him.

Ivan sighed, "Taylor, I don't know about this."

CHAPTER 3
TAYLOR CALLAHAN

October 3, 2015
Four Hours Before The Switch
I arrived at the pier. Fog rolled in off the waves and lightly coated the abandoned boardwalk. My boots made a thumping noise as they hit against the wooden planks. I knew I shouldn't be pacing; movement only draws attention. I knew I should never turn my back to an area where someone could come up behind me, but I was nervous and if I didn't pace I'd explode. My thoughts were racing. *Where are these kids?* I occasionally glanced back at Ivan who sat in the parking lot as my getaway.

I looked down the pier, every shadow looked like it could be Zeke hiding, ready to strike. I was dying for a cigarette, but smoking would only draw attention and distract me. I turned to look back the other way towards the parking lot. No movement. No cars. Nothing.

I paced down the pier twice until I turned around to see three teen girls standing behind me.

One of them let out a laugh and then asked, "Hey, you T?"

"Yep," I replied, my nerves a tangled mess.

All three of them smiled with a Stepford grin. The first two were typical brunettes, pretty but nothing interesting about their faces or their attire of Northface Jackets and UGG boots. But the third girl. She looked just like me.

We had the same short heart-faced face, slim and pointed nose, and olive upturned eyes. Her wheat blonde hair curled in soft but chaotic waves just like mine. It was as if she was a living (and I'll admit it, more well-groomed) Madame Tussauds figure of myself.

"What?" the girl asked, feeling uncomfortable by my stare.

I pulled my hood down.

All three of the girls stepped back.

"Jamie, what's going on? Do you have a twin we don't know about?" one of the brunettes asked.

"What? No, I don't. She doesn't even look like me," Jamie replied.

"You've got to be kidding me, she's a dead ringer," the other brunette said.

Jamie seems embarrassed and confused, but I could tell she saw her reflection in me too.

"Weird, right? I guess our families must be from the same village or some shit," I said.

The girls laughed again. It seems like anything would tickle their funny bone.

No longer having any patience for them I said, "Do you have my money?"

"Yeah," said one of the brunettes, "if you have our shit." She stood up straight, trying to act tough by borrowing my way of speaking. But it was clear she wasn't used to saying *bad words* openly.

I opened my bag and showed them the merchandise.

They handed over my money but just as I handed over the drugs, my phone dropped out of my pocket.

"Fucking Hell," I cursed as I crouched on the ground looking over a shattered screen.

The girls giggled at my distress and I could hear them begin to walk away.

"Taylor motherfucking Callahan!" The familiar voice of Zeke sliced through the silence of the pier.

I froze, still hunched over in the shadows. I was certain my death was near. Any second a knife would plunge into my back or a bullet would rip through my chest.

The girls screamed.

"Don't you think I won't fucking kill you and your little friends after what you did to me," he continued.

"No, please don't kill us. Please put the gun away," Jamie begged. I could hear tears in her voice.

"I never thought you were the crying and begging type, but I guess we all aren't so tough in the end." He lets out a snort of a laugh.

"Please don't—" Jamie tried to speak again but she was cut off by the sound of three shots being fired. I heard Zeke's feet pounding the wooden planks of the pier as he sprinted away. Then three thuds of dead weight hit the ground.

CHAPTER 4
TAYLOR CALLAHAN

October 3, 2015

Four Hours Before The Switch

I gathered the strength to turn around and stand up. In front of me, I saw each of the girls lying flat across the ground. Their blood soaking through their clothes into the wooden planks of the pier. My heart pounded as I knew it would have been me lying dead on the ground if Zeke had seen me first instead of Jamie.

But somewhere between my horror and fear, I could see this tragic event as an opportunity for me.

Ivan came running up from the parking lot, his eye swollen from Zeke's fist. "Taylor, I'm sorry." His voice was shaking. "He had a gun and told me he was going to kill us both if I didn't say where you were and that he just wanted to talk to you. I'm so sorry," he said as he pulled me into a hug.

I hugged him back even though I was pissed at him for cracking so easily.

I pulled myself away from his hold.

"What do we do about the girls?" he asked, wiping a tear away from his good eye.

He looked at the bodies then knelt down by Jamie. The bullet blasted through her eye socket, causing the right side of her face and back of her head to explode with blood and gore.

"Holy shit, Taylor, I feel sick." Ivan knelt on the floor and started dry-heaving. He took a breath and calmed himself down before asking, "Why did he even bother to kill them when he was after you?"

"This girl, Jamie. She looks exactly like me. That's why he killed her, he thought I was her."

Just to be sure, I felt for her pulse. Nothing. The same with the other two girls.

Ivan crossed his arms across his chest. "Looked exactly like you? I don't believe it."

I reached into the pocket of her hoodie and pulled out an iPhone with a bright orange case coated with stick-on jewels and a pink leather wallet with a plastic display area for an ID. I handed him her driver's license.

"Damn, you're right. She could be your twin." But the sight of three dead bodies started to overwhelm Ivan. He began breathing heavily and shaking. "What do we do? Should we call the police? They shouldn't just be left here. Who knows the next time someone will be out here?"

"You're right but—" I flipped through her wallet and found her school photo ID. The colorful logo of a purple and yellow bear mascot was on the side.

Here's my chance, I thought. *I can go back to high school and start over. When opportunity knocks, I might as well answer the door.*

I stood up and threw my jacket and shirt to the ground.

"Hey, what the Hell are you doing?" Ivan shouted.

"Switching places." I unzipped my pants and peeled them off my legs.

Examining Jamie's body, I noticed that she fell in such a way that all the blood and goop from her brain ran away from her body down towards the crashing waves at the end of the pier, leaving her clothes unstained.

I lifted her legs, heavy like I suspected. I wrangled off her skinny jeans which was as hard as skinning a python.

"What! Why?" shouted Ivan.

"Shh. Keep your voice down." I told him, "I've been thinking about it. I want to start over. Go back to high school. Do it right this time."

He crunched up his nose at me and opened his mouth in exasperation. "Seriously?"

I stopped trying to undress Jamie and knelt next to him on the ground.

"You know what our lives have been like. But you got to finish high school and you had parents around. Zeke fucked up my life at sixteen. I'd do anything to go back in time and have a do over."

Ivan stared at me for a minute. He nodded his head and gave me a small smile which I knew meant he understood me.

He stood up and helped me remove Jamie's pink hoodie and slid her white tank top down her body to avoid getting any blood on it.

"I feel so perv-y doing this," I joked.

Ivan lets out a laugh, "You don't even like women."

"It doesn't matter how I feel about it, it matters how it looks."

I put on her clothes in a panicked frenzy, trying to get her top over my head while pulling up her pants. I almost tripped and fell on to the bodies below as I shoved my feet into her pink converses.

Ivan lifted Jamie's heavy legs and torso up as I pulled on my black Ramones T-shirt over her chest. We both shimmied my jeans up her legs. We got one sleeve of my black hoodie up one arm then, Ivan rolled her to one side, so I can wedge the fabric under her body and get the other sleeve on. I claimed her keys, wallet, and phone as my own while stuffing her pockets with my identification. I took out my phone to do one last thing.

"What are you doing, now?" Ivan moaned.

In a text saved in draft, addressed to nobody, I write:

"I don't want to go through with this. I'm afraid Zeke is going to find me. He's out tonight and he could kill me for what I did."

"If these poor girls had to die because of me, I want their killer to be found," I told him.

Dressed in Jamie's fabric-softened clothes that were still warm from her body, we returned to Ivan's car.

CHAPTER 5
TAYLOR CALLAHAN

October 3, 2015
Three Hours Before The Switch

"Are you sure you want to do this?" Ivan asked me.

"Yes, I'm sure. I want a chance to start over."

"Alright," he let out a heavy sigh. He scratched his head for a minute then grabbed Jamie's phone from my hand. "If you're going to hijack this girl's life, you're lucky she's the type who's got loads of pics on Facebook and Instagram."

We scrolled through her photos. She took hundreds of selfies almost every single day. There were at least fifty shots of her in a bathroom wearing a white lace top with a skater skirt and brown leather jacket. She had attempted to contour her face, but it turned out patchy with pink and bronze hues. And if she wasn't taking pictures of herself, someone else was.

She was tagged in a photo from the football game last night, Jamie beaming a blindingly white smile in a cheerleading uniform made up of a white skirt with purple band lining the bottom, a highlighter yellow top with "Bears" written on a purple iron-on patch. She received over thirty comments on that picture alone all from people stroking her ego with various compliments.

She would be tagged in tons of those basic-girl memes like the ones of Marilyn Monroe saying, "Well-behaved women rarely make history." I rolled my eyes at that one.

Once in a while, she would post something religious like this picture of a weeping Jesus with text in Papyrus over his face saying, "He gave his life for you, what have you given him?"

"She is conceited, popular, and religious. Pretty much everything I hate," I said to Ivan.

"Now you have to become conceited, popular, and religious." Ivan beamed at me.

I made a snarled face at him and went back to my social media research.

I found a video of her.

"So, it's the first day of school, what do you think?" asked the girl holding the camera.

"Oh, my God, I hate it," replied Jamie.

I scrolled through her timeline and found quite a few videos. They mostly are of her and her pretty friends talking celebrity gossip or singing along to their favorite songs in the car before they break out into laughter. The more I watched the more I learned how she behaved. I noticed the way she moved, her habits, and her nervous ticks. She always tucked her hair behind her ear with the opposite hand, she pinched the sides of her bottom lip together when she was bored. She smiled quickly and brightly, and her face seemed to exude confidence, yet she slouched her shoulders in a way that made me think that her confidence was a lie. She spoke quickly and sprinkled her sentences with the word "like" every chance she got.

I turned away from Ivan for a second. I took a deep breath and pinched my lower lip like Jamie. I turned towards him, tucking my hair behind my ear with my opposite hand, obstructing his view of my face.

I hunched a little forward, beamed at him and say "Hi, I'm Jamie MacKenzie, I'm, like, a junior at Southfield High" as quickly as I can.

Ivan shuttered. "That's freaky. You sound just like her."

"That's the point," I said in my normal voice.

Ivan pulled over into the parking lot of an Easy Drug Pharmacy. He took Jamie's phone from me and he scrolled through her pictures. "I hate to break it to you but if you're really going to take this girl's place, you're gonna have to freshen-up a bit."

Inside the drug store, he collected hair dye, teeth whitening gel, and brown eye liner. The eyeliner wasn't for make-up. You see, Jamie and I don't look 100 percent alike as I thought. While my young-looking face makes me look like a teenager, if you looked hard enough, you could see that Jamie and I weren't the same person. Her nose was slightly rounder, her bottom lip was a little fuller, and she has a noticeable flat mole on her right cheekbone.

We approached a stocky middle-aged woman with a choppy haircut. I could see her entire body tense as we walked in. Ivan was right, I did look a little rough around the edges and we were now in the nice part of town.

She rang us up and Ivan flopped two twenty-dollar bills down on the counter.

"Can I have a key to the bathroom?" I asked her.

With a barely audible groan, she removed the key that's attached to a big "W" on it from behind the counter.

In the bathroom, we rushed to get the metal beads out of my hair and comb out my half-hearted attempt at dreads but they really just looked like loose curly ropes. Then, we wet my dark blonde hair with streaks of teal blue running through it in the sink. Ivan painted my head with the dye and we let it sit for thirty minutes. While we waited for the dye to work, I forced layer after layer of whitening goop onto my teeth until I achieved the pearly white smile of Jamie.

I spent what felt like forever drying my hair under the hand dryer until my new straw-colored hair was almost dry.

With a fresher blonde sheen to my hair and a newly drawn mole on my face, Ivan said, "All right, Jamie, let's get you home."

Just as we're about to leave the bathroom, someone thuds on the metal door.

"Miss, are you in there? I need the key back," the clerk called out.

"One minute," I said as I rushed to get all my things together.

I opened the door and the woman jumped back. She was not expecting to see Ivan in there with me.

"What were you two doing in there together? You know I can have you arrested for that!" said the clerk, waving a fist at us.

"Relax lady, we weren't doing the dance with no pants. I don't even like the ladies. I was just giving her a fabulous make-over." Ivan played up his words to give off the sassy gay friend impression.

"Oh, I—" The woman stammered.

"We bought all this stuff, and we didn't do anything else in here. Back off. We're leaving." I pushed past the woman and Ivan followed.

We rushed out of the store as the woman waddled behind us ringing her hands.

●　　　●　　　●

In the car, I rolled down the windows to let my hair dry a little bit more while Ivan punched Jamie's address into Google Maps. The app said she lives twenty minutes away from our current location and showed us a red brick ranch in the street view.

During the drive, I looked deeper into her Facebook account. Apparently, she loved peanut butter—she's seen eating it out of a jar with a spoon in several pictures. She also has a penchant for playing Dance Dance Revolution—Lame! I guess I'm gonna have to learn to like this stuff too. She is into Country music, Lady Antebellum and Florida Georgia Line in particular. She went to their concerts last year. I found a photo from a year ago, Jamie's mom, Joan MacKenzie, her dad, Phil, and little sister, Faith smiling for the camera on a road trip.

Her parents are a bit on the larger side. Her dad has a Santa Claus belly with blonde hair and beard, but he is always wearing a baseball cap. Her mom has a blunt short brown hair cut, a large round face with a few wrinkles around her lips and eyes. Faith looks shy as she rarely looks into the camera. She has long brown hair and is always seen wearing long sleeves and full-length skirts even in photos dated in July and August.

Word of those two other high school girls' deaths was going to spread quickly. I needed to have my story straight about how this night played out from Jamie's perspective.

I scrolled up Jamie's timeline to the present. At four o'clock, she was tagged in several photos with the other girls I recognized from the pier. Their names are Ali Everette and Courtney Wilson. I jumped to their Facebook accounts, so I can learn more about who these two girls are. Courtney wore heavy makeup for a teen girl. Her sharp but delicate features were highlighted with pointed eyeliner, bronzer and matte lipstick. Ali had darker brown hair than Courtney and had a natural beauty to her. She had a round face and was slightly bigger than the other two girls, mostly because she seemed to always be eating. Courtney and Jamie posed with their food, smiling next to pieces of pizza, fake eating a handful of popcorn or candy corn while Ali never smiled or posed because she was always truly eating. In one picture, she even commented right after it was taken, "No pizza next time or I'm going to get fat! LOL!!"

All three girls were in their cheerleader uniforms last night. *So that's how they're all connected.*

A few hours later in the timeline, a bunch of other girls are starting to show up in these pictures. I didn't think anyone could have so many friends. All of them smiling for the camera or fake kissing each other's cheeks. Around eight o'clock the pictures stop. That's when I met the girls.

Ivan parked a block away. He grabbed me and kissed my cheek. "You crazy girl. Be careful," he said.

I smiled and told him, "Of course."

"How can I reach you?" he asked.

"You can't."

"But how will I know you're alright or if you need me?" A worried look spread across his face.

"I'll call by pay phone every week just to check in."

"Okay. I hope this makes you happy," he said.

For a moment, my excitement faded. I had no idea what kind of an effect this would have on Ivan.

"Are you gonna be alright?" I asked him.

"Of course, plus I'll take on your clients after the news gets out. Double my income."

I laughed. "There's always a silver lining with you."

"Now go and good luck."

I get out of the car and walk across a few freshly watered lawns before I get to her house.

I approached the brown oak door with a mat that reads, "Welcome to Our Home" in cheerful script. I reached for the doorknob and froze. A terrible flash of memories ran through my head and my whole body broke out in goosebumps.

CHAPTER 6
TAYLOR CALLAHAN

February 17, 2011
4 Years, 7 Months, 16 Days Before The Switch

I had goosebumps all over my body the night my mother threw me out. She found little brown baggies of heroin and my three ounces of weed nestled in a shoe box underneath my twin bed.

My room was a disaster zone, clothes in piles on the floor, shoes thrown in every direction, belts, and jewelry hanging on the door knob and chair, nail polish from three years ago splashed across my small desk.

I thought she would never find it. It was a good hiding spot for Zeke. I didn't know she had scored a hot date and would go trolling through my room looking for my black boots with the zipper up the sides.

I came home, and she was hiding behind the door. She rushed out and grabbed me by the neck screaming, "What in the Hell is this, Taylor Elizabeth Callahan?"

I wrestled her French-tipped claws off me.

"Are you using? Are you just some druggy-whore now?" she screamed as she pulled up my sleeves to inspect me for track marks.

"No," I screamed back. "I don't use. I deal."

Her eyes widened. She clutched her chest. "You deal? What the Hell for?"

"For money, so I can leave this place."

I looked around at my home, a tiny vomit green duplex with bars on the window and chain-link outside. My little brother, Neil, sat on our wilting blue couch playing video games. But the flickering of his little thumbs on the controller froze and he looked right at us, eyes watering.

When my mom looked down at the box for a second, I mouthed, "It's okay" at him.

She clutched my wrist and said, "Well this is what's going to happen to your life if you keep dealing."

She dragged me to the bathroom. She tried to flush one of the little baggies down the toilet only to see it rise up again with water spilling over the bowl.

"Oh, shit!" she shrieked, her mustard-yellow curls bouncing into her face and sticking to her make-up.

I couldn't help but laugh a little.

"You think this is funny. You think that I'm happy that you repay me, your mother, for busting my ass day in and day out to put food on the table for you to disrespect me and say you don't want to live in my home."

"I wouldn't call guilt-tripping one of the three men who you say is my father for cash as busting your ass," I told her.

Her eyes filled with cobwebs of little red veins and her lips parted into a growl. She took me by the neck again and pushed me out in front of her. I almost tripped on the long draping black shawl she was wearing.

She opened the front door and threw me out into the snow. My knees and wrists slammed against the frozen concrete below. I screamed in pain as I felt a twisting pop and my left wrist hung over, unable to move.

She rained the little baggies of heroin down over me, but kept the weed for herself, and screamed, "Now get off my property."

I shoved the bags into my oversized purse with my good hand. I looked over to see Neil sobbing at the window with his little hands pressed against the glass. Before I could say goodbye, my mom pulled him away and closed the curtains.

At that moment, I missed Drew. I knew he would have defended me. He was the man who I thought was my father until I was twelve years old. He wasn't great, he was an angry drunk who used to throw empties at the TV when the Rangers lost a game, but he was good to me. He always brought home a treat for me like gum or a new pack of crayons when he had the money.

Right after my tenth birthday, he told me it was about time for a growing girl like me to learn how to defend herself. He bought me a rifle almost too big for my hands and took me to a make-shift shooting range on his buddy's rural property. The first shot scared me and almost knocked me to the ground. But I got up again and fired a hole through the middle of every one of those torso-shaped cut outs. After that, he would brag about his girl being the next Annie Oakley to all his friends.

He took me to the range in secret every few weeks until my mother found out. They both were sloppy drunk, yelling and screaming at each other.

Drew called her a controlling bitch and a bad mother. My mom fired back with "Well, it don't matter what kind of a father you are, cause the kids ain't yours." I remember he took one last sip of his beer, placed it down on the kitchen table and said, "That ain't fair Nadine, that ain't fair."

A few weeks later, I was at the courthouse with an old woman with mildew breath who rubbed a dry cotton swab on the inside of my cheek. I never saw Drew again, so I assumed the DNA test showed that I wasn't his daughter. I still don't know who my father is and neither does my mom. She told me he is either her old boyfriend who is now in prison for creating a Ponzi scheme or her old co-worker from the restaurant, Don, the cook. Since I can't cook a damn thing, but I can lie through my teeth without a moment of hesitation, I'm pretty sure the Ponzi scheme guy is my father.

It didn't matter who my father was because neither Drew nor my real dad was there to protect me from my mom or from Zeke. That night, I was a sixteen-year-old girl out in the freezing cold on a school night with a purse full of heroin and Zeke was my only lifeline. He lived about twenty blocks west. With my head down, and my feet freezing, I waded through inches of snow towards his place.

I muttered curse words to myself calling Nadine "a bitch," "a slut," and "a terrible mother." Then I stopped hating her and started hating myself for getting caught, for not wearing warm clothes, and for not being rich enough to buy a real cell phone. I envied the few well-off kids at school with their state-of-the-art smartphones while I was left to play Snake on my ancient Nokia.

I knocked on Zeke's door. He lived in a little manufactured home with a white metal shell. The TV was blaring, and Zeke yelled out, "What is it?"

"It's me, Taylor. I'm hurt," I said.

Zeke opened the door and pulled me in with a big hug. I showed him my wrist.

"Oh shit, babe, what happened?" he said gently, taking my hand in his.

"Nadine threw me out," I told him.

"Why?"

"Because of this" I opened my purse to show him the goods.

He reached for my bag and took it from me. "Fuck, it's a good thing you took them with you."

"She took the weed for herself," I grumbled.

"That's okay, you can earn it back," he said.

Zeke rushed into action. He pulled some of his old clothes from the back of his closet, smaller sized t-shirts and sweatpants for me to change into. When I came out in dry clothes, he called me to the kitchen where he created a cast out of wooden sticks, gauze, and tape.

"My parents were really big into hunting and camping. My dad made me learn how to do all this survival shit."

"I'm glad he did," I said with a smile.

He leaned in, grabbed the back of my head, and kissed me hard until my head was ringing. The short-trimmed hairs on his face that matched the hairs on his head in both length and black-brown shade scraped against my chin.

He picked me up and pulled me to his chest. My legs reached around him. He took me to his bed and laid me down in his messy flannel sheets.

He tore off his clothes showing off tan muscles and perfect plumes of masculine body hair. He slid my pants down and entered me. Gently, he pulled my hurt arm away from our bodies, taking extra care not to hurt me. Though our usual style of sex was rough, he took things at a slower pace that night.

Afterwards, he made us Mac and Cheese off the stove, and we fell asleep while watching reruns on cable.

That night I thought that was all our relationship was ever going to be: tenderness, good sex, and a warm place to call home. But that only lasted for a few days and abruptly ended when Zeke left me in a motel room he never intended to pay for or return to.

CHAPTER 7
TAYLOR CALLAHAN

October 3, 2015
The Switch

I blinked my eyes and forced myself to focus on what I was about to do. This opportunity was new and shiny, and it wouldn't involve Zeke abandoning me or my mom throwing me out. All I had to do was walk through that door and start a new life, a better life.

I took a deep breath and put the keys in the door. My first step inside was greeted by a deafening alarm that radiated through the house.

The people I recognized as Jamie's mom and dad rushed out both aiming shotguns at me. I threw my hands up out of fear.

"My goodness, Jamie!" yelled her mom over the blaring noise.

She walked over to the alarm and turned it off. "Did you forget the code again? It's Aunt Wendy's birthday, 1-8-59. Remember?"

"Sorry everyone," I said.

"Why did you come home early? You never come home from a sleep-over early." Faith poked her head out from the hall.

"It's nothing. I just needed to come home," I told them.

"Sweetie, what happened?" asked her mom, handing her gun to her husband before coming over to me.

"Oh, leave her alone," said Phil, "you know how many fights those girls get into. I'm sure someone just upset her."

"It's nothing. I'm fine," I said.

Joan yelled behind her, "Phil. Faith. Go back to bed. I'm going to have a talk with Jamie."

The two of them listened to her orders and they stomped off down the hall.

I called out "Sorry" again and beamed a Jamie-esque smile at them.

In the kitchen, Joan was microwaving something. I sat down on the bar stools that were in the '90s style kitchen with cream-yellow Formica countertops and wood grain cabinets. She placed two mugs of heated milk next to me and she joined me on the neighboring bar stool. "So why don't you tell me what this is all about?"

Remembering I had to be a secretive teenager I repeated, "It's nothing. I'm fine."

"No, no. It isn't. Now, I know my daughter and you haven't vacated a sleep-over on your own free will since you were nine years old. For Heaven's sake, remember your first sleep-over when I had to drag you from that girl, Madison's house? Both of you were in tears like you were going off to war." She laughed.

I let out a small laugh, too.

"So, spill," she said while poking me in the stomach.

"Alright, Mom. I just," I paused, and I looked away for emotional affect and to give me time to think up an explanation. I took a swig of my hot milk and it burned my mouth causing tears to bubble up in my eyes. Perfect timing.

"I just didn't want them to get in trouble," I blurted out as if it was a long-held secret.

"Who?" she leaned in closer.

"Ali and Courtney," I sighed.

"Why? What did they do?" Her eyes widened with excitement.

"So, they were talking about turning the sleep-over into a real party...you know...with boys, alcohol, and drugs. I pretended to be fine with it because I didn't want them to think I was lame or anything but then they wanted me to come with them to get the drugs and I panicked and left."

"Oh, no, honey. You did the right thing. I'm so proud of you for turning down that temptation." She hugged me, and I left a few believable tears soaking into her purple pajamas.

"How did you get home then?" she asked.

"You're gonna get so mad at me," I moaned.

"What happened?" she persisted.

I knew I couldn't name anyone who would have actually taken me home and even if I did, it would have been too easy for her to ask them. "I started walking but I forgot how far it was on foot, so I hitched."

"You hitchhiked? How could you put yourself in such a dangerous situation? Don't you ever do that again!" Joan shouted slamming her mug down onto the counter. "He could have been a rapist or murderer."

"But he wasn't. He was nice and by the way he talked I think he wasn't into women, if you know what I mean." I smiled.

"All that truly matters is that you got home safe and sound. But if anything like this happens again, make sure you call us. We'll come get you."

"I didn't want to wake you then I forgot about the alarm." I put my head down as if I was overly ashamed of my actions.

"Do you think Ali and Courtney are alright or do I need to call work?" she asked.

Call work? Why would she call her work?

"I don't know. They're probably mad at me for ditching the party. I think they might've bailed on the deal because they were so upset at me," I answered knowing they didn't bail and that their bodies were still and cold outside on that pier.

"I'm going to have a talk with their parents about what those girls have been up to. But in the meantime, give them a text and if they don't answer soon. I'll call my boys."

My boys? I turned to my left to see the family dining room surrounded with pictures on every inch of the walls. In the middle, I saw Jamie's mom standing at attention in a blue uniform and a badge on her shoulder. Panic stung my stomach at the realization: my new mom is a cop.

•　　•　　•

I entered my new bedroom. It was dimly lit by a Mickey Mouse night light near the entrance to the room. I flopped myself down on the empty bed in front of me. Before I could relax into a nice night's sleep, I felt eyes on me.

Faith was staring at me from her bed on the other side of the room. "What happened?" she whispered.

I jumped. My heart raced. I had no idea they shared a room. I blurted out, "Nothing, don't worry about it."

"But you never come home early from anything," she continued, with her soft voice floating over the darkness.

"Whatever, just forget about it. It's none of your business," I said with my most convincing teenage snark.

Her voice quaked, "I was just checking that you were okay. You don't have to be so mean to me."

Oh shit, maybe Jamie and Faith didn't have the typical attitude-laced relationship other teenage sisters have.

"Hey," I said, sitting up in my bed and meeting her glare. "I'm sorry. It's just that my friends might be in trouble and I'm worried."

"Oh no, what happened?" she asked, leaning forward.

I shook my head. "I'm not sure. I don't want to think about it right now. Let's just go to sleep."

"Okay," she sighed.

I rolled on my side away from her, but I could feel her eyes pressing into my back until I finally fell asleep.

CHAPTER 8
TAYLOR CALLAHAN

October 4, 2015
One Day After The Switch
"Wake up, we're gonna be late for church." Faith shook my shoulder.

"Do we really have to go?" I asked.

"You know what the answer to that question is in this house." She pulled up the blinds casting sunrise into the room.

The walls were baby girl pink. The duvet covers on the two twin beds matched the color perfectly. Each mattress was held up by white headboards that each girl decorated with magazine clippings and twinkle lights. To the side of the room, there was a white desk and dresser next to a closet with clothes popping out of the sliding doors. I noticed that around the border of the room faint stencils of Cinderella next to her pumpkin stagecoach and Fairy Godmother poked out from behind the furniture. These people really needed to redecorate.

"Hurry and shower before Dad hogs all the hot water." Faith giggled.

I did as she instructed and I came back into the room wrapped in Jamie's pink robe with my hair neatly straightened and the freckle freshly redrawn on my face.

I opened the closet door, but I didn't know which side of the closet was mine.

Panic froze my blood and my thoughts raced. I couldn't get made so soon, I've only been here for a night. Plus, I'll lose major street cred for getting caught by a ninety-pound teenager.

"Can't decide what to wear?" asked Faith from behind me.

"Yeah, nothing's, like, speaking to me." I placed my hand on my hip and pretending to be some valley girl picking out an outfit.

"What about that blue and yellow dress? The one that matches your hair," said Faith reaching into the closet in front of me and pulling it out.

She holds out a baby doll style dress with lace at the collar, something a girl several years younger than Jamie's age would wear.

I beamed a famous Jamie smile at her and took it. "Good choice."

Faith and I walked out to the family room to see Joan waiting for us. "Have you heard from them?" she asked me.

I took out my phone from a brand-name knock-off purse I found in Jamie's closet. I pretended to scroll through my texts. I shook my head no.

"It looks like it's time to check in with the boys." She took out her cellphone and paced back and forth, her taupe kitten heels digging into the brown fuzzy carpet.

"Hey Pete, It's Joan. Look, my daughter is really concerned about two of her friends, Ali Everette and Courtney Wilson. They were —"

Pete's muffled voice cut her off and her face tightened. She shot me a glance but quickly turned the other way.

"I see. Call me when you have any updates," she said then snapped her phone shut. Of course, she still had a flip phone.

"What happened?" I asked, allowing my voice to shake a little too much.

Joan's voice was steady and matter-of-fact. "Ali's parents called in earlier this morning when they noticed she didn't return home. They have units out looking now."

"I'm so worried about them," I whimpered.

Faith hugged me from the side, her long, lean arms reaching around my shoulders. "It will be okay, I'm sure they'll turn up."

Their mom sighed, I assumed she was annoyed by her younger daughter's naivety. As a cop, I was sure she knew that girls who go missing usually don't get found and on the off chance they do, they aren't still breathing.

Phil came down the hall, his big belly rolled over his khaki pants which prevented his blue blazer from closing. Even though he looked uncomfortable in his clothes, he walked with a spring in his step like he didn't have a care in the world.

"Everybody ready?" he asked with a big smile, clearly unable to read the sullen faces of the three women in front of him.

● ● ●

I walked down the center aisle of a church with a high ceiling that came to a point at the altar. Dark wooden arches created the skeletal structure of the building. Sconces casts tiny pools of orange light over certain sections of the church. Where the light couldn't reach, it was almost pitch black. I didn't understand why people dressed so brightly only to come to a place that was so dark.

During the service, I faded in and out as Bible verses were read aloud by shut-in looking women and overzealous teens. I learned when to shout, "Amen" and easily mouthed the words to songs that contained the words "Lamb," "Shepard," and "Forgiveness" in many different combinations. So far, having to sit through this boring crap every week was the worst part about being a MacKenzie.

But I soon learned there was something far worse than church: chore day. Upon returning the service, I was instructed to get my work clothes on. Faith had pulled some paint-splattered jeans and baggy t-shirts out from a basket in the bottom of our closet. The four of us proceeded to clean every inch of the house.

Joan assigned me to the bathroom where I had to bleach every centimeter of the grout between the tiles on the floor and in the shower with a toothbrush.

Halfway through the job, she popped her oversized head in and asked, "How's it going?"

I wanted to respond with, "Seriously regretting stealing your daughter's identity" but instead I simply offered, "It's going."

She smiled. "It's good practice."

I didn't realize I was getting myself into housewife-training when I got here.

● ● ●

I was in the middle of heaving a sopping ball of laundry from one machine to the next when Joan answered a knock at the door.

"Jamie, can you come out here please?" she called.

I came into the living room to see two policemen in the same uniform as Joan's picture in the dining room.

"Hey Jamie, how's it going?" asked one of them with a brown jarhead haircut.

"Alright, just, like, doing my chores," I responded in Jamie's fast-paced voice.

The other officer stepped forward. He was black with no hair except for a thin beard.

"We're here to ask you about Courtney Wilson and Alison Everette. Can we sit down?" he asked.

I nodded and sat myself down in the middle of the couch. Joan pulled in two chairs from the dining room.

The officers sat across from me on the other side of the perfectly polished wooden coffee table.

The black officer cleared his throat. "This isn't easy for us to tell you. We've known you and your family for a long time, and we don't want to upset you. But unfortunately, your two friends were found dead this morning."

I let out an airy "What?" and covered my mouth and made sure my eyes gave off the look of fearful surprise.

"I know this is some really hard news to hear but we need you to tell us what you know about the night they were killed," said the jarhead officer.

I knew I needed to start crying soon or they were going to get suspicious of the teen girl who doesn't cry when she hears her friends are dead. I bet these girls were the type to cry when they learn their BFFs aren't going to be in the same homeroom as they are. This isn't the time to skimp on the dramatics.

I cupped my nose and mouth with both hands and keel over, letting out a few short blasts of sobs. Joan came over to pat me on the back. During this time, I shoved a fingernail into the side of my nostril just hard enough to cause me to tear up without getting a nosebleed. I popped back up with my eyes watering. Joan ushered me in for a hug.

The black officer pulled a tissue from the box on the table and handed it to me.

"I'm sorry," I whimpered at them.

"Don't be sorry, we understand," said the jarhead officer.

I took a few exaggerated deep breaths and calmed down.

"Are you ready to answer some questions?" asked the black officer who opened a small note pad.

I nodded.

"Where were you last night?" he continued.

"I was at Courtney's house, there was going to be a party with the rest of the cheer squad," I said, remembering the pictures of the girls that were tagged on Facebook, some of them were in their cheer uniforms in the photos online.

"What time did you arrive at the Wilson home?"

"Ali picked me around..." I looked at Joan.

"Around four," she filled in for me.

"We got there early, and it was just me, Ali, and Courtney until about seven when everyone else showed up."

"What were you doing during this time?" asked the jarhead.

"Before everyone else got there, we just hung out and talked, and ate a few snacks."

"Then what happened?"

"Well," I took a deep breath, "Ali told me that some of the boys were going to stop by and they wanted to turn it into a real party," I said quoting Derek. "They wanted me to come with them to get drugs. I got in the car with them to meet the dealer but then I got freaked out. Courtney wouldn't take me back home, so I got out and left."

"What did you do after that?"

"It's really stupid and my mom already knows about it. I hitched a ride home."

"Jamie, I shouldn't have to tell you how stupid and dangerous that is," The jarhead cop barked at me.

"Relax," said the other officer. "What time did you return home?

"Almost midnight." Joan laughed. "She came barreling in here and set the alarm off."

"You must have been pretty scared to leave the party and come home the way you did."

I nodded, "I was. I just had this little voice in my head that said, *get out now* and I knew I had to leave."

There was a pause and I decided it was time to ask the question: "How did they die?"

"They were shot," said the black officer. "Their bodies were found on the pier next to the body of a known criminal."

That's me!

"It seems to be a drug deal gone wrong, but we aren't sure who could have done this since the dealer was also found dead. We will do everything possible to track down their killer."

"Thank you," I said with the most grateful smile I could muster.

After they had left, I fake-sobbed into my mother's arms. Both Faith and Phil had wandered into the living room to see what was the matter.

Joan mouthed the news to them and they took turns hugging me.

Even though I was fooling these people, I couldn't help but feel thankful to them for giving me more hugs in one day than I've had in my whole life.

CHAPTER 9
TAYLOR CALLAHAN

October 4, 2015
One Day After The Switch
I flopped my body down on my bed, face first. First church, then chores, and a police questioning, I had no idea that being the good girl would be so exhausting. My arms dangled past the side of my bed brushing past the rough edges of the mattress. I felt something hard and pointy poking out from the mattress. I pulled out a notebook covered with pink fuzzy faux fur. I opened it up. It's Jamie's diary. Jackpot.

I flipped through it and landed on a random entry:

4/13
Brandon wanted me to cut class today and make-out with him in the empty chem lab. I told him I would go but as soon as Mrs. Romano saw me I chickened out and went to class last minute. Brandon was mad that I left him there but I just couldn't do it.

4/25
Courtney made fun of me in front of everybody today. She said that I was too lame to go to the cheer sleepover tonight because I've never tried alcohol. She said "you care more about what your Youth Group thinks about you than us." It's not true. I care about all of them. She said if I cared about them then I should come over tonight but it was Friday night youth service at church and I was doing a reading. I couldn't let the church down.

5/12

I stayed over at Ali's house and didn't finish the assignment that was due in biology today. Ali gave me the number of this Asian kid in the senior class who does homework for money. She said he could get it done by the end of the day. I texted him and he said he would do it for forty bucks but I never got around to texting him back.

I read a few more entries but they all are the same. Someone wants Jamie to do something rebellious but she backs out. On the rare occasion that she gives in, she is riddled with guilt for weeks.

I turned the page, but I don't see a date of entry and there are only a few sentences that read:

When they take me out to the killing fields I feel that vengeance is on my side and the Lord at my back. My rifle is the instrument of God's Word and the defender of the innocent. I feel that it is my calling to rid the world of the unrighteous and the sinners.

Creepy. On the opposite side of the page, there was a tally that counted to six.

I heard voices down the hall and I put it back in its hiding place.

"You know I can't stay home tomorrow. I've got a big shipment coming in and I'm the only manager on duty to sign for it," Phil huffed.

"I don't think she should go to school tomorrow after all of this. I see stuff like this all the time and it tears people apart. We should go easier on her," said Joan, her voice had a flustered tone to it.

"Fine, she can stay home, just not with me." Phil insisted.

"You know I can't get out of my shift either," Joan replied.

"She's a big girl, she can stay home alone, she has before," said Phil.

"I know but in such a state, she may not want to be alone all day."

"Well then go and ask her."

God yes, I would love to stay home tomorrow. I don't think I can fool hundreds of teenagers into thinking I'm Jamie just yet.

Joan's footsteps thumped down the short hallway and she poked her head into my room. "Hey hon, do you want to stay home tomorrow? I can call in for you given the circumstances."

I turned around.

"Yeah, Mom, that would be a good idea. I don't think I can face school tomorrow." I sniffled.

"And you think you'll be fine alone? You won't get too lonely or depressed?"

"No, I think I need the time to just think."

She nodded, "Then we'll do that."

She left, and I lay down on Jamie's bed again. My mind filled with memories from my first time in high school and how it ruined my life.

CHAPTER 10
TAYLOR CALLAHAN

November 1, 2010
4 Years, 11 Months, 2 Days Before The Switch

Chanel was my best friend, more like my only true friend, in high school. I was so grateful to her for including me in her friend group. Her boyfriend, Manny, was especially welcoming to me. They both knew I was shy and pushed me to open up and be more adventurous with them. This was anything from cutting class to playing pranks on our friends to attempting to dread my frizzy-for-a-white-girl hair. It never looked great but I wore it that way on and off throughout my life because it reminded me of them. Even though their heart was in the right place, it was their desire to get me out of my shell that led me to the worst turning point in my life: meeting Zeke on my sixteenth birthday.

Chanel, ignoring my desire to have a small birthday celebration at her house, threw me a huge sweet sixteen birthday party. Her hands were on my back as she guided me blind folded through the long corridors of the abandoned elementary school we took over for the evening. I heard the echoing screech of the metal door opening before she pulled the scarf from my eyes to see the old gymnasium lit up with thousands of strands of lights. In the far end of the room there was a table set up with snacks and a birthday cake that was next to a small dancefloor Chanel had arranged with a light machine and a stereo blasting Drake's *Thank Me Later* album.

"You did all of this for me?" I asked.

"Of course," she beamed.

"Where did you get all this stuff?"

"Let's see, the lights are mostly Christmas lights I *borrowed* from my neighbors. Don't worry, they'll get them back before it's time to start decorating. And the disco lights and sound system I legitimately borrowed from my cousin who is a DJ and—"

We heard noises of what sounded like a stampede of footprints and laughter coming down the hall.

"Wait," I said. "How many people did you invite?"

"About everyone at school and my whole neighborhood," she said before she rushed up to the group coming into the gymnasium and gave several girls I didn't recognize hugs and kisses.

I was overwhelmed by the amount of people coming in and by the thought of being the center of attention. Feeling shaky and sick, I backed away into the corner, hoping not to be noticed by anyone.

Chanel left the girls she was talking to and rushed to my side.

"What's the matter? All these people are here for you," she said.

"I know," I gulped between short panicky breaths. "That's the problem."

Chanel scooted a large cooler out from under the tablecloth of the snack table. She fished out a beer, screwed off the top, and handed it to me.

"This will help," she said as she grabbed me by the arm and pulled me closer to the dance floor. "Now drink up so you can have some fun."

She pulled me to the middle of the floor and shouted, "Hey everyone, this is the birthday girl, Taylor. Now, who wants to dance with her?"

A bunch of the guys in the room cheered.

"Let's get this party started," Chanel said as she turned the volume on the stereo up as high as it could go. She turned to me and pushed the beer bottle up to my face and tipped it forward until I had swallowed the whole thing.

A short but cute Hispanic guy who was standing next to me said, "I'll get you another." He rushed away and back to me in a matter of seconds with two fresh beers in my hand. He introduced himself as Mateo and asked if we could dance together. The beer must have started working as I didn't hesitate to start dancing with him.

As the songs continued to play we danced and drank until the colors and the lights began to swirl. I was starting to feel nauseous and was going to tell this guy I wanted to sit down when another guy, about fifty pounds heavier and a foot taller approached Mateo and yelled over the music, "You've been hogging this blonde bitch all night. Enough is enough."

The bigger man pushed Mateo to the side and tried to grab me by the wrist. I maneuvered myself away from him. Before he could continue to pursue me, Mateo, who had been hit with a case of false courage from all the beer, punched the bigger man in the face. In return, the big man punched Mateo. Suddenly swarms of other guys jumped in. Some defended Mateo while others fought alongside the bigger man. Most of them just started punching each other for no damn reason.

The sight of the fight scared me enough to sober me up. I rushed towards the exit with tears running down my face. I was about to turn the corner to leave the gymnasium and escape down the corridor when I slammed myself against the muscular chest of a man.

"Sorry," I said as I wiped tears from my eyes.

I was about to brush past him and continue on my way home when he said, "Hey girl, what's wrong? You okay?"

His voice was so deep that it was almost startling but at the same time was strangely comforting to me.

"There are a bunch of guys fighting in there and I'm scared," I told him.

He peeked his head around the doorframe. "Oh shit, you're right. We better get out of here before the cops show up or worse."

"Worse?" I whispered.

"A lot of those guys in there have beef with each other. I'm surprised a fight didn't start sooner."

"Shit." I was starting to feel even sicker with worry than I felt before the party began. I took a few steps down the corridor until the man caught up with me.

"You should come with me. I'll keep you safe," he said.

"I don't even know you," I said.

"It's safer with me out here than back in there," he said.

I nodded.

"I know a really nice spot. Just trust me." He took my hand and I smiled.

We rushed out of the building and down several streets, twisting and turning through apartment complexes and disused government buildings. He pulled me through a run-down apartment compound until we were at the back of the building.

At the top of a small hill, there was a playground that looked over a river. Still holding my hand, he guided me to the swing set where we both took a seat on the squeaky metal swings.

"Isn't it beautiful here?" he asked me.

It really was. Since there were almost no lights from this worn-down section of town, we could see all the stars in the night sky, and they reflected in the tiny river that ran past the playground.

"It is. It's so peaceful and quiet." The nervous feeling in my stomach still lingered even though I was in a calmer place.

We sat in silence for a few minutes before he said, "You looked worried."

I laughed and began to slowly rock myself on the swing. "That's because I always am."

"Why? What do you have to worry about?" He leaned in close and looked deep into my eyes.

I couldn't handle his intense stare, so I looked down at my feet instead. "Everything. I'm nervous all the time. Chanel always tries to drag me out of my shell but it doesn't work. I never know what I'm doing or what's happening around me. I never know when my mom is going to scream at me or when some random girls at school are going to beat me up," I flushed a little as I told him this.

"That's how they get you," he said.

"Who?" I asked him.

"Society. The Man. The government. Other people."

I furrowed my brow. "What do you mean?"

"Everyone around us is always telling us what to do. The government says we can't do this and parents say we can't do that and the school system says we have to learn only what they tell us to. So, the more you worry about other people, the more they can control you. What does your mom tell you?" he asked.

"That I'll probably amount to nothing and that I might need to see a shrink because I don't have a lot of friends," I said looking down at the ground, secretly hoping that he didn't agree with my mother's opinion of me.

"Fuck what she thinks! You can be anything you want to be. What does school tell you?" he asked me.

"That I have to be there almost every day until I'm eighteen," I answered

"Fuck them," he said louder, his voice echoing over the abandoned landscape. "You can go where you want and do what you want."

"Really?" I asked.

"Hell yeah," he shouted, almost rising to his feet with excitement. "I found a way to make a shit ton of money. At fifteen, I was able to move out on my own. Haven't needed to rely on my parents or school for anything. I'm a self-made man all because I didn't listen to them or to what the government had to say. People want to feel a certain way and I have the stuff that will do that for them. It ain't nobody's business except mine and my customers. They don't have the right to tell me how I can or can't make my money."

I didn't know how to respond to him. On one hand, I knew being around a drug dealer was bad news but on the other hand, I wanted to believe him. I wanted to have a life outside of the control of others. I wanted to be as free and as brave as he was.

He took notice of my uneasiness and leaned in closer to me. "I realized I'm telling you all this stuff and you don't even know me. I'm Ezekiel Warren-Hernandez but everyone just calls me Zeke."

I smiled. "I'm Taylor Callahan."

"Well, Taylor Callahan, I have to tell you that I think you're beautiful, strong, and fearless. And you shouldn't listen to anyone who tells you differently."

He leaned in and kissed me.

At that moment, I was hooked. My anxiety was cured just by being around him. It felt as if my bones were growing stronger and the ball of tangled nerves that lived inside me straightened itself out. With him by my side, I feared nothing. That is why it was so easy for Zeke to push me to do more and more intense shit. It wasn't just because I wanted to please him, he made me feel invincible enough to get away with anything.

As much of a Grade A asshole Zeke turned out to be, he was right. I was strong and fearless. Even prison couldn't hold me for long. I always slid my way out one way or another. If there is anything I'm good at, it is not getting caught.

CHAPTER 11
TAYLOR CALLAHAN

October 5, 2015
Two Days After The Switch

The next morning at the MacKenzies' I stayed in my pajamas as I watched my new family rush out the door with each one of them giving me looks of pity and random hugs. The house was cleared out by 8 a.m. and it was prime time to do some snooping.

I went into the parents' bedroom at the end of the house. In the middle was a queen-sized bed with two broad built-ins shelves running along its side. Two rifles hung over the bed. I guess I now belong to one of *those* families.

I glanced up and down the shelves until my eyes rested on two white plush-covered books. One read, "Jamie" and the other, "Faith."

Jamie's book was filled with pictures from when she was born through kindergarten.

The first image was of Joan looking sweaty but proud in a hospital gown holding Jamie in a light-yellow blanket while Phil leaned into the picture. Pink puff paints spelled out, "May 27, 1999" underneath the photo. My new birthdate. I definitely should memorize that.

The next few pages were filled with little Jamie being held by various members of the family. Grandma Harrison had big thick bifocals with permed stacks of white hair almost like Marge Simpson. Next to her, Grandpa Harrison wore a green golfing sweater and smiled with no teeth.

A pleasant-looking woman with a kind smile, thick glasses and puffed out 90's blonde hair held baby Jamie next. "Aunt Wendy and Jamie" was written in looping handwriting just below the picture.

Multiple pages in the album were dedicated to photos from summers spent down on the shore. The last photo showed Jamie building a sloppy sandcastle with bright orange and blue buckets. The photo next to it captured Phil burying Jamie's legs in the sand and shaping it into a mermaid tale.

Faith's photo book begins with a three-year-old Jamie holding her new baby sister with the help of her Aunt Wendy. "September 22, 2002" was spelled out in more puff paint. Good to know my sister's birthday too.

I flipped to a new page and saw a photo of the girls with their backs to the camera, staring at a shining black coffin that is in between two large mounds of white lilies. The handwriting below the image said, "Aunt Wendy's Funeral - December 20, 2006." I didn't understand why they put this in a scrapbook. I thought most people only wanted to save happy memories. Whatever their weird reason was I was happy to have educated myself on their family history.

I put the books back and gazed at the other framed photos. In separate photos both Joan and Phil appear in Army uniforms with the American flags at their back. I bet that's how they met. There was nothing new for me to discover in the other rooms of the house. I went outside to see the rolling hill of a backyard.

The grass was freshly cut by Phil during chore day. In the back stood a thick plastic shed that was poorly fabricated to look like wood.

Without thinking, I rushed out of the house and went over to it.

Inside, I found normal gardening supplies: a lawnmower, a weed whacker, a rake, and a shovel. Out of the piles of gardening junk, a large dog cage stood out. It looked big enough to house a German Shepard. I haven't seen any dogs since I've been here. I didn't even see a dog dish or a chew toy. Even if their dog had died, there were no photos of a dog anywhere and Joan was not the type of person to skimp on photos.

I moved closer. Next to it, there was a black trash bag. I opened it up and found a pair of handcuffs, rope, ratty towels, and a bottle containing a clear liquid with the label torn off.

Please let it be vodka.

I took the cap off and sniffed it. It smelled dense and sweet like wine. I took another whiff, and everything went dark.

•   •   •

I woke up on the ground with my feet toppled over the lawnmower. My neck ached, and dirt was pressed into my face. *How long was I out?*

The sun was now higher in the sky, and it was a few degrees warmer. I dragged myself to my feet, closed the doors to the shed and hustled back to the house.

The clock on the stove read 10:05. I had been unconscious for almost an hour and a half.

My mind fogged up with a million questions: Why did these people have this stuff? What are they going to do with it? And are they going to hurt me?

No, they aren't going to hurt me, I told myself. *I'm their "daughter" and as long as I keep it that way, I'll be fine. That's right, I'll be fine.*

I spent the next hour eating cinnamon sugar cereal and pacing around the house trying to shake what happened in the shed from my mind.

Pacing is the only thing that calms me down in situations like this. When Drew left, when my mother almost got arrested for food stamp fraud, when Ivan's dad threatened to shoot our landlord, and when I was about to be released, I remember pacing back and forth across the room or as far as I could pace in my cell.

The only thing that will ensure my survival is if I can play a convincing Jamie right now. I won't have to be like her forever. As the years go by, they will forget more and more about how the real Jamie acted and the two of us can morph into one person and no one will know that this "Tamie" or "Jaylor" — no, I don't like that one — this Tamie is not how the old Jamie would have been.

For example, what if in a year, I stop saying "like" every two seconds, then in a year later I can "suddenly" get really into classic rock and Tarantino movies. I'll say that I'm maturing, that I'm really finding myself. And if I can get into college and leave them behind, I can be anyone I wanted to be — anyone except Taylor Callahan.

This could be easier than I expected. All I had to do was make sure I was playing the part right. That's when I remembered the diary. I rushed to the bedroom and pulled out the fuzzy notebook from the bed and flipped to entries from this past week.

9/28

Mr. Reynolds is the worst. He thinks that everybody should be so fascinated by History when really it's lame and boring. He gave me a C because I couldn't remember the dates to all this crap that happened in the Civil War. I don't care when and where these battles took place, it's sad and boring all at once. Can't we just move on? Then Michelle wanted to copy my homework for Algebra, but I worked really hard on it. It took me like three hours on Sunday and I finally figured it out. I let her look at it anyway even though I was so pissed she even asked. She should do it herself.

And Brandon keeps putting pressure on me. He thinks because we've been dating since The Valentine's Dance that we should be going all the way by now. I told him I'm saving myself for God and he just laughed at me and said 'we'll see'. I don't know if I should still be seeing him if he's like that but he is so cute and everyone likes me more now that we're together and I don't know what people will think if I break up with him especially for that reason. Courtney, Michelle, and Ali told me to just do it already. I'm not sure what to do.

9/29

OMG While we were doing the pyramid, Michelle fell on me and farted. It was so gross and so embarrassing for both of us. I feel so gross having her fart on me. But other than that, I think we are getting a hold of the routine.

Bombed another one of Mr. Reynold's History quizzes, and almost cried when I got the grade back. I don't get it. I aced the pop-quiz in Algebra yesterday and Mrs. Romano loved my short essay. Why can't I get History?

Great, now I have to learn all this class bullshit, too. I guess this is the life I signed up for. A pink backpack came into my side vision and I rushed over to it. Unzipping the compartments I found comp notebooks, an Algebra book, and a History book. One of the notebooks has her schedule written on it. I knew the only way I would continue to keep up this act and graduate with that diploma I wanted so badly was to get up to speed on Jamie's homework. But first, I need to know more about her. I skipped further back to catch up on Jamie's summer.

6/15

I'm so excited school lets out in a week! Courtney keeps making fun of me for being a camp counselor at my church's Bible Camp. She says I should come visit her at her parents' summer house in Florida, they'll buy us booze and we can walk on the beach and meet cute guys. I told her I couldn't go. My parents wouldn't let me. I couldn't tell her that I would have much more fun at Bible camp. I loved teaching the little kids how to make friendship bracelets and singing songs around the campfire as we roasted marshmallows. I'm really looking forward to it but I don't know if that's lame or not. Does that mean I'm doing Jesus's work or am I being immature by wanting to go? I don't know. This whole thing is confusing.

She continued in several other entries to talk in detail about what she did that day at camp and how Courtney and Ali keep putting pressure on her to "grow-up". In between entries I find another poem.

It's You, Oh Lord, that fills my spirit with righteous rage. The weak and the sinful will tremble before me as I bring forth Your Will. I shall honor my family and secure their place in Your Heaven. Fill me with Your Spirit and I shall obey whatever You command.

The creepiness of these poems seemed a little out of place — okay, a lot out of place. Sure, this family was religious, their church is a little too serious for me, but they aren't that different from any other Christian family. They didn't spend all their time praying or talking about the Rapture. I haven't even seen a Bible or a cross save for one picture of Jesus in the dining room.

I told myself that everything was fine as I got out her books and notes, preparing myself for a serious study session.

CHAPTER 12
TAYLOR CALLAHAN

October 6, 2015
Three Days After The Switch
I walked to the front entrance of Southfield High School. The building was tall and made of concrete brick. It loomed over me casting a heavy shadow across most of the parking lot.

As I made my way towards the forest green front doors, I felt a little nauseous like the world around me was expanding and contracting at the same time. Just as I was about to turn around and run back to the car, I heard someone call "Jamie!"

A set of twins rushed up to the side of me. They're Asian with straight black hair down to their waist.

"Jamie, I'm so sorry," one of them squeaked and threw a big hug around me.

I hugged her back.

The other twin joined in making it an awkward three-way love fest.

They pulled away and smiled. The second one said, "If you need anything let us know. I'm sure you're missing Ali and Courtney a lot."

I nodded, "Yeah, it's like, the worst thing that could have, like, happened to them."

The girls put a sympathetic palm on my shoulder.

"Well, I'll see you in Art class," said the first one and they half-hopped away.

They didn't suspect a thing. Good.

I needed to find my homeroom. Thankfully Jamie detailed her schedule inside her comp books, so I knew I had to get to room 205 by

8:15 a.m but I couldn't ask for directions or look at the map of the school in the foyer as if I didn't go here.

I made my way down the halls and passed room 102, 104, 106, and 110 but the hallway came to an end at an emergency exit door. Next to it was a staircase full of kids rushing up the steps. I figured 205 had to be on top of 105 so I followed the stream of kids upstairs. I walked in the room and two girls, one was a white girl with a frizzy brown 'fro and the other a black girl with a business-woman's bob waved at me and pointed at a seat behind them that was empty. I scuttled my way into the one-sided school desk and whispered a happy-to-see-you-but-I'm-still-in-mourning, "Hi".

"Oh my God, Jamie, you look terrible," said the white girl.

Shit, maybe she can tell.

"Geni, leave her alone, you know what happened. Wouldn't you be sad looking if I died?" the black girl said.

"I can't believe you're back at school so fast. I don't think I would ever come back," said Geni. She had an over-the-top sad look on her face, like she was in a play about someone's friend dying, not actually living it.

I explained to them, "I don't think they would want me to stop, like, living or anything. I think they, like, would say, you know: *Go on without me, you only live once.* That's like how they would want it."

"YOLO!" both girls shouted, dropping their grieving facade for a moment. I had forgotten how loud high school girls can be.

The teacher walked in and told everyone to "settle down."

Geni turned back to me and whispered, "We're studying after school at Shawna's house, if you want to come."

"My parents would love to see you," the black girl who I assumed was Shawna added.

I whispered, "No thanks. I'm not feeling up to it."

The bell rang, and the principal read the morning announcements in between bits of static on the loudspeaker. After he announced the victory of the wrestling team and today's lunch of cheese pizza and carrots, he said, "Once again, anyone affected by the recent loss of two of our students, can go to the safe space in the counseling center."

Everyone including the teacher stared at me.

"Jamie, do you need to?" whispered Geni.

I replied, "I'm fine right now, maybe later."

I found myself in a note-taking frenzy in my next two classes. My hand ached from scribbling about how DNA reproduces and why Jane Austen was a literary renegade for her time.

At first, taking notes would keep people from looking at me directly in the face, it only took one person to say something for this whole thing to unravel but no one noticed a thing. I got a few pitiful looks from the teachers as I entered their class and some random hugs from girls I was supposed to know. After a while, I was actually enjoying learning, which was unusual for me. I never had more than a C average when I was in high school the first time and never cared. I couldn't believe I was starting to like it here.

CHAPTER 13
TAYLOR CALLAHAN

October 6, 2015
Three Days After The Switch
The bell blared its now-familiar screech across the campus, it was time for lunch. After a woman with peach fuzz slapped a previously frozen piece of pizza and scoop of soggy carrots on my tray, I turned to face the socially-complicated jungle that is the cafeteria.

Just the smell of this place made me feel sick. The scent of canned marinara and processed cheese that mixed with bleach-laced vapors was unholy yet awfully familiar. I remember sitting at a round table in the corner of my high school's cafeteria with Chanel and her friends making stupid jokes about partying as I pretended to know what they were taking about.

Now, I was in high school again but this time, I was going to be at the cheerleading table in the center of the cafeteria where Geni, Shawna, and a few other girls waved me over.

As I sat down each one of the girls took turns running up to me and squeezed me with hugs. They mostly wore yoga pants with the waists rolled down and loose tank tops flowing over their bird-boned torsos. Their long hair got in my mouth as they embraced me. They all talked over each other, a few of them were crying with mascara and glitter eyeliner running down their cheeks.

One girl with a bright pink shirt that read "Namaste in Bed" asked, "Why didn't you tell us you were going home?"

Another said, "We thought you were with them, that you were missing too. You scared us."

"Sorry guys," I replied. "I just had a bad feeling when we left, and Courtney wouldn't take me home, so I got out of the car and hitched a ride home."

"Jamie," said the Namaste girl, "that's so unlike you."

"I know, I just had to get out of there, I knew something was wrong and they wouldn't listen to me." I looked down at my lap and slowly bit my tongue until tears pooled in the corners of my eyes.

A few other girls at the table start to cry. "I'm gonna miss them so much," the Namaste girl muttered in between sobs.

"I'm so sad that cheer practice and the game are cancelled this week. I don't think Ali and Courtney would have wanted it that way," one girl moaned as she dapped her eyes with a tissue.

"Oh, hush Michelle," said Shawna, "you only want to get back to practice so you can try to sweeten up Coach Andrea for Courtney's spot on the top of the pyramid."

"Well, it's important," said Michelle, flipping back her long brown-gold ombre hair.

The rest of the girls continued to bicker over who should take Courtney and Ali's old positions on the cheer squad. I tuned them out as I slowly made my way through my soggy pizza and carrot smush.

The bell rang again, and we scattered in different directions. In the hall, I passed a boy with brown hair that was styled into a pointed wave like a cockatoo. He had hollow gray eyes that made my stomach hurt when he looked at me. My gut told me he was a threat.

"So, you're gonna just walk past me, is that where we are now?" he asked.

I turned around, mentally kicking myself for forgetting to look up Brandon on the internet.

"Sorry, I'm just in a bad place right now," I told him.

His face turned red and the veins in his neck looked like they might bust, "Look, I know your friends are dead and everything. And I know I should have checked in with you yesterday but, like, coach is riding us real hard and my dad is up my ass about my grades so I, like, don't have time to be the *perfect boyfriend* right now but you shouldn't just ignore me like that."

I calmly said, "I'm sorry, I'm just kinda in a fog. I don't know how to feel right now."

"Whatever," he huffed and walked away.

I didn't have time to think about some teenage relationship fight. I had to get to History class, the class Jamie was on the brink of failing and since she was on the brink of failing that means so was I.

I rushed upstairs to room 213. I was two minutes early, but the room was already filled with other students. I took a seat in the front row and I got out my textbook, opened it to the page that the syllabus told us we would be studying and placed my notebook on top of it.

Mr. Reynolds sat at his desk, glancing over something at his computer. He had red hair that was fading into a light horseshoe pattern on top of his balding head. He had thick black glasses and a Satan-looking goatee.

He darted a look at me. "Jamie? In the front row today? Don't you want your usual spot in the back corner?"

I didn't know she had a "usual spot." I hate how high schoolers are so territorial about their seats. I simply shook my head no.

"And you actually came to class prepared?" He stood up from his desk and walked over to me.

My mouth felt frozen. I knew if I spoke, I might give myself away.

"What is causing this sudden change of heart? Are you suddenly going to play *the good student* after what you did last class?"

Shit, what did Jamie do last class that is fucking me over right now?

Mr. Reynolds stood over my desk and glared down at me. I could see his eyes scanning my face like a laser. He contorted his mouth and several creases in his brow appeared.

I knew he was noticing something about me.

"What's different about you?" he asked.

My heart pounded, and my mouth gaped open. I had no idea what to say. Seconds passed, and I couldn't come up with a single word to say.

"Cat got your tongue?" he asked me.

A voice erupted from the back. "Her best friends were shot, that's what happened."

"Oh, I'm so sorry, Jamie. I didn't know you were close with those girls." His face flushes with embarrassment as he steps away from me.

My eyes began to tear up.

He hunched over to get closer to me. "Listen, I didn't mean anything by it. Do you want to go to the counseling center?"

I whimpered a "yes," and shoved my things into my bag and took off.

I didn't know which way I was supposed to be going but I marched down the hall like I had been there a hundred times before.

Everything looked the same: long white-brick corridors with a dozen of forest green doorways leading to God knows where. My feet hurt from walking, but it seemed like I hadn't even gone anywhere and was just walking in circles.

The bland off-white color of the building materials looked familiar. Where did I see them before? That's when I remembered, these bricks were the same material used to form the inside of my prison cell.

I felt a sudden swelling of fear as if someone turned on a tap inside me and I was filling up like a bathtub, getting heavier and heavier.

The smell of bleach and the dining hall slop were rising out of the walls. The metallic echoing clank of a cell closing rang out in the hall. *Did I actually hear it or was it just in my head?*

Expecting to see a police officer ready to arrest me and send me back to prison, I almost collapsed with fear and landed on the floor.

I wasn't faking it now. I really was crying.

CHAPTER 14
TAYLOR CALLAHAN

October 6, 2015

Three Days After The Switch

Light footsteps tapped against the linoleum floor, followed by a voice exclaiming, "Oh my goodness, dear, are you alright?"

An older woman with bushy brown hair and a pair of pointed red glasses attached to a beaded chain around her neck.

Swallowing hard, I remembered I needed to stay in character. "Ali and Courtney, they are really dead," I uttered at her between broken sobs.

She put a hand to her cheek. "I'm so sorry, dear, it is such a tragedy. Were they friends of yours?"

"Yes, best friends," I told her.

She bent over and put her hands on her knees as if she was talking to a kindergartener and said, "Now, why don't you come to the safe space? Let me take you there."

I didn't protest. I followed the lady towards the front entrance of the school and turned into the administrative offices.

In the back, they transformed a conference room into a "safe space" with crayons, coloring books, and lined paper I assume is supposed to be used for writing about my feelings. Chairs had been pulled out and the coloring materials were in slight disarray. Other kids had been here earlier but none were there now.

The woman with the glasses let me in and asked if I wanted to see a counselor. I told her, "I will when I've calmed down."

Alone in the safe space, I wiped down my face with tissues only to rub my fake mole off. Crap.

I rubbed down my cheek until it was completely clean of any left-over make-up knowing it's important to start with a clean slate. I rifled through my things before I found my eyebrow liner hidden among my pencils. But I didn't have a mirror. I combed through the backpack two more times and no compact. The walls in the safe space were bare. I couldn't sneak out to the bathroom without someone seeing me.

Then I noticed that one wall in the conference room was made up of windows hiding behind dust-covered blinds.

At one corner of the room, I pushed the blinds to the side and caught my reflection in the window long enough to redraw the birthmark perfectly. Just as I clipped the little lid down on the eyeliner, the door to the room opened.

In the doorway, a thin woman in her thirties wearing a pristine black pencil skirt and jacket appeared. "Hi Jamie, I'm Ms. Solberg. Brenda mentioned you might need a counselor."

"I'm not really sure," I said.

"That's okay. How about we go into my office for a little talk? And don't worry about your make-up, hon. You look fine." She motioned at me to follow her.

I smiled and shoved the eyeliner into my back pocket.

I followed her into her office, thanking God or my lucky stars or whatever I believe in, that she didn't come in the room thirty seconds earlier.

I sat down opposite of her desk. The room was painted a buttery yellow and both her walls and her desk are filled with pictures of her two beagles frolicking through various fields.

"Now I hear that you, Ali and Courtney are, um, were very close," she began.

"Yeah, we were best friends and we did, like, everything together. Which is why I feel bad about what happened." I let out a sniffle.

"Why do you feel bad about that?" Ms. Solberg leaned in closer.

"I should have stopped them from going. They wanted me to come with them and I almost did, but I chickened out and didn't go," I told her.

"Why did you *chicken* out?" She rested her head on her hand.

I continued, "I just had this really bad feeling in my gut like I knew something bad was going to happen. I told them that, but they thought I was just being lame."

"Listening to your gut is not chickening out. You did the right thing." She sat back in her chair, proud of herself for giving this fragile teen girl some good advice.

"I know but I feel like I didn't try hard enough to get them to stay behind with me," I said.

"Do you really think anything would have gotten them to change their minds?" she asked.

I shook my head no.

"Then, don't blame yourself for what happened. I know that it's hard, very hard, to lose a friend, let alone two like that. But I want you to understand that the grieving process can take a long time and that you might feel a whole range of emotions: sadness, guilt, anger, denial. Let yourself feel those things and try to work through them," she said, softening her voice to what was supposed to be a soothing whisper.

"I feel like I'll never get away from the guilt," I said.

"I know that right now all of this seems daunting and the idea of ever feeling better seems like a million miles away, but you will feel better. I'm surprised you made it to school today, it must have been rough coming back here seeing all the places you used to be with Ali and Courtney."

"It's not the memories that upset me today, it was Mr. Reynolds." I figured I'd throw the bastard under the bus. He pissed Jamie off. Now, both Jamies.

A deep wrinkle appeared in her brow. "Mr. Reynolds?"

"Yeah, I'm supposed to be in his class right now. Let's just say I'm not his favorite student and he got all weird at me for not sitting in my normal seat and he kept asking me over and over, "What's wrong with you? What's different? Why are you acting so strange?" He was leaning over my desk and staring right at me. I was so scared and upset all I could do was cry. It was only when another kid in class told him about me being friends with Ali and Courtney that he backed off."

Ms. Solberg's face went flush. "I'm sorry you had to go through that, Jamie. In my opinion, his behavior was inappropriate. Given the recent incidents he should be sensitive to his students." Her knuckles turned red as she gripped her pen to make a note of my comment.

"I don't want him to get in trouble," I lied.

"That's not for you to worry about, Jamie. It won't reflect on you. Do you think you might want to stay home again tomorrow?"

My mind was flooded with images of the shed, the weird smelling liquid, and my face smashed in the grass.

"No thanks, I like being here. It feels normal," I said.

"Ah, I understand," she smiled.

We both smiled at each other for a moment, not knowing what else to say to one another.

"Would you like to go back to the safe space or are you able to get to class?" she asked.

I looked at the clock, almost time for Art.

I nodded, "I think I can make it through my next class."

"Good." Ms. Solberg stood up as I exited the room.

•   •   •

In the art room, the teacher told us to take the half-finished watercolors we were working on off the drying racks at the back of the room. I had no idea what Jamie would have been painting so I fiddled with my backpack until everyone else in the class had their painting.

I picked up the only painting left and set it down in front of me. On the thick, bumpy watercolor paper lay a forest scene that was only halfway colored in. A clearing laid out before the forest in almost a perfect semi-circle of brown grass. Two large bare trees stood close-up on the far left and right sides, only the left one had been painted-in yet. In the back, there was a small hill covered with pine trees that spilled down the hill and ended at the clearing with the two large trees.

I picked a deep chestnut paint color with my brush and mimicked the way Jamie had filled in the first big tree. I don't have the best artistic skills, so I made myself work slowly. By the time the hour and fifteen-minute class was over, I only finished one tree and a little bit of the grass.

The teacher who had her long blond-slowly-turning-gray hair tied up in a bun came by and lightly stroked my back. "Oh Jamie, I'm so sorry to hear what happened."

I gave her a mournful look and said, "Yeah, I'm not feeling too great."

"That's okay, sweetie. Take as long as you need to finish it. I'll extend the due date for you."

I smiled and thanked her.

As I placed the painting back on the drying rack, a bit of light reflected off something in the background. In the forest part of the painting, where Jamie had already painted over her original sketch, I made out the shiny pencil outline of a man in between two trees. It looked like Jamie painted over him instead of erasing him. Regardless, it gave me the creeps and made my body feel cold. I wondered who he could be.

As the final bell rang, I walked out of the school and rushed to get in Jamie's car. In the sanctuary of the little Hyundai, I felt a weight lift off my shoulders. The hardest part was done. The first day passed and no one noticed I was not Jamie. Mr. Reynolds was the only one who seemed to know something wasn't quite right about me. But I won't have to worry about him. I bet that Ms. Solberg is going to make him feel like shit for talking to a grieving student that way.

CHAPTER 15
TAYLOR CALLAHAN

October 6, 2015
Three Days After The Switch

I pulled out a chair from the oak dining room table. The wooden legs squeaked as I dragged it across the floor.

Phil came in, stroked the back of my head and said, "Hey kiddo, feeling okay?"

"It still, like, doesn't feel real to me. I still expect to see them again soon," I replied.

His face saddened, and he said, "I know what you mean, honey."

"I hope this will make you feel better," Joan exclaimed from the doorway. She held a red ceramic casserole dish in her hands. The smell hits me right away.

"I made your favorite: tuna casserole." She grinned at me and placed the congealing fish dish right in front of my face. I almost threw up at that moment.

I hate fish, especially tuna. It's the worst food on the planet. But it was just my luck that I'd have to pretend to love that shit for the rest of my life.

I mustered all my strength and said, "Yay! Thanks, Mom."

She scooped three big globs onto my plate before she called Faith to come to the table.

As she slopped the casserole onto Faith's plate she said, "Phil, honey, why don't you lead the prayer tonight?"

"Sure, sweetie," he replied as he clasped his hands and bowed his hands over his plate.

I imitated him which caused the tuna smell to waft farther up my nose.

"Dear Lord," he began, "thank you for the bounty that you have provided us with at this table. Thank you for my wife and two loving daughters. Dear Lord, we understand that it was your plan to call away two young lives this past week. Though we are saddened by their passing, we pray that they live forever with you in your Glory in the Kingdom of Heaven. And those that are responsible for the brutal slaughtering of such young souls face the harshest punishment that you see fit. In your name, we pray. Amen."

Taking a tiny portion of the casserole with my fork, I forced the gray-white mixture of fish, noodles, and what I hope were peas into my mouth. *Disgusting.*

I choked down three more spoonfuls of the stuff before I felt Jamie's phone vibrate in my pocket. It was a text from that douchebag Brandon. "Hey babe. Sorry about today, I was just real upset. Have lunch with me tomorrow. K?"

I had enough crap on my plate, literally and figuratively, without some moody boyfriend hanging around. I'd have to break it off tomorrow.

"Yeah, sure." I texted back knowing teenage girls are always super vague right before they're about to break up with someone.

I took another bite of the casserole, this time the taste caused tears to arise.

"Jamie, no phones at the table," said Joan as I ducked the phone back into my pocket.

She noticed my tears and asked, "Oh honey, are you crying? Is it about Courtney and Ali?"

I sniffled and nodded while pouting my lower lip.

"Sweetie, I'm sorry. This must be so hard on you."

Faith got up from her chair and threw her arms around me, something I still wasn't used to.

"I hate to see my girl like this," said Phil, "I hope they find the bastard that did this and string him up."

Joan laughed. "Sadly, no one gets strung up anymore. These thugs just rot in prison eating away at our tax dollars. It's not real justice if you ask me."

Faith let out a heavy sigh. "Not this again. I don't think Jamie wants to hear this right now."

Joan nodded. "You're right. All Jamie needs to focus on is moving on, one day at a time."

CHAPTER 16
TAYLOR CALLAHAN

October 7, 2015
Four Days After The Switch

I walked into the school's front doors again, this time I felt like the weight of the world had been lifted off me. At this point, I've passed for Jamie with every single person who has ever known her. Well, almost everyone. I still haven't had a real conversation with this so-called boyfriend, Brandon, and I didn't want to.

I was able to fly under the radar for the first three periods of the day but just as I'm about to turn the corner towards the cafeteria, Brandon came down the hall and spotted me. He wrapped his arm around me and smiled. "Hey babe, I thought I'd find you here. I have an idea. Let's have lunch alone."

"Alone? Where?" I asked, hoping the chaos and chatter of the cafeteria wouldn't allow him to really pay attention to me.

"Shop class is empty, and Mr. Griswold is cool with me chillin' in there sometimes," he shrugged.

"Shop class, really? It's, like, all dusty in there," I said scrunching my nose.

He rolled his eyes. "Oh, come on, I'm trying to be romantic here."

I sucked in my breath and agreed.

I soon discovered that the shop class is not in one of the many classrooms of Southfield High but in a large shed outside behind the school.

Brandon set down our lunches after clearing off a workbench. I took big heaping bites of my peanut butter and jelly sandwich to prevent me from talking to him and to get this lunch over with as soon as possible.

When we finished eating, he turned to me, ran his hands up my legs and said, "Listen, I know you've been going through a lot right now and I want you to know that I'm here for you 100 percent if you'll be here for me, too."

He slammed his chest up against mine and kissed me. My head hurt from the smell of his potent body spray.

I pried him off me. "Listen, Brandon, I've been thinking, and I don't think this is working anymore."

His face flashed red. "What do you mean?"

"I've been through a lot with Ali and Courtney, and I don't think I can be anyone's girlfriend right now," I replied.

He bottled up his fist and slammed it down on the bench. "You know this is fucking bullshit."

"Look, I'm sorry but I just can't do this anymore." I did a quick scan of the room in case I needed something to defend myself.

He stood up and tossed the stool he was sitting on to the ground. It kicked up a bunch of saw dust when it hit the floor.

"You made a promise to me and I think you should keep that promise."

"What promise?"

"Don't play dumb with me. You said when you were ready, we would finally do it and it looks like I've been waiting around for nothing. I don't even care if you're *ready* or whatever, you kept me waiting around, leading me on and you should have to keep your promises. And knowing what a timid little church mouse you are, I doubt you'll stop me."

He grabbed me and kissed me again but this time it was vicious with the whole of his mouth pushing against mine, making my neck hurt. He then ran his hands all over my body, feeling for the zipper on my fly and pushing it down. He was about to force his hands into my pants when I hit him with a knee to the groin.

He fell to his knees, both hands clutching his nuts. He got to his feet using a table leg as leverage.

"You little bitch." He came rushing towards me with both fists clenched. As he was about to bring a punch down on to my head, I blocked it with my left arm and threw a punch into his gut.

Before the douchebag had a chance to retaliate, I swiped a circular saw from another work bench.

I grabbed him by the neck and held the saw to his face. I flicked a switch and the saw buzzed to life.

"If you ever touch me again, or even talk to me again I will not hesitate to cut you up like a piece of beef, do you understand me?"

He nodded frantically trying to distance his face from the blade.

I pushed the blade an inch closer. "You sure?"

"I'll stay away for good," he whimpered.

I let go of my hold and yelled, "Then, get out of here before I change my mind."

Brandon burst out the door muttering "psycho bitch" under his breath.

I turned off the whirring of the saw and sat in silence for a second. Being "the good girl" was starting to be too much work.

CHAPTER 17
TAYLOR CALLAHAN

October 8, 2015
Five Days After The Switch
It had been almost a week since I became Jamie MacKenzie and I was dying for a smoke. Jamie didn't smoke so therefore I couldn't either. That totally sucked. The girl was willing to go buy drugs from a stranger but no cigarettes because they're too dangerous.

I was out in the school parking lot in her car. It was a rainy morning and there was fog covering the tops of trees and obscuring people's faces in the distance. I didn't want to run into that asshole Brandon again. I might have scared him off, but I didn't know if he would try to pull something one me. I didn't want him showing up with his daddy's gun seeking revenge like some Columbine loser.

I watched as kids parked their cars and strolled into school. Some of them have their heads down and seem to be beaten down by the day that hasn't even started. Others walked in clumped little groups, laughing at God knows what.

I stared at the digital clock in the Hyundai. Four minutes until class starts but I couldn't find motivation to move from the car.

I buried my head in my hands. *I can do this,* I thought. Everyone believed me so far. But I felt that at any minute, someone would materialize before me and call me out for being the imposter that I was.

Tap. Tap. Tap. I almost jumped out of my seat. There was a man knocking his bulky walkie talkie against my window. He was an old black man with a stern face with many sags and deep wrinkles like a bulldog.

I rolled down the window. "Yes?"

"Miss MacKenzie, what do you think you're doing?" he asked me.

What could I possibly be in trouble for?

I shrugged. "Um, I was just about to go to class."

"Yes, I got that," the man took a deep breath. "Why are you parked in a teacher's spot?"

I leaned forward and saw "RESERVED" spray painted in all capital red letters on the parking block in front of me. *Shit.*

"Oh sorry, I didn't notice."

"You've been going here for almost three years and you're telling me you just *forgot* where the teachers park? Don't you remember the assembly where I told all you kids not to park here or you'll get a ticket?"

"It must have, like, slipped my mind," I told him with a shy smile.

The man took out a tiny notepad from his back pocket and scribbled something on it. "One afternoon detention."

"Are you serious?" I took the piece of paper in my hand and stared at it.

"Rules are rules, Miss MacKenzie." He leaned in further, his head passing over the window seal. "Look, I know what happened to your friends and I'm real sorry to hear it but I've been told that I have to issue detention for anyone who parks in a staff member's spot. I wish I could help you out, but I can't."

I nodded. "My parents are gonna, like, kill me or something."

"Sorry about that but I've got Mr. Daniels waiting."

A white station wagon was lingering right behind me.

"Fine, I'll move." I slammed the car into reverse.

"Thank you," he smiled.

I slid into my seat for first period just as the bell rang. Panic was welling up in my gut. That ticket was too obvious. Jamie wouldn't have forgotten where she wasn't allowed to park. That guy was right. How could I have gone there for almost three years and suddenly not know where to park? It was a big red flag flying in the wind and I was afraid everyone would see it.

•   •   •

My fear of being discovered didn't get any better in biology as I sat down next to Shawna and Geni. They both waved at me like it had been years since I saw them.

"Hey, how are you feeling today?" asked Geni with her usual pep.

"A little better but I'm still so sad."

"You still look a little worn down," noted Shawna.

"I'm still really upset," I said but what I wanted to say was "That happens when you're five years older than the age everyone thinks you are."

"Awww," moaned the two girls as they threw their arms around me.

"It'll be okay," said Geni. "I'm just glad both our moms didn't let us come over that night. I can't imagine what it must like to have been there with them just minutes before they —"

The teacher got up from her desk at the side of the room and put her finger to her lips to quiet us down. "As I hope you're aware, we have our midterm exam in two weeks. In preparation for the exam, we will be having a semi-pop quiz tomorrow."

The whole class grimaced.

"Come on people, it's not so bad. We're going to review the topics we learned today. You'll have tonight to study. So, we'll have the quiz tomorrow and Friday, I'll put on a video."

"Yeah!" a few kids in the back called out.

"Okay class, let's get right to it. What is the difference between DNA and RNA?"

I forced myself to listen and take notes through all I really wanted to think about was how Joan and Phil were going to react to the detention. But it would be an even bigger red flag if Jamie failed a quiz on a subject she normally does well in.

By the time the bell rang for the next class, my hands ached from writing so many notes. I filled up eight whole pages of notebook paper. As I packed my stuff, Shawna looked at all I had written. "Geez, Jamie, why did you take so many notes? Don't you have them from earlier this year?"

I did have Jamie's old notes, but I just wouldn't remember them the same way if I hadn't written them down myself.

"I'm just worried I'll, like, fail or something," I told her.

"When have you ever failed?" laughed Geni.

"Once, I think," I said, making it up.

"Okay, overachiever. Don't make us all look bad," said Shawna with a laugh.

I walked out of there feeling annoyed. It was as if nothing I did was right. If I took good notes to ace the quiz like Jamie would, it was suspicious. If I didn't take notes and failed the quiz then that would be suspicious, too. But I figured it would be worse to be busted by her parents than by these two idiots so, out of the watching gaze of Geni and Shawna, I studied like a champ in my next two classes.

Unfortunately, I couldn't avoid them all day as birds of a feather must have lunch together.

It was insane how attached these girls were to each other. Just after I sat down with my tray of cafeteria slop, one girl announced she had to go to the bathroom and as if she snapped her fingers, two other girls instantly got up from their seats and left their lunches to escort her to the bathroom.

One of them turned around and smiled at me. She had big teeth that were chained together by braces decorated with pink bands. She tossed her straight-iron damaged blonde hair back and asked me, "Jamie, do you have to go?"

She wanted me to travel in their pack with them.

"No, I'm good. Thanks." I threw a cheesy smile at her. In reality, it didn't matter if I wanted to use the bathroom or not, I didn't want to be alone with those girls for fear they might realize I don't know anything about them, not even their names.

"Oh, okay." She smirked at me then ran away to catch up with the other two girls.

Michelle sat down at the table next to Geni and Shawna. "So, I've talked to Ms. Solberg from the counseling office, and she is helping me put together a candlelight vigil for Ali and Courtney."

"Oh my God, Michelle, that's so sweet of you," cooed Geni.

Then everyone at the table looked at me.

"Jamie, what do you think?"

As the best friend of the dead girls, it was clear that they were treating me like next of kin and wanted me to approve of everything they did regarding Ali and Courtney. Truthfully, I think vigils are stupid. Candles and nice words aren't going to bring anyone back, but I knew I couldn't say that. The real Jamie probably would have loved that sort of thing.

In a peppy tone, I forced out, "It seems like a great idea. I'm sure they would love it. When is it?"

"Sunday night at the United Methodist Church. Ali, Courtney, and I go there. But you should say something. Pick out one of your favorite passages, like the ones you sometimes read before cheer practice."

"That's a great idea. There are just too many to choose from. I feel like nothing I say will be enough," I said, hoping to get out of it.

"Of course, it will." Geni reached across the table and stroked my hand. "You know how much that would mean to their families."

I nodded.

"We are going to my house after school to make the flyers and print them out. Can you come?" asked Michelle.

"Yeah I think so. What time?"

"Around five. I have a student council meeting tonight, so I can't make it home until after that," Michelle answered.

"Perfect," I told her.

"Wait," said Shawna, "how are we going to print hundreds of copies of flyers from your house? That'll take forever."

Michelle replied, "No, it won't. My dad's an accountant and works from home. He told me we can use his office printer."

"Then we're all set," said Shawna.

As painful as hanging out with these girls after school would be, it was the perfect excuse that would keep me from telling Joan and Phil about detention.

I pulled out my phone and texted, "Hey mom, I'm gonna go over to Michelle's house after school to make flyers. There's gonna be a vigil for Ali and Courtney and I promised I'd help. Is that okay?" I added a few cute emojis to soften her up.

This would explain me not coming straight home from school as I could go to detention for an hour then head over to Michelle's without the parents knowing anything about it. My red flag waving in the wind wouldn't be so big after all.

• • •

I finished the school day and pushed my way like a salmon swimming upstream down the hall as every other student in the school was walking the other way to exit the building. The place cleared out in a matter of minutes, and I was left alone in a pale-yellow hall lined with rows and rows of dark green lockers.

I had a sick feeling in my gut and my vision blurred for just a moment. The lockers, the smell of bleach from an old janitor in the hallway and the sound of teenagers laughing convinced me for a moment that I was in school again. Not Southfield High, my real high school.

CHAPTER 18
TAYLOR CALLAHAN

February 26, 2010
Five Years, 7 Months, 8 Days Before The Switch
The halls of my real high school were a war zone and the teachers acted like disgruntled prison guards instead of educators. The grounds were bare and often littered with empty Gatorade bottles and Doritos wrappers. We had to file in one by one through metal detectors each day. Inside, staff would regularly crack open lockers to find drugs and weapons inside. Afterwards, my teachers would scream at their whole class for the found contraband even though no one in the room was responsible for bringing it to school. My History teacher got so angry once, he threw a textbook at a student who was friends with the kid who most recently got in trouble.

As each year went by, more and more of the faces I got used to seeing in my classes would vanish. A few girls would get pregnant, a few boys would get suspended or thrown in jail. The kids that stayed became increasingly hostile towards each other like rats that would tear each other apart because they hated their cage.

I was a few inches shorter back then. I wore my hair in two pigtails that draped down the sides of my back and a pair of glasses sat on my nose. With my eyes cast to the ground and my books clutched to my chest, I'd make my way through the school with the anxiety of someone walking through a minefield.

I was one of a few dozen white students at the school and the only one in most of my classes. I knew I didn't fit in. It wasn't just a race thing. I'd see other white girls who were popular. They always knew all the words to the newest rap song, wore the sexiest fashion trends, and weren't afraid to cut class to drink vodka out of water bottles in one of the abandoned buildings in town.

On the other hand, I didn't know anything about the latest music, wore the shabby clothes Nadine bought for me and was too shy to hang out with anybody. Not exactly the makings of a cool kid.

Of course, this made me a target. I avoided going to the bathroom at school because some girls told me on my first day of high school that if they saw me in there again they would kill me. So, I'd have to sneak in once a day to use the toilets inside the women's locker room at lunch because it was the only time it was empty.

But on this one day, I really had to go. It felt like the lining of my bladder would rupture at any second so, raised my hand and the teacher let me go. I darted into the nearest bathroom and to my relief, it was empty.

As I pushed the handle down to flush the toilet, it must have masked the sound of footsteps because when I opened the stall, two girls were staring right at me.

"You know this is our bathroom, right?" asked one girl in a booming voice that echoed in the tiled bathroom. I quickly recognized who they were. Tiffany was one of the cool white girls. She and her best friend, Alyssa were two of the most feared girls at school.

"No," I whispered, knowing it was a lie.

"Speak up, girl, I can't hear you," Tiffany shouted. She wore a cut-off jersey that proudly displayed her toned midriff.

"I didn't know," I insisted.

Alyssa rolled her eyes. "Bullshit. Everybody knows."

"I'm sorry," I told them, putting my hands up to show I wasn't trying to start shit.

Tiffany took a step toward me and said, "Well sorry ain't good enough. If you want to use this bathroom, you're gonna pay for it. How much do you have on you?"

"Nothing," I replied

Alyssa let out a laugh, "Nothing? Your parents let ya starve?"

"No, I make my own lunch." For some reason I pulled my sack lunch out of my bag to show them. I guess I was trying to prove to them I wasn't lying.

"What's in it?" asked Tiffany.

"A ham and cheese sandwich and some goldfish."

"Mmmm, that sure sounds good. Much better than the shit they serve here. Take it, Alyssa," Tiffany commended.

Just as she was about to rip my lunch out of my hand, Chanel came into the bathroom. She was about six feet tall and towered over the three of us.

"What's going on here?" she asked, pointing her nose down at the two girls.

"Mind your business," shouted Alyssa.

"Why don't you leave my girl alone and find something better to do?"

"She's your girl? Yeah right," said Tiffany.

Chanel walked over to me and put her arm around my shoulder.

"Damn straight, me and—" She looked at me and I whispered, "Taylor."

"—me and Taylor go back a-ways. We've been tight since third grade."

"She's a sophomore, you're a junior. How could you have been in the third grade together?" Alyssa folded her arms across her chest.

"She's smart." I chimed in. "She skipped a grade."

Chanel beamed at me.

"She's telling the truth." Chanel laughed. "Now why don't you two get on out of here?"

"This ain't over," huffed Tiffany and they both stormed away.

"Thank you so much," I told Chanel.

"It's nothing," said Chanel as she dug around her backpack and pulled out a deep red lip gloss and gilded it over her lips. "Want some?" she asked, holding out the wand.

I waved the make-up away. "No, I could never pull it off."

"Don't doubt yourself. You know, I bet you'd look real good if you tried a little."

"What do you mean?"

"Let's see here." She pulled the rubber bands off my pig tails. "Now bend over and flip your hair back."

I did as she said, and long dark blonde hair crowned my face.

She pulled the glasses off my face and asked, "Do you really need these?"

I nodded.

"That's too bad. That means we got to up the sexiness somewhere else. Take your backpack off."

I let the bag fall to the floor. She took my t-shirt and twisted it into a knot at the base of my spine and tied it up with one of my hair bands. This tightened the shirt, causing it to cling to my breasts and stomach and it showed a gap of skin and hip bone between my jeans and shirt.

"What are you hiding this body for?" she asked with her voice raised higher. I could tell she was genuinely excited for me.

I shrugged. "I don't know."

"Well, I got to show you off. You should come sit with me at lunch."

"Really?"

"Yeah, of course." She took my hand and we rushed out of the bathroom, down the hall and into the cafeteria.

She dragged me over to the lunch table that was overcrowded with her friends laughing at some joke one of them just told.

"Everyone, this is Taylor," announced Chanel.

One of the guys got up and offered me his seat. I took it and he squished in close next to me.

"You new here?" he asked.

I laughed, "No, I've been here for two years."

"How come I've never seen you?"

"Guess you weren't looking hard enough."

The rest of the group got riled up at that.

From then on, I was one of the group. I went to parties with them, ate lunch with them, and cut class with them. We had each other's backs when other people tried to start fights with us. I miss that feeling, feeling like I belonged.

CHAPTER 19
TAYLOR CALLAHAN

October 8, 2015
Five Days After The Switch
As I sat in a classroom surrounded by other kids in after school detention, I never felt more alone. I was living the life I thought I should have had but it felt like I was suffocating every time I had to hide something about myself. I couldn't let anyone know my true likes and dislikes or tell them crazy stories from my past. I was going to have to spend the rest of my life with people knowing me only as Jamie and never have anyone know me as Taylor again.

For some reason, I had this longing, this burning urge to see someone who knew me as my old self as if my existence as Taylor didn't exist unless there was someone out there who saw me as myself, not as Jamie. I couldn't see Ivan, not yet. I lost touch with Chanel and everyone else I knew was connected to Zeke or Saul. There wasn't anyone left.

The door to the classroom swung open and in walked Derek. The guy who set up the deal between me and Jamie's friends. Relief came over my body. Someone who met me as Taylor Callahan did exist. I wasn't losing my mind because I did exist as Taylor.

I knew I couldn't tell him who I really was. He never saw my face, so he couldn't recognize me. But at least there was someone left from my old life regardless of how shitty that life was.

Mr. Turner, the man who busted me in the parking lot, stared over the classroom of kids as we all sat in silence for about fifteen minutes. We weren't allowed to read, do homework, draw or even move. So, I just watched the secondhand tick around the clock over and over again.

After about twenty painful minutes, Mr. Turner stood up, stretched his arms over his head and yawned. "I'm gonna get something from the vending machine. You all stay in your seats and stay quiet." He left the room with the door open.

As soon as he disappeared from our view, the classroom erupted into a noisy jungle. Boys threw things at each other, jumped over desks, and began yelling swear words at each other. A few other girls pulled out their phones and began texting away with lightning-fast fingers.

Derek hopped two seats over and sat next to me. "Hey, I've been dying to know. Are you mad at me?"

I scrunch my forehead. "Why would I be?"

"Because the whole Courtney and Ali thing. It was kinda my fault," he said.

"How?" I asked.

"I'm the one who set them up with the connection." He looked at me with a facial expression that said "duh?"

I looked away from him. I wasn't in the mood for his attitude.

But he continued anyway. "I thought she was safe. She seemed pretty chill when I met her. I had no idea someone was gonna go after her."

I quickly steered the conversation away from the dealer who was indeed me. "I'm not mad at you. I'm kinda mad at them," I told him.

"How?" He looked at me almost disgusted. I guess that was something Jamie wouldn't say.

I explained, "They're the ones that took the chance. They knew that buying drugs was risky and they did it anyway."

He let out a small laugh, "Yeah, but you seemed all excited about it. Finally, a chance to rebel against your perfect Christian family. But no, you had to chicken out."

I leaned away from him, "Screw you, Derek."

"Relax, I'm only telling the truth." He threw me an annoyed look. I never liked this kid, not as Taylor, not as Jamie.

"No, I was smart. I decided one party wasn't worth messing things up for me."

Derek shrugged. "Look, I just wanted to say I'm sorry for what happened, okay?"

"You're forgiven," I said.

"Good." He hopped back to his original seat just as Mr. Turner strode back into the room with a KitKat in hand.

CHAPTER 20
TAYLOR CALLAHAN

October 8, 2015
Five Days After The Switch
Out of detention, I walked as fast as I could to my car. I was just about to leave the parking lot when I realized I had no idea where Michelle lived.

Shit. Shit. Shit. This is something Jamie would know. There was no way I could ask for directions without giving myself up.

I pulled Jamie's phone out and scrolled through Jamie's contacts. I tapped on "Michelle Brown." There was no address listed under her name. *Crap.* I am just about to text her some lame excuse which would blow my cover for detention when I remembered that her dad works from home. I searched for accountants nearby. I flick through the different results, passing up every listing that was in an office building until I see Thomas J. Brown, CPA. There was a picture of a white colonial that appeared next to his name.

That's it! I turned on my GPS and I arrived at Michelle's house in fifteen minutes. As I got out of the car, I saw Michelle open the front door. "Jamie, thank God! I need your help."

Inside the house, she led me to a Mac with a large white monitor. On it, she was using some fancy software to make these flyers. She had a grid pattern up and was making sure the border and writing on the flyer were all perfectly aligned.

"I've been working on this flyer for over an hour and it still doesn't look right. I don't think anyone is going to like it." She sounded like she was almost in tears.

I attempted to comfort her. "It looks good. I like it."

She snapped, "You're lying. I'm not good at anything even when I try my best."

"That's not true." I lightly patted her on the back.

She clasped onto me crying. "Yeah right. I never made cheer captain. I'm terrible at gymnastics, which is why I'm never picked to be at the top of the pyramid. I can't get straight A's. I only have a 3.7 GPA. No college is going to want me. And now I can't even make a flyer to honor my two friends."

She fell over into my lap, her tears soaking through my jeans. *Oh man, what a nutcase.*

"Hey, you are so good at a lot of things. You're really good at cheer and a 3.7 is a great GPA," I told her.

"Yeah right, what's yours?" she sodded,

Frick, I didn't know my GPA. "3.8," I blurted out.

"See, everyone is better than me."

"Oh, stop it now. You're doing fine."

She sat up and stared at the flyer. "Then why doesn't this flyer look right?"

The flyer is only in black and white. "Well how about some color?"

"I thought color was too joyous, like we're celebrating their death," she said with a dramatic emphasis on the word "death."

"No, no one would think that. Now do you remember Ali and Courtney's favorite color?"

"Duh, they both loved pink."

Of course, they did.

"See, why don't we make the background pink. And since it's a candlelight vigil after all, can you find an image of a candle?"

Michelle scrolled through Google images and found a picture of a white candle in the hands of a small child and was able to add it to the flyer.

"Wow, you made this so much better." She hit print and her dad's printer in the next room buzzed to life. As she got up to get the flyers, the doorbell rang. "I need to get the door. Jamie, can you get the flyers?"

I walked into her dad's office. He had a large mahogany desk with built-in shelves displaying boats and anchors with ocean maps hung up all throughout the room. There was a picture with him on a small yacht with his family. By the way he smiled, I could tell boating was his true calling.

The printer continued shaking and buzzing as it spat out pink paper after pink paper. I looked over the room again to see a pack of Camels sitting on top of a mountain of paperwork.

I walked over and stuffed three cigarettes into my jacket pocket. Just imagining the taste of smoke and nicotine running through my veins made me feel lightheaded.

I scooped up the stack of flyers and brought them out to the girls.

Geni, Shawna, and two other girls who I pretended I knew were now in the next room.

Shawna took a flyer from my hands and admired it. "Oh pretty. I love the pink. Hey, you know what would be fun? We could decorate them with glitter glue. Do you have some?" she asked Michelle.

I could see Michelle's face twitching as her mind runs over the idea of her perfectly symmetrical flyers being ruined by craft glue.

"I don't think that would be a good idea. It's a vigil, not a bake sale," she told them.

"I think they'd like it," declared Geni, "Mrs. Brown, where's your craft supplies?" she shouted up the stairs at Michelle's mom.

Knowing I couldn't handle all the glitter and high school drama that was about to go down, I pulled out my phone and to my surprise there was a real text on my phone from Jamie's mom: "Please get home soon. The boys need to ask you a few more questions."

"Hey guys, I gotta go. My mom wants me home," I announced, almost too happy to leave.

"Boo," Shawna called out.

I waved goodbye and told them, "I have to go. I'll help you guys put them up tomorrow."

It's sad that I'd rather spend the rest of the day with the police than with these people.

CHAPTER 21
TAYLOR CALLAHAN

October 8, 2015
Five Days After The Switch

Police always revisit people on a case. I knew that this was normal but it still was unnerving to have to speak to them one more time and pull off this charade yet again. But after I finished with them, I could sneak away and enjoy the contraband I lifted out of Michelle's dad's office.

I parked Jamie's car curbside as a police vehicle was hogging up the driveway. Before I could get the keys in the lock, Joan opened the door and pulled me inside. She was still in her uniform even though she has been home for a few hours now. Her hair was pulled back into a tight ponytail that tugs at the edges of her face like a bad facelift.

"Jamie, Detective Fisher has a few questions for you." She angled her body back to show the detective sitting in Phil's armchair. Standing next to him was the same black officer from before but his jarhead counterpart was missing. He gave me a polite nod of recognition.

The detective rose from his seat. "Hi Jamie, nice to see you again. Why don't you sit down so we can have a little chat?" He sat down on the sofa and patted the cushion next to him like he was beckoning a little dog to jump up on the furniture.

"Okay," I responded, shooting him a polite smile.

I sat down and in response the black officer took a seat on the armchair and leaned forward ready to listen intensely.

"How have you been holding up since your friends' death?" Detective Fisher asked.

I looked into his face. He was mid-forties, with deep creases running down the side of his mouth and his dark brown hair was combed back with too much gel. Unlike the other officer, he was in a navy suit and tie, not a uniform.

I cleared my throat and answered his question, "I'm alright, I guess. I mean, I was, like, super depressed at first but I'm starting to feel better. I was just with a few of our friends from the cheer team planning a vigil for Courtney and Ali."

"That's awfully nice of you girls. I bet their families appreciate the effort," he replied, crossing his legs in an attempt to appear more casual. "Now, if you don't mind, I'd like to ask you a few questions about that night?"

"Yeah, that's fine with me but I thought I already gave a statement," I said, flicking a long blonde strand back and behind my ear.

In a patronizing tone, he told me, "I know, honey, I know. No need to worry. We're trying to get as much information about what happened that night in order to solve the case. So, we want to make sure we didn't miss anything from anyone."

I nodded and sucked in my lower lip in such a way that conveys I'm grateful to him for explaining such a big and scary thing to a dumb little girl like me.

He continued, "On the night of October third, you were at Courtney Wilson's house, correct?"

"Yes, I was," I said.

"How did you get there?" he asked.

"Ali picked me up around four that afternoon and we both went to Courtney's house."

"Ali Everette?" he asked.

"Yes, of course," I said. "I don't know any other Ali who was killed."

He ignored my last sentence and asked, "Once you arrived at the Wilson residence, what happened?"

I answered, "It was just the three of us for a few hours. Courtney's parents were at some event and weren't supposed to be back until the next morning. So, Courtney invited all the girls from the cheer team over to have a party."

He paused to scribble on his notepad before he asked, "What time was this party supposed to start?"

I shrugged. "Not really sure but I remember a lot of people started coming over around seven or eight that night."

"If there were so many people at her house why did Courtney, with Ali, decide to leave?"

I bit my lip and looked away to seem embarrassed. "Well, they kept talking about turning this party into, like, a real party. I thought at first, they just meant finding some alcohol but then they told me that they found a hook up for some weed, cocaine or ecstasy. They wanted me to come along with them to pick it up."

"Did you?" he asked.

"I did get in the car with them. You see, Courtney has always given me a hard time about being too much of a good girl and sometimes I just go along with what she wants to do so she would stop picking on me. But as we drove on, I panicked and told her I didn't want to go anymore. I told them that I believed doing drugs was morally wrong and I didn't want to be a part of it anymore. But she refused to take me back to her house, so she stopped the car and let me out."

Detective Fisher leaned in, "Where did you go after that?"

"It would have been a really long walk from where I was back to her house or to mine so I decided to hitch back home. And before you get mad at me, I know it was unsafe and I won't do it again."

He scolded me anyway, "I'm glad you admit that it was stupid. You should never put yourself in harm's way like that. Why didn't you just call someone to pick you up?"

I looked down at the ground and said, "I didn't want to wake anyone in my family, and I didn't want to tell them about what my friends were doing."

His face stiffened and he picked up the pace of his questions. "What about the friends at the party? Why couldn't you call them?"

"Because I was too embarrassed that Courtney kicked me out of the car," I said in a matter of fact way like he should know teenagers care more about what their friends think of them than their own safety.

"Who picked you up?"

I answered, "A guy in his twenties with red hair. He was nice and he kinda talked and acted like he was gay, so I figured he wouldn't be interested in me."

He breathed out a small sigh. "You're lucky that he found you and not someone else."

"I agree. I thanked God in my prayers that night for letting me get home safely," I said with a smile.

He wrote more down on his pad. "Do you know who set your friends up with the drug connection?"

I shook my head. "No, I have no clue."

Leaning in closer he asked, "No clue? No idea about which kids in your school would do something like that?"

"I mean there are lots of people I know who are into sinful things like drugs at my school. Trust me, I smell it in the halls sometimes, but I can't think of which person in particular would be the one Courtney went to. She was the most popular girl in school, she could have gone up to anyone and they would have helped her out," I told him.

He barely acknowledged my answer. "Do you know Derek Jenkins?"

"A little bit but not well," I said, keeping my innocent act up in spite of his impatience with me.

"Do you know anything about him dealing drugs?" he asked,

I paused, pretended to think, then answered, "I've heard that he's a stoner but nothing else."

"Uh-huh. I guess I can assume that you don't know anything about him having any possible connection to the deceased Taylor Callahan?"

A lump swelled in my throat and forced myself to swallow it down. "I barely know anything about him. I have no clue if he was friends with some drug dealer."

"I see. Alright Jamie. Thank you for your time. I've got all I need." The detective got off the couch and walked over to Joan.

"Thanks for letting us come by," he said to her.

"No problem. See you at the office," she replied.

"Don't forget it's your turn for the coffee run tomorrow." He laughed and swung a fake punch at her shoulder.

"How could I forget?" she grinned.

"You folks have a good evening," said the officer as he followed Fisher out to the car.

As soon as they pulled out of our driveway, Joan rushed over to me. "I have exciting news about the case, but you have to promise me you'll keep it a secret."

"Of course," I said.

"It looks like that Taylor girl's ex-boyfriend was mad at her. He had been in jail for a while, but he got out right before this happened. They found a text on her phone saying she was worried he would come after her. As soon as we can find him, we can finally give your friends the justice they deserve." She then wrapped me up in a hug.

"That's so amazing! I was afraid they would never know who did this." I wasn't acting this time. I couldn't contain my joy at the thought of Zeke sitting in a jail cell for the rest of his life.

Joan continued, "I have to say, it doesn't always work out this way. Stuff like this doesn't always have a clear lead."

"I don't understand," I lied, "if they know who did this, why did they question me again and why did they ask me about that kid, Derek?"

"Well, it's good police work to question people involved several times, especially the last person to see them alive, to make sure all the details are ironed out. Also, Taylor's phone received texts from Derek's phone requesting orders, so it looks like Derek is going to be in some serious trouble soon."

I frowned, "That's terrible. I don't want him to get in trouble."

She let me out of her grasp. "What do you mean? He is guilty and he needs to be punished. I thought you didn't know him anyway."

I told her, "But I still don't want his life to be thrown away just because he made a stupid choice as a teenager."

She stared down at me. "That doesn't sound like you. You of all people should know once someone becomes a sinner of that nature, there is no hope for them. They need to be locked up or put down to save the rest of us. I thought you knew how important this is, to keep these dangerous idiots out of our society. I don't want you getting soft-hearted just because you go to the same school as the boy."

I felt tense from her tone. "I'm not. It's just weird to think of one of my classmates getting in that much trouble."

"It may feel that way but if he wasn't around both of your friends would be alive and well."

I wanted to scream at her, to tell her that's not how crime works. If you want something illegal, there is a way to find it. You can lock up all the Dereks in the world but there always will be someone there to take their place. As a cop, she should know this. Badness isn't something that springs up in a few people, it can be found in all people. It just has to be managed. But I couldn't let my feelings out. She would have known right away that it wasn't her daughter screaming at her.

CHAPTER 22
TAYLOR CALLAHAN

October 11, 2015
Eight Days After The Switch

Jamie's family and I sat down on a hard wooden pew in a dark church. We each held a long white candle that was stuffed into a mutilated Dixie cup to catch the wax. I knew I had to say a few words. Thankfully, Jamie wasn't short on Bible Verses. All I had to do was thumb through her Bible that was in her room and find one of her favorite verses which she highlighted in pink and yellow that would work for the vigil.

A man was on the stage or altar or whatever religious people call it. I assumed he was some kind of minister. Both sets of parents of the deceased girls made speeches. I zoned out through most of it.

Then, it was Michelle's turn to speak which meant I'd be up next. As she finished and wiped a tear from the corner of her eye, she said, "And now Jamie MacKenzie, one of Ali and Courtney's best friends is going to say a few words."

I walked up the center aisle and felt the eyes of the crowd hit me like a thousand tiny spotlights. I tightened my muscles, forcing myself not to shake with nervousness. I gave myself a quick pep talk in my head: I've stolen drugs from inside an abandoned building. I've run an identity theft ring. I've been to prison for Christ's sake. I can make a dumb little speech.

I put on a sweet but humble smile and began, "Hello, I'm Jamie. I've known both Courtney and Ali for what feels like forever. They were both so much fun to be around. They filled my days at school, at cheer practice, and on the weekends with so much joy and laughter. I never thought there would be a time when I wouldn't see them every day. I want to be mad and I want to be sad for losing them, but I must remind myself that they are in the Kingdom of Heaven now. They are safe, and they feel no pain or suffering. While we will all miss them, we must rejoice in their place with our Creator.

"I'd like to read you a short passage. John 14:1-7: "Let not your hearts be troubled; believe in God, believe also in me. In my Father's house are many rooms; if it were not so, would I have told you that I go to prepare a place for you? And when I go and prepare a place for you, I will come again and will take you to myself, that where I am you may be also. And you know the way where I am going." Thomas said to him, "Lord, we do not know where you are going; how can we know the way?" Jesus said to him, "I am the way, and the truth, and the life; no one comes to the Father, but by me. If you had known me, you would have known my Father also; henceforth you know him and have seen him. Amen."

I stepped down from the podium and took my seat with my family. Faith and Joan wrapped their arms around me.

Phil said to me, "Honey, that was beautiful."

"They are smiling down from Heaven right now," said Faith. I was surprised that they didn't notice that I wasn't crying.

After the service, the MacKenzies got caught up talking to Ali's parents. Faith went off with friends from her grade and *my friends* were gathered in a circle at the front of the church.

I slipped out the doors and made my way to the back of the church. I sat down next to a drain pipe on a dry piece of concrete. I was finally alone. Still holding my candle, I fished out a cigarette that I was hiding in my bra. I placed it in my mouth and watched the white paper crackle as I lit it with the candle's flame. I puffed the smoke out into the air and the wind carried it away. I couldn't tell which was worse: the family that knows their daughter is dead or the one that doesn't. Either way, their loss lights the way of my future.

CHAPTER 23
TAYLOR CALLAHAN

October 13, 2015
10 Days After The Switch

It was a Tuesday again, over a week since I took Jamie's place, and no one knew a thing. Life carried on for the MacKenzies: Their daughters got up to an old-fashioned looking alarm clock with its face painted with a scene from the Little Mermaid, they shuffled in their fuzzy bathrobes into the kitchen and brewed their coffee and popped Eggos out of the toaster. Faith and I argued over who gets to shower first and we'd rush to shove our homework and books into our backpacks and make it out the door. To them, everything was normal, and October third was just a sad incident that everyone, even Jamie would recover from.

But really a stranger with a criminal past was in their daughter's clothes, taking their daughter's classes, and driving their youngest child around. But if I had made it this far without them noticing, I could make it for the rest of my life.

I was feeling good that day. I passed that quiz from last week with an A. I seemed to be fitting in and getting into a routine. It was easy, predictable, and almost boring, especially when I had to talk to Jamie's friends at lunch but I could handle it.

• • •

I placed my lunch tray of two corn dogs and a side of peas down inside the circle of pretty girls. Sometimes I was amazed at how many straight smiles, pimple-less complexions, and flat-ironed hairstyles I would see all around me. I remembered how Chanel and I had to steal

Clean and Clear Spot Treatment from Target to fix our acne. And there was no way we could have gotten away with taking a $200 ConAir straightener that Michelle boasted about using every day. Luckily, I had been born with straight teeth because my parents would never have paid for braces.

"Oh, my God, guys!" Geni busted out.

"What?" asked Michelle.

"We get to go back to cheer practice today!"

The girls around me let out a chorus of excited screams. I'm still not entirely used to joining in on this teen girl bonding activity yet.

Shawna turned to me and asked, "Jamie, are you not excited?"

I pinched my lip like Jamie used to do and said, "I am but it won't be the same without them."

"Aww, I miss them too, but life has to go on. Remember, you said they would want us to," she replied.

"Yes of course. I can't wait to go back," I said. Then the reality of this hit me. Why hadn't I thought about this before? I would have to pass as a cheerleader to continue this charade. A knot twisted and grew inside of my stomach as I realized I didn't have the strength, flexibility, or training to pass as a cheerleader. But I would have to go because Jamie would go. Sure, I could back out but that would ring alarm bells. I'd have to go to cheer practice in just a few hours and pray that no one noticed I was not the athletic teenager I claimed to be.

•   •   •

In the last period of the day, I had just cleaned off the paint from my workstation in Art class as the bell rang. School was over, and I would have to pass as a cheerleader. I was fucked that I felt dizzy with anxiety. I could barely listen to the teacher babble on about how we were starting pottery next class. My identity was going to get blown in a matter of minutes. I might not even be here for the next class anyway.

Am I actually getting sick? I thought. *No, this is nerves.*

I haven't felt nervous in years. Most people have never questioned the lies I've spun for them like how flies don't think about the structure of a spider's web before they are caught in one. But this, this was my limit.

I walked to the locker rooms like I was heading to the gallows. Thankfully, Jamie wasn't one to keep security measures tight, so I found her cheerleading locker combinations in the back of one of her notebooks. I opened her locker and pretended to be getting ready while I observed what was going on around me. A few of the girls I saw at lunch were already there. Most of the girls were half-naked and out in the open. I knew that Jamie probably had the same nonchalant attitude about changing in front of others and so I couldn't hide in the stall like I did when I was in high school the first time around.

I had found Jamie's practice outfit in her locker. I slipped into school-colored sweatpants and a way-too-tight t-shirt that read, "Go Bears" across my chest.

I locked up my bag and followed the group of girls out to the football field.

We lined up in front of a short muscular woman with "Coach Andrea" stitched above her pocket in her polo shirt. She had a long horse-like face with foundation and bronzer that was caked into her pores and wore glimmering pink lip gloss that was meant for a girl half her age.

First, she instructed us to do various forms of "warm-ups" that involved a serious amount of jogging and jumping. I was out of breath and hiding my physical pain as Coach Andrea told us it was time to start something called "tumbling practice." These girls would spring off the mat, rotate in the air then land in a perfect Y shape position at the end. Others did a series of cartwheels and landed in the splits. I'm able to bang out a cartwheel and a handstand. I thanked God I was able to do them without tearing a muscle, but I knew I couldn't do the rest.

Next, we were told to practice this awful routine for half-time. It looks like a combination of your typical innocent "Go-Team" cheer moves with the body shaking gyrations of a music video. Because of Courtney and Ali's death, they had to change up the routine to accommodate the lower number of girls on the team. Since everyone was new at this particular dance, my lack of experience didn't stick out like a sore thumb.

As I was starting to feel like maybe I could pull this cheerleader thing, Coach Andrea called everyone to circle up around her.

"Because of the recent tragic events," she said with her eyes watering, "we need to change up the positioning for the pyramid as well. Now, no one can replace either Ali or Courtney, but we have to move on. So, we've decided that Jamie MacKenzie will take Courtney's place on the top and Shawna Marshal will take Ali's place."

The girls squeaked and hugged me, all crying with both sadness and joy.

In the center of it all, I stood terrified. I wouldn't be able to pull this off and there was only one way out of this.

The girls got into formation. The group supported Michelle and Shawna as they stood on top of the group of girls like a flamingo with one leg bent at a right ankle facing inwards. I was supposed to climb and stand on their legs making a perfect Y shaped cheer stance all the way at the top.

I took a deep breath and put my feet on the hands of two girls who created a little basket with their fingers to scoop me up. I placed my sneakers firmly on the shoulders of the girls under me and then I lifted them to the out-stuck legs of Shawna and Michelle. They grabbed my wrists and hoisted me up to my position.

I pretended like I couldn't find my balance. I let go of their hands and I rocked back and forth and circled my arms as if I was frantically trying to steady myself. I closed my eyes, prepared myself for the pain and let myself fall.

CHAPTER 24
JOAN MACKENZIE

October 13, 2015
10 Days After The Switch

> Dear Lord,
>
> There is something wrong with my daughter.
> I know it.
> It happened the night she came back from the party.
> Something is off.
> Her features are slightly distorted, her eyes have a sadness, a worldliness to them that wasn't there before.
> At first, I thought it was worrying over her friends because teenage girls can be so attached to each other but no, something else has changed.
> Her voice, it's slower and more forced. It's like she is remembering how to speak.
> I've been kind to her.
> I've been so scared of what might be wrong that I can't question her.
> Oh, dear Lord, it's making me think about those things again.
> The things I used to think about as a child.
> I know they are sinful and it's wrong to believe in anyone other than you and what is written in your Holy Book, but those things, I still can't explain.
> Those dark shadows of people I saw in the woods, my reflection in the mirror that moved when I didn't.
> And the Tommy incident.
> Dear Lord, the Tommy incident.
> Seeing that boy who looked just like Tommy sit on my bed in the middle of the night when the real Tommy was away at camp miles from home.

Could this be another?
An empty shell of my loved ones, following me around.
Please Lord guide me in what to do.
Please give me the strength to have faith in my daughter and put my suspicious mind at rest.

Amen.

I pulled myself off the floor. My elbows and knees ached from kneeling at the foot of the bed. I heard Phil gargling Listerine in the bathroom. I got my phone out to kill time while waiting for him to come out.

I checked my email and got my Biblical passage of the day: "Colossians 3:13 NIV. Bear with each other and forgive one another if any of you has a grievance against someone. Forgive as the Lord forgave you."

I left the house in uniform before the girls got up. They're used to my hours. With my hair tied tight, a badge on my chest, and a gun on my hip, I was no longer afraid of those things, those questionable things that may or may not hide in the dark. There's an explanation and I'm going to find it.

•   •   •

My shift was over at four o'clock. I got home before the rest of the family. I'm about to put chicken in the oven when the landline rings, never a good sign.

"Mrs. MacKenzie?" a youthful but nervous woman's voice asked.

"Speaking," I replied.

"This is Coach Andrea from the cheerleading team. Jamie fell off the Pyramid and we think she may have broken her ankle."

"Oh, my goodness, I'll be right there," I told her.

I ran scenarios in my head as I made the fifteen-minute drive to the high school. In all Jamie's years of dance, tap, soccer, and cheer, she only sprained her arm once in middle school. She has stellar balance and a natural grace I'm envious of. Though, I'd never tell her that. My talents lie in the way of softball, straight shooting, and investigating a crime scene, not in dance or cheerleading.

When I got to the school's football field, I saw Jamie sitting on the ground, closely studying her right ankle.

"Hi, Mom," she called out, letting out a sliver of a smile.

That's not like her. She usually brushes a situation like this off with a big white smile or she is in tears totally overwhelmed. She is never cool and casual.

• • •

After two hours of waiting in the hospital, the doctor showed us a grainy X-ray.

He lowered his wire-framed glasses and said, "No fracture but I believe you have a second-degree sprain. No cast. Don't worry. You'll just need a boot and some crutches."

"How long before she can cheer again?" I asked the doctor.

"Probably not for at least three months, maybe even longer if she pushes herself to put weight on it before it's ready," he answered.

No cheerleading, she'll be devastated. I braced myself for the waterworks.

Jamie frowned. "Oh no. That's too bad."

I was stunned.

The doctor continued, "You'll need about three weeks in the boot for it to heal right. After that, you have to be very careful. That means no high heels and definitely no running, jumping, skateboarding, or whatever you kids are into these days."

Jamie nodded, still not visibly upset at the news. Her whole world should be shattering right now. *Why isn't she freaking out?*

I tapped the doctor on the arm, "Can I speak to you privately?"

He nodded and ushered me into an empty room next door.

"Listen, I've been noticing strange things with her lately," I told him.

"Such as?" he asked, pushing his glasses up further on his nose.

"She seems like a completely different person. She used to be either enthusiastic or melodramatic. Now she doesn't seem to care about the things she used to love, and she doesn't get upset by anything either."

"She's sixteen, right?" he asked.

I nodded.

He let out a small chuckle. "Well, we all go through huge changes when we are at that age. She could just be maturing."

"What about her face?" I blurted out.

"Her face?" His forehead wrinkled.

"I noticed her features are slightly...off," I said.

"That can happen too. All these hormones that are circulating inside teenagers can often cause facial changes. With boys, it's more obvious. We get big ears or a big nose before the rest of our face catches up. Smaller changes can happen to girls. I'm sure it didn't happen overnight; it just may have taken a while to become noticeable." He sympathetically patted me on the shoulder.

I know my daughter's face, I thought to myself.

"I still don't see why she is acting so differently," I muttered to myself.

He heard me and asked, "Are you concerned about drugs?"

It hit me like a stack of bricks. Her friends were trying to buy drugs when they died. I knew Jamie would never do anything that stupid. She got out of that situation before it became dangerous. But maybe she had been using this whole time and she's been lying about being pushed into going along with the other girls that night.

"Yes, I am," I said.

Dear Jesus, help me. I've lost my mind. I'm a cop and I didn't suspect drugs. What is the matter with me?

"She didn't give me that impression," said the doctor. "She looks well-rested and isn't irritable. She didn't even ask for pain meds. But she's your kid. If you think something up, you should talk to her about it."

Something was wrong. And it was my job to find out what it was.

CHAPTER 25
JOAN MACKENZIE

October 14, 2015
11 Days After The Switch
At work, I decided to do some digging on the circumstances surrounding Ali and Courtney's deaths. I rolled my office chair up to my computer and placed my morning coffee down next to several stacks of paperwork. Those other cases could wait.

I opened the girls' files. Both Ali and Courtney were shot in the gut with one bullet a piece. The other girl, Taylor, they found at the scene was shot in the head, her brain erupted out of her skull and most of her face was shattered and unrecognizable. The fact that she was shot in the face and the other girls in the stomach, indicated that the killer was angry with her and the other two just got in the way.

She was identified by the driver's license in her wallet. Her family didn't even come in to claim the body.

I clicked on her profile: Taylor Callahan. DOB: November 1, 1994 in Union, New Jersey. Several arrests but only one conviction for felony robbery. She pleaded it down to a misdemeanor in 2013. I clicked on her mug shot to enlarge it.

The sight of it took my breath away. She had ratty blonde hair, smeared make-up, and a swollen lip. But if you ignore those things, the face of my daughter looked back at me. The small heart-shaped face with a pointed nose and plump lips. The same sharp green eyes just like my sister's, God rest her soul. But something about Taylor's smirk was sinister.

I took a deep breath. I was so grateful that this lowlife died instead of my Jamie. But she could have easily been there with them and died alongside her friends.

If there was a chance Jamie did use drugs with Ali and Courtney, she could be putting herself in even more danger. What could she be using? What if she overdosed? What if she got arrested for possession? I had to give her a drug test as soon as possible. And I'm going to get her fingerprinted just in case she ever does anything, she'll come up in the system and I'll know about it. That will make her think twice before she does anything stupid.

•   •   •

I got home from work to see the light on in the girls' room. Jamie was hunched over her desk, reading a textbook. She really should improve her posture.

"Hey, Mom," she said, only looking up for a second.

"How's the foot feeling?" I asked her.

"It hurts a little. What's worse is the armpit pain from the crutches," she said, rubbing her underarms.

"Listen, I was thinking about you taking a day off school tomorrow to let it heal and you can visit me at the station," I said to her.

"At the station?" she asked.

"The boys want to see how you're doing," I lied.

"But I can't go tomorrow," she said with a pouty face.

"Why not?" I asked.

"I have a test tomorrow morning in Algebra," she told me.

"Let me see your syllabus," I demanded.

She gave me a weird look then took two pieces of white paper out of her folder. She was right, it said, "Midterm exam on October 15th."

"That's okay. I'll take you after school." I turned around and didn't give her time to protest.

CHAPTER 26
JOAN MACKENZIE

October 15, 2015
12 Days After The Switch

I ignored my piles of paperwork once again and made a quick trip down to the lab. I saw Martin, one of the geeky lab guys, standing over some equipment.

"Hey man, can you do me a solid and run the drug test for me as soon as I bring it to you?"

He looked up from one of his cultures and said, "No."

"Why not?" I prodded him.

"We shouldn't use supplies on non-police business," he said without looking up from his work.

I laughed. "Martin, I think you're forgetting that I looked after your new girlfriend's terror of a cat for two weeks, so you could take her to Barbados. He scratched up my poor Faith and broke three of my great-grandmother's china plates which you never paid me for. I think you can do this one small thing for me."

"How much were they worth?"

"Probably over 300 dollars," I fibbed.

He pursed his lips and scratched at his thin mustache. "Fine," he replied.

Back at my desk, I busied myself with some mindless paperwork until the phone startled me with its sharp ringtone.

I picked it up. "This is Officer MacKenzie."

"Hello, um, Mrs., um, Officer MacKenzie. This is Mrs. Stevens, the nurse at Southfield High School." The nervousness in her voice was palpable.

"What happened?" I asked.

"There was a bit of a mishap in Art class today," the nurse said.

"What kind of mishap?" I snapped. I have no patience for anyone beating around the bush.

"You see, they were making pottery, a mug actually, and Jamie went to take her mug out of the kiln and she touched it before it was cool and burnt her hands," the nurse explained.

"I'll be right there."

•   •   •

I found Jamie laying in one of the little cots in the nurse's office. Her hands were heavily wrapped in gauze down to the middle of her palm.

"What did you do?" I asked with my arms crossed.

"I'm so sorry, Mom." Her eyes were red and puffy from crying.

I turned to the nurse and yelled, "I've ought to sue this school. How dare you let this happen to my daughter?"

"No, Mom, it was my fault. I was being stupid," she started to cry some more. Now this was more like the Jamie I know.

I signed her out of school for the day and helped her get into the car. But an inkling of doubt was still lingering in my mind.

In a few minutes, we pulled into the station's parking lot.

"Mom, why are you taking me here? I need to go home." Jamie's eyes widened with panic.

"We need to do something first," I insisted.

I got her inside of the bathroom as quickly as I could. She can't use her crutches with her burnt hands, so I pulled her through the station as she limped behind me.

I left her in the bathroom and told her, "Don't move. I'll be right back."

I got the drug kit from the lab and met her back inside.

"I need you to pee in this," I said.

"What? Why?" she asked in that snotty teenage tone.

"I just need you to," I yelled, shoving the cup at her.

She looked down at her jeans' zipper and said, "I don't know how I can get this open with my hands."

I huffed and helped her pull her pants down.

"Are you going to stay here?" she asked.

"Yes," I said, "I'll turn around but I'm staying in the room. Just go."

"Mom, this is gross," she whined.

"Do as I tell you!"

"Fine." She sat down on the toilet and filled up the cup. I helped her redress herself then I rushed the sample back to the lab.

In the car, she yelled, "What in Hell was that about?"

"Don't use the H-word," I scolded.

She let out a grunt of frustration. "Why did I have to pee in a cup?"

"Your friends were buying drugs and it wasn't their first time. I just want to check to make sure you didn't use with them," I told her.

"Mom, I've never done drugs. You know me," she said.

I turned on the engine and started to drive away from the station. "I know but you're a teenager and teenagers do stupid things sometimes even if you think you would never do those stupid things."

"Fine, you just wasted your time." She turned away from me.

Since I couldn't fingerprint her now with those burnt hands, I hoped that the drug test was enough to scare her away from drugs for good. But if she doesn't start behaving more like her old self, I'm going to wait and let her heal before I put her to the real test.

CHAPTER 27
TAYLOR CALLAHAN

October 16, 2015
13 Days After The Switch

I sat alone in Jamie's bed for hours. Joan spent quite a while in the morning on the phone with the school, explaining why I shouldn't be expected to come in for a long time. Thankfully, the school administration saw her side after mentioning that the school might be at fault for my injuries. I had three weeks at home to recover. We set up an arrangement where my teachers would email me assignments and Faith would drop them off for me at school.

Soon after, she stuffed her bloated middle-aged body into her blue uniform and tied her hair into a stiff bun and left for her shift.

I must have dozed off as I was startled awake by the sudden vibrating of Jamie's phone on my nightstand. A phone number that wasn't saved in Jamie's contact appeared on the screen. I winced as I used my burnt fingers to swipe the screen to answer the call.

"Hello?" I asked.

"Hey, it's me," a voice whispered.

"Who?" I asked.

"Ivan," the voice replied.

"Is it safe for you to be calling?" I said, sitting up in bed.

"Don't worry. It's a payphone. You can say it was a prank call or a telemarketer if they see it on the bill," he said.

"Why are you calling? Is everything okay?" I asked him, panic swelling in my veins.

"I had to talk to you. You're worrying me sick. You said you'd call."

"I know. I'm sorry. Things got weird here. I couldn't just disappear to a payphone as easy as I thought I could. How did you find Jamie's number anyway?" I asked.

"I know a guy," he replied.

"Do you mean Max?" I asked knowing he was the only hacker we both knew.

"Yep."

We both laughed.

"So, what has happened since you got there? Do they suspect anything?" he asked me.

"Her mom's a cop," I blurted out.

"No way. That's too much for you to handle. Taylor, you gotta get out of there."

"I think I'm alright for now. I can't tell if she is on to me or not. Last night she wanted to take me down to the station to say hello to her cop buddies. I freaked out and burnt off my fingerprints in the kiln at school."

"You did what?" His voice crackled over the static on the payphone.

"But she took me there anyway and made me do a drug test. But it turns out that because Jamie's best friends were killed at a drug deal, she got this wackadoo idea in her head that Jamie must be doing drugs. Which means I had to get tested."

"Have you been using?

"Jesus, Ivan. You know I've been clean since I left Zeke. Plus, I never really liked the stuff anyway. There is nothing in my system except nicotine. You have no idea how hard it is to sneak in a smoke in this household."

"Are you sure you want to stay there? I can come and get you out of there in thirty minutes."

"I'm not running this time. I don't think this is something the average mom—cop or no cop—would suspect. Sure, teenagers get into trouble all the time, but they don't have their bodies switched and their identity stolen every day, now do they? I only have to put up with their weirdness for another year or so and I'll be eighteen—

again—and can do what I like. This time, I'll have an education, a clean record, and a good reputation. You can't buy those things, Ivan, not with all the drug money in the world."

There was silence on his end which means he knew I was right.

"You know," he started, "I'm not just going to stop being your best friend just because you have some other girl's name and Social Security number. If you really want to stay and be Jamie MacKenzie, then I won't stop you. But, quit trying to get rid of me."

My heart sank.

How could he think I would ever not want him in my life?

I reassured him, "I'm not trying to get rid of you."

"Good," he said sternly, "Now I'm going to call you again at the same time next week to check up on you. Take care of yourself, Taylor."

He hung up.

I don't know what I did to deserve such a good friend.

CHAPTER 28
JOAN MACKENZIE

October 16, 2015
13 Days After The Switch

Clean. Jamie's results were clean. Well, not all the way. We found nicotine in her urine in small amounts, meaning she must have smoked three to five days ago. Typically, I would be livid with her, but relief washed over my body instead. She wasn't using. She wasn't coping with our family ritual or the pressures of high school with illegal substances.

I tossed the lab paperwork on my desk and leaned back in my chair. Then something out of the corner of my screen catches my eye, The autopsy for Taylor Callahan was still up on my scene, obscured by other tabs. Clicking on the mouse, I closed everything else until the mug shot of the deceased came back into view. I shivered at the sight of her, this degenerate version of my daughter with messy tangled hair and smeared make-up under tired eyes. Were there any other secrets this corpse was hiding?

I scanned her chart. No nicotine or other substances were found in her body. I got angry at Jamie again. How come this street rat could stay clean but my Jamie was smoking? In and out. In and out. I forced my breath to calm. I need to cut her some slack, her friends have died. I looked over the autopsy one more time before glancing at Jamie's urine analysis results on my desk. I filled out the remaining pieces of information Martin asked for. Height: 5'9. Weight: 135 lbs. Blood Type: O+. All these details about Jamie matched what was on Taylor's file.

•   •   •

After my shift, I pushed through the door of Jamie's room. She was still laying in bed like I left her.

"Get up," I commanded her.

"Mom. My ankle?" she reminded me.

"I don't care, I want you up!"

She pulled herself, putting all her weight on her uninjured leg and kept her bandaged hands always from her body so the burnt skin wouldn't brush up against anything.

"There was nicotine in your urine. Have you been smoking?" I asked her.

"Yes, just the one time. After the vigil. Someone offered me one. I was really depressed and thought it might help for some reason. I know it was stupid and I won't do it again." She looked down at the floor.

I narrowed my eyes. I got closer and grabbed her face in my hands and turned it side to side.

"Mom, what are you doing?" she squeaked.

I saw the same short but pointed face, olive green eyes, and puffy-lipped pout. She was the right height and weight, but something was off. Something I couldn't put my finger on.

In a flash, I suddenly found myself embarrassed. Of course, this was my daughter. This was the same face that always came home with a smile. The same person who understood and lived our values. I was just being overprotective. I tend to get carried away when I feel like someone has wronged my family. But now, I'm going above and beyond.

"I'm sorry, honey," I said while releasing my grip. "Just promise me to stay away from cigarettes, okay?"

She looked down and shook her head in agreement.

"I'll leave you be now." I exited her room feeling guilty for making my crazy hunch get the better of me.

CHAPTER 29
TAYLOR CALLAHAN

October 17, 2015
14 Days After The Switch
I was sitting wide awake in Jamie's bed. Joan's little break down rattled me and I couldn't get to sleep. The burning in my hands and the aching of my ankle weren't helping either. I was so close to being caught that if it weren't for Joan's own self-doubt I'd be at the police station right now. Would this be identity theft? Or maybe it was fraud? They could maybe get me on tampering with a corpse or failure to report a crime. Even if I couldn't pin down what laws I actually had broken, I knew what I was doing couldn't be legal.

I felt like an idiot. Smoking was too out-of-character for Jamie. I had to quit for good this time. Thankfully, I would be home alone for most of the time so I could withdraw without anyone noticing why I'm suddenly irritable as all Hell.

After a few more minutes of restlessness, I couldn't take the insomnia or the pain in my hands anymore. I stumbled out of bed and limped on my good foot to the bathroom. In the medicine cabinet, I popped the lid to a prescription container. The label read, "Take one every four hours as needed for pain. May cause drowsiness."

Good.

I tossed two into my mouth and drank a gulp of water from the sink. As the pills ran down my esophagus, I checked myself in the mirror.

Was I too old and worn down to be pulling this off?

My forehead was still smooth and there were no smile creases at the corners of my mouth. My eyes could get a little puffy, but it usually goes away after I'm awake for an hour. I didn't think anyone would notice it.

I took out the eyeliner pencil again and filled in the fake freckle even more for good measure.

"I'm Jamie MacKenzie," I whispered to myself. I had to believe it or they'd see right through me. I could do this. I only had a year and half left living here and then I could move out and live a better life.

I got back to the room and tripped on my way to the bed. Faith woke up and asked, "Jamie, are you okay?"

I wanted to say, "No, I'm not because I'm not Jamie and I think your mom is going to find out."

Instead, I replied, "Yeah, I just tripped on my way back from the bathroom. My hands are killing me."

She pushed the covers off her and came to my side. She pulled back my sheets and ushered me to lie down.

She took my left hand in hers and gently unrolled my bandages. I hissed from the pain.

"It's okay," she said in a soothing voice.

She grabbed a dollop of the white anti-burn cream from its tube on my bedside table and lightly rubbed it into my sore fingertips. She then covered my healing wounds with fresh gauze.

She motioned for me to give her my other hand, but I said, "You don't have to do this. You should be in bed, getting your rest for school tomorrow."

She lifted my other hand anyway and unwrapped my fingers.

"Seriously, why are you being so nice to me?" I asked her.

"Because you're my sister and you need me," she whispered.

She finished wrapping my other hand and told me to get some sleep.

"Thank you," I told her as she climbed back into her bed.

I didn't stay awake for much longer. The medication was a lot stronger than I thought it would be. I fell into a nightmare-drenched sleep that was plagued by the memories of my terrible former life.

PART 2

CHAPTER 30
TAYLOR CALLAHAN

February 19, 2011
4 Years, 7 Months, 15 Days Before The Switch

I could feel the rush of excitement as Zeke and I walked along the alleyway behind the casino. It was our first deal together. In a narrow dark alley that smelled of rotting cabbage, I was bursting with anticipation. An energy buzzed in my body making me feel alive in ways I never felt before.

Zeke banged three times on a metal door next to the dumpster. We waited a few minutes in silence sucking in the putrid air before Zeke slammed an open fist on the door once more. A man much shorter than Zeke with a pencil-thin mustache poked his head out of the door. "What the fuck, man? You're late."

"No, man, you're late. I've been waiting in this hellhole for ten minutes."

The man pushed the door open more, holding it open for us. "Shit, calm down. Just get in."

The door led to the back of a kitchen where a scrawny teen huddled over a sink filled with mountains of dishes.

"Julio, why don't you take a break?" The thin mustached man said to the boy.

He turned his acne-covered face around and said, "Nah, I'm almost done."

"Julio, take a break," the man said again.

Julio nodded and rushed out of the kitchen.

"You got it?" asked the man.

Zeke nodded. "Half a kilo. That'll be 28,000 dollars." He swung his backpack to the side and showed the man a small square package covered in silver tape.

"Yeah, yeah, yeah." The man reluctantly handed Zeke a large brown envelope filled with stacks of cash.

"I need to count it first." Zeke laid the envelope down on a cutting board. After thumbing through the bills, he declared the money to be the correct amount and handed the silver package to the man.

"Good luck," Zeke told him as he placed the money in his bag.

"You too, man, you too," the man said with a laugh.

Zeke took me by the arm and led me out the door.

"Holy fucking shit, that was the most insane thing ever," I told him.

My heart was pounding with excitement. I'd never been a part of anything so cool, so badass, so illegal before.

"I can't believe you got all that money," I squeaked.

Zeke turned around with his hand raised and I took a step back.

"Shut the fuck up," he shouted in short breathy bursts.

"What did I do?" I asked him.

"Don't talk about money until we're behind closed doors. Do you want to attract every pick-pocketer in the city? Or worse, the cops?"

"No, I don't. I haven't seen that much money at once before and I just got excited," I explained.

"If you're gonna roll with me, you've got to learn a few things. I'm such an idiot, taking a newbie like you out with me. If I didn't like you so damn much, I would have left you at home." He grabbed me by the arm and jerked me towards him. He gripped the back of my head and kissed me hard.

When he let go I said, "I'm sorry, I don't know the rules. You'll have to teach me."

"I will. I've got a lot to teach you actually." He smacked me on the ass and motioned to me to get going.

•   •   •

Back at the house, he told me to sit next to him on the couch. He took the envelope out of the bag and counted out 6,000 dollars for himself and sealed up the rest for the boss.

"Get up and push back the coffee table," he said, rising to his feet.

"You just told me to sit down," I protested.

He sighed, "Why don't you just do what I ask you to do, 'ight?"

I scowled at him and pushed the table across the floor with a screech.

He tossed the two couch cushions out of the way to reveal a pull-out mattress.

He tugged on the black metal bar on top until the mattress gave way and sprung up.

Zeke had taped and hot glued plastic bags filled with smaller plastic bags, each containing a different type of drug, to the mattress. Tightly wrapped joints gave off a skunky odor. Next to them, sat three more of those silver packages we had given to the man in the kitchen. Various forms of white powders and colorful pills in small dime bags ran along the sides of the mattress. In the middle, Zeke had stored several brown envelopes with what I assumed would be more wads of cash.

"Holy shit babe, I had no idea this was here," I said.

"That's the point," he laughed.

"What are those?" I pointed to a clear bag that contained several chucky plastic devices. They looked like pagers but with one large slot and no buttons.

"Skimming machines or skimmers as some people call them." He took one in his hand and tossed it over to me. "You pop them over an existing credit card port and they collect all the credit card numbers of the people who use it. You can either keep the info and use it yourself or sell it to someone online."

"Cool."

He sighed and took the skimmer back and started packing up his collection of contraband.

"It's too bad your old lady found our shit, I was counting on using your place as another storage facility, but I guess I have to be creative now."

"You know I didn't mean for that to happen," I said, feeling guilty.

"I know, babe. It's not your fault your mom is a bitch, but right now you still owe me 300 dollars' worth of weed so I'm gonna have to have you do some runs until you make up that money."

I shouldn't have agreed with him. I should have said, "That was your shit and you're liable if it gets taken even if it was taken by my mom." I should have run out of there fast, so fast that he couldn't chase me. Maybe I could have asked my mom to take me back. I would promise I wouldn't go near Zeke or drugs again. Or maybe I should have tracked down Drew and told him that even though I wasn't his daughter by blood, I was still his kid in a way and that maybe we could be a family of our own. But all the "maybes" and "shoulds" in the world couldn't change my past.

I was scared and I didn't want to disappoint Zeke or get him in trouble, so I stayed and I took everything he told me as gospel.

CHAPTER 31
TAYLOR CALLAHAN

February 19, 2011
4 Years, 7 Months, 15 Days Before The Switch
Zeke reached into one of the larger bags and pulled out a dime bag of coke and another smaller bag of weed. He took his time patting down his merchandise, making sure everything was secure in its place. It almost seemed like he was petting them, like they were little precious animals.

He slowly folded the "mattress" back up and replaced the cushions for us to sit on.

"Alright, let me teach you what you should know," he began. "Never give them the merchandise until they show you the money and you have a chance to count it. Always carry at least one weapon, especially something small and easy to hide like a knife. Never let them know your real name and use one of these," he pulled a thick black cellphone out of his pocket, "a burner phone, so no one can track the calls and texts to you. I'll see if the Boss can get you one."

Zeke pulled a tiny mirror off the side table and placed it in front of us. He poured a little baggie of coke on it. Around his neck, there was his razor blade as always. He took it off and tapped the powder into thin white lines.

"What're you doin'?" I asked him.

"Sampling." He bent down over the line, pushed one nostril closed and sucked the coke into his nose.

He let out a "woo" before snorting some more. "Good shit, I don't have any issues selling this."

"I thought dealers were supposed to stay away from the stuff they sell so they don't end up addicted," I said.

"That's just bullshit from *Law & Order*. Everyone I know samples. You see, I don't use, I test. I have to provide quality to my clients or they may not come back. If you're gonna get in this game, you got a sample too."

"Can't I just take your word for it?"

"Fuck no, you gotta try." He pushed the mirror closer to me.

"I'm afraid I'll get hooked," I said.

"No, nothing can hook you. You're too strong for that. We're too strong for that. As long as we're together, we can do anything, nothing can hold us back!" His voice was getting louder and louder. I felt a rush pour through my veins, I felt alive. I felt unkillable.

I leaned down towards the mirror. I was panting with nervousness. My breath scattered the white line.

"Shit, Taylor, don't breathe out when you're near it," he scolded. "Just take one big inhale."

He straightened the lines and I drew in one long inhale of powder that burned my nostrils. It felt like I was getting water up my nose at a swimming pool times a million. I held my aching sinuses and shouted, "Mother of fuck, that hurts."

"You'll get used to it," said Zeke as he did another line of blow.

My heart began to race as my body buzzed alive with energy. All the fears and "what ifs" that were swirling around in my head instantly shut up.

"Oh, my God! This is amazing." I jumped to my feet.

Zeke stood up too with a smile on his face. "I knew you would like it."

"I feel incredible, I feel like we could take over the world, like I'm not scared to deal anymore, I'm not scared of anything anymore."

"Yeah, that's it!" cheered Zeke as he scooped me up in a big hug. "I knew you would come through. I knew you would be my partner in crime."

"Exactly, that's who we are, we're Bonnie and Clyde, We're Natural Born Killers. No one can stop us," I told him.

"Fuck yeah, we are, baby!" Zeke slammed the button to his stereo system and Ludracis' "Money Maker" came on.

Zeke and I danced around our house feeling like the stars of our own movie. Eventually, we found ourselves on the floor, going at it like animals.

Afterwards, Zeke pulled me to the couch again. "I forgot to give the rest of your lesson but first I need to mellow out."

He went to the kitchen and returned with some pre-rolled joints and lit them.

"Here, it will help bring you down" Zeke passed the joint to me.

I took a hit from it and the smoke filled my lungs. I lunge forward into a huge coughing fit.

"It's okay, you know it always hurts the first time." He winked at me and I playfully rolled my eyes at him.

"Continue with your lesson, professor." I nudged him with my elbow.

"Right, let's see." He paused. "Don't smoke in the dark. The light from the cigarette can give you away. And don't ever turn your back on them during the deal. They may want to get their shit for free and pull a knife on you so keep your eyes forward. They might want to negotiate a lower price, don't say a thing and just pack up your shit to leave. If they're using, they can't go too long without it and if they're selling, they've got clients breathing down their necks. They need your merchandise and yeah, they could call up someone else to get it but it's gonna be more of a hassle. You have the advantage. You got it so far?"

"Yep, of course," I answered, curling up deeper into his arms.

He went on. "If they are trying to be intimidating, which can happen if they are insecure or if they want to pick on you because you're a chick, don't back down. Be tougher. Show them that you own the room, do something big and aggressive that gets their attention."

"Like what?" I ask.

"I don't know, anything that makes a loud noise, like slam down a glass of water or scream at them, something."

I heard a faint buzzing and Zeke reached for his burner phone, still pressed against his ankle.

Zeke answered the phone, "Yeah, what's up?".

After a few seconds of silence, he asked, "Okay, how much? Eight ball? Got it. Be there in twenty."

He hung up and motioned for me to get going.

•　　•　　•

We parked the car in the Hotel across the way from where we're going. I wish I could remember which hotel it was, but the pot tainted my memory. All I know is that the place had red, orange, and yellow neon lights flashing all over the place.

The hallways had some red and gold gaudy design that was on both the wallpaper and the carpet. I was hungry, so hungry that this ugly paper looked like spaghetti and marinara sauce that I wanted to lick up.

Zeke pounded on the door and a short guy with sandy hair and thick glasses opened the door.

He pushed his way in before the guy had a chance to ask what he wanted.

Inside the room, a topless redheaded woman wiggled around on the lap of a man with thick black hair and a prominent chin.

About six other guys sat in a circle around her tossing dollar bills her way. They all looked like clones of each other. They wore suits that were wrinkled and messy with their ties missing and buttons loose. They all had varying shades of brown hair that must have been gelled back at the start of the day but was now falling out of place. Most of them had a drink in their hands.

Behind me to my left, there was a cabinet that held the TV, the mini-bar someone forgot to close and the stereo blaring out Aerosmith's "Walk this Way." I haven't been able to listen to that song the same way since.

The man who opened the door turned the music down a few notches before asking, "Are you the guy?"

"Yes, I am. You have the money?" Zeke asked.

The man pulled out a wad of cash but before he could count it out for Zeke, one of the guys called out to me, "Who is she? Another stripper? Come over here, honey and sit on my lap."

I was silent, racking my brain for something to say but then the man continued, "It's only fair that the groom's brother gets a lap dance too."

The other men in the room shouted and "woo'd" at me as the brother of the groom grabbed me by the arm.

Then I remembered the big aggressive gesture Zeke was talking about.

On the dresser to my right there was an unopened bottle of champagne. I picked it up and threw it over the groom's head. It crashed into the opposite wall and erupted with fizzing alcohol and green glass.

I screamed, "I'm not here to give you assholes a good time, I'm here to get my fucking money. We've got the shit, now pay us before we leave you bitches with nothing."

"Jesus, calm down," said the brother of the groom, dropping his grip.

The man from the door counted out 500 bucks with shaking hands. "Is that enough?"

"I should charge you assholes a fee for harassing my girlfriend, or worse get my boys over here to fuck you guys up. But you ain't worth my time. Take your shit and get out of my sight," Zeke barked at the man while tossing him the package of baggies.

I flipped them off before I let the door slam behind me.

Zeke rushed down the hall before he turned to me and said "Babe, that was fucking amazing. I know you're tough enough to handle this. Let's get you started on solo work soon."

CHAPTER 32
TAYLOR CALLAHAN

March 21, 2011
4 years, 6 months, 12 days
I didn't realize that Zeke had been grooming me like some psychopath pedophile who gives treats and compliments to the little boys he wants to wank off. But Zeke didn't realize what I would become. He'd tell me I was perfect and surprise me with little romantic gestures. One time, he told me that he needed a safe place to hide something he didn't want the boss and other guys to know about.

He dragged me to the abandoned elementary school where we had first met at my birthday party. We entered the long narrow building that had classrooms on each side. In one of the rooms with toppled chairs and decaying alphabet wallpaper, he pulled me and kissed me.

"I wanted to hide this here as a way to honor our love, the greatest love story in history," he said.

I swooned like a girl in a Victorian romance novel. "Really, baby?"

"Really, now help me find a good place for it," he said, his eyes scanning the little room.

The tossed-about furniture wouldn't provide great cover, and neither would the rotting walls.

"How about up there?" I pointed to the ceiling.

Zeke smiled, put his feet on a tiny chair and pushed the tile back, making a little hiding nook for our secret stash for both of us to use or sell without anyone else knowing about it. Or at least, that's what I thought.

CHAPTER 33
TAYLOR CALLAHAN

January 25, 2012
3 Years, 8 Months, 9 Days Before The Switch

Over the next year of our relationship, Zeke's mind games got sicker, and he put me in real danger. He made me hungry for compliments and terrified of disappointing him like I was some stray he took in off the streets.

On one particular night, he asked me, "Do you love me?"

"Of course, I love you." I was eating a TV dinner while watching Jeopardy.

"Then you'll go on this run, a delivery out to MAGIC's house," he said, not missing a beat.

"I told you, I don't want to go near him," I replied.

He moaned, "Oh, you are overreacting. It was a joke, even a compliment."

"Asking you how much you'd sell me for isn't funny. MAGIC is a pimp, a gross white trash Piney pimp," I said.

"That's just how he is, okay? So, are you going to be a whiny bitch about this or are you gonna make me proud?" He looked me dead in the eyes.

I was quiet and turned back to the TV.

Zeke grew frustrated by my silence and threw the remote against the wall. "I don't know why you watch this boring shit. Do you think it's going to make you smart all of a sudden? You don't even have a high school degree."

"Neither do you," I replied.

"What did you just say to me?" he growled.

"Nothing," I whispered.

"That's right. Now go bring MAGIC his shit." Zeke shoved a large bag of weed, a gram of coke, and a few dime bags of meth into my backpack and tossed it at me.

"If you were actually smart, you wouldn't have given me a hard time about this. You would just go," he said as I opened the front door to leave.

I didn't respond. I just left and made my way on foot to MAGIC's house. It was already dark, and I felt fear stirring my stomach. I was afraid of showing up at MAGIC's house, but I was more afraid of Zeke's rage if I didn't. Only when I was terrified like this, I would take out a little container from the side of the bag. It had a little mirror and just enough blow to have me feeling invincible for about thirty minutes.

•   •   •

When I got close to MAGIC's house, I snorted the coke as fast as I could. Music with a low bass was pounding from the house. It was an old Victorian house in shabby condition. Shingles were missing from the roof where satellite dishes were propped up. The paint was peeling from the side and the majority of the wood looked rotten. If MAGIC was such a great pimp, he should have been able to afford a better house.

Inside, there was a room to my left with nobody in it. It had leopard print covers over the couch and chairs. To my right, I peeked through a crack in the door. MAGIC was surrounded by three of his buddies playing video games. They all had that scrawny tweaked-out look to them. They cursed at each other as shots were fired on what was most likely Grand Theft Auto.

Down the hall, a sliding glass door that was falling out of its threshold. Outside there was an above ground jacuzzi humming away. Two guys with topless women on their laps were laughing and chatting in the hot tub.

"Hey, who's that?" I heard a man yell from inside the room where MAGIC was.

Before I had a chance to decide what to do, one of MAGIC's boys opened the door.

"Come on in, girl. What're you waiting around outside for?" called MAGIC from the middle of the faux leather sofa.

"I didn't want to interrupt your game," I told him.

"This one I like, she got manners," said his friend to the left of him.

"Why don't you offer our guest a seat?" said MAGIC to his friend.

The man who opened the door, motioned for me to take his empty chair to the left.

I sat down, swung my backpack off and held it in front of me. I proceeded with my usual opening line of, "You got my money?"

MAGIC replied, "Sure do, but why don't you relax a bit, socialize, enjoy yourself?"

I replied, "I'm not in this business to socialize, I'm in this business to get paid."

Two of his friends let out howling noises at me.

"And I respect that but maybe I wanna know you a little bit more," said MAGIC.

"Why do you care?" I asked.

"Because I want to offer you a business deal," he said.

"What kind of deal? We already bring you what you ask for," I said to him with a stern voice.

"Nah, not that. How about you work for me?" He leaned forward.

"No thanks."

"Think about it. You'll make all sorts of money with that fine white ass. I'll take care of you, protect you, give you a place to stay. I know hundreds of dudes who would pay through the teeth for a piece of that. But the first thing I gotta do is fix that hair."

He reached up and pulled on my dishwater blonde hair that was thick with the beads and feathers I had placed in it.

I smacked his hand away.

"Easy honey, you don't behave like that with me," he warned.

Rising to my feet, I replied, "How about you pay me, take your stuff and I never have to look at your ugly face again?"

"Listen, I don't think you're understanding me. Working for me ain't a choice."

Two of his friends got up and blocked the door. He took a gun from his side and pointed it at my chest.

"Ask me why they call me MAGIC," he commanded.

With a smirk, I asked, "Why do they call you MAGIC?"

"Because I can make a woman disappear."

I smiled. "You promise?"

In one quick motion, I slapped his wrist with my right hand and twisted the barrel of the gun to face him. With a strong yank, I pulled the gun from his grip. MAGIC might have been able to fight me off if years of drug abuse had not whittled his body down to a skeleton with skin.

In a solid stance, I pointed the gun at MAGIC's head. MAGIC and his friends put their hands up. I backed out of the room and down the hallway until I got to the front door.

I rushed out of the house as fast as I could, but I sensed the presence of someone following behind me. Just as I was about to leave the yard, two of his buddies came after me.

I realized I still have his gun and I pointed it right at them. They stopped in their tracks, and I made a mad dash back to the front door. Glad they knew how to pick their battles.

I was a few blocks from Zeke's house before I remembered to dump the gun. I lifted the lid to someone's trash can, untied their trash bag and buried it under a mound of eggshells and coffee grounds.

I walked in the door and Zeke was there, startled by my presence. I fell to my knees sobbing.

"What happened?" Zeke barked at me.

"MAGIC tried to kidnap me and turn me into one of his girls," I said.

He sighed. "Are you sure?"

"Yes, I'm sure. I had to take that motherfucker's gun to get him to let me go," I cried.

"You pointed a gun at one of our best clients?" Zeke stared at me with his eyes bulging with rage. "MAGIC ain't some bachelor party of bros we'll never see again. He pays thousands every month."

I shrieked, "Zeke, you're not listening. He was going to keep me there."

He rubbed his face. "I doubt it. I bet he was just playing with you. He's like that."

"He wasn't, Zeke. He wasn't!" I yelled.

Zeke brought his face down to mine. "Did you at least make the deal?"

I wiped my eyes and said, "No, I had to get out of there as fast as I could."

"Taylor, you've got to be fucking kidding me." Zeke stormed away from me, reached for his empty beer bottle on the coffee table and threw it inches above me. When it made contact with the wall it rained brown glass over me.

"I never thought you could fuck up so much in one night. You threatened a client, ruined my reputation, and you didn't even get paid on the deal. I would have given you some slack when you first came here. You were such a hurt puppy with your broken wrist and mommy issues. Not now. It's been almost two years and you're still just as pathetic."

"No. I'm not. You don't understand. He could have killed me," I said to him.

"Don't be so over dramatic and clean that shit up," he said, pointing to the shards of glass covering the floor around me.

With shaking hands, I picked up the sharp pieces in my palm.

A few seconds or so later, Zeke walked by me with his coat in his hand.

"I need to go out. I can't be near you right now." His heel crushed a sliver of glass into tiny fragments as he walked out the front door.

CHAPTER 34
TAYLOR CALLAHAN

May 1, 2012
3 Years, 5 Months, 3 Days Before The Switch

Jesus took three days to rise from the dead and it took me three days to realize Zeke wasn't coming back.

I was home watching a rerun of Dr. Phil when Zeke burst through the door, his shirt stained with sweat and a look of fear in his eyes.

Before I could greet him, he blurted out, "We've been raided! We need to move. Now."

"What happened?" I asked, rising to my feet.

"I'll explain later," he said as he began rooting around our hallway closet. He threw a black duffle bag at me. "Fill this up."

We ran around the house bumping into each other and shoving t-shirts, toothbrushes, and pairs of sneakers into our bags.

In ten minutes, we were in his little blue Scion burning rubber down the turnpike. I can't believe I thought his car was cool at the time.

When Zeke finally calmed down enough to drive the speed limit, he told me, "I don't know exactly what happened, but I got a call from Manny. He was all panicked and said he was just about to go to the drop zone only to find DEA vans parked outside. As far as he knows, none of our boys were inside but until we know what they know about us, none of us are safe."

"What are we gonna do?" I asked him, attempting to sound cool and collected.

He replied, "Drive for a few more hours, find a cheap place to stay and figure it out from there."

· · ·

A few hours later, we pulled up to a motel that doesn't have a name. We got a key and walked past the exterior orange halls with blue railing up to our room on the second floor. We threw our bags in the closet and had passion-less sex on the creaking mattress before falling asleep.

In the morning, he was awake before me which was surprising. He mumbled some excuse about having to meet up with the boys to deal with the DEA situation and how I shouldn't call him for a few days until it was sorted out.

I've replayed this day over and over in my mind that I've worn out the actual details like a VHS that has been rewound too many times. I can't remember what was actually said and what I did during that time, but I do know for certain that he left me there for three days, eating crap from the mini-fridge and vending machine with the Motel owner banging on the door demanding payment.

Just as I was about to lose my mind with anxiety, pacing around the musty dark room picturing him getting busted and thrown in jail, I got a call from Manny. He had broken up with Chanel some time ago but still worked with Zeke all the time.

"Hey girl, I'm outside. Let me in," he said.

I looked out of my motel room peephole. The outside hallway stared back at me. No one was there.

"No, you're not." I laughed.

"I'm outside your house. Hear me knocking?" he asked.

"No, I'm not there. Zeke took me to a motel somewhere close to Jersey City," I told him.

"Why the Hell would he be doing that?" he asked.

"He said that we weren't safe. That the drop zone was raided by the DEA and that you saw it all happen."

"I don't know what you've been smoking but I was just there. No DEA or nothing."

"You mean he—"

Manny took a panicked breath. "Hey Taylor, I got to go." Dial tone rang in my ear.

Zeke lied to me and left me stranded in a town I've never been to before with no way to get home. *Shit.*

I took stock of everything. I had a duffle bag filled with mostly dirty clothes, no food left in the mini fridge, twenty dollars to my name, and a motel clerk who is going to be up my ass if I try to bust out of here. My back was up against a wall, and I had to come up with a plan.

•   •   •

The sun started to set around seven o'clock, the motel's busy time. All the couples who were having affairs would get off work and meet here. With all the comings and goings, I'm sure I could sneak away.

At 7:15 that evening, a tall man with a go-tee and sunglasses who was built like a house, met up with a chubby curly haired woman in the room next to me.

I listened to two uncomfortable hours of grunting noises before I heard them exit the room. I threw my bag over my shoulder and popped out of my doorway.

I hung back and walked four or five paces behind the big man using him as a shield. The woman got into a black Escalade and the man drove off in a Miata. *Go figure.* I slid up behind the Escalade and used it as cover. I paced next to it until it had completely left the driveway.

I scurried my way down the street, thanking God the motel managers didn't see me. Two blocks over, I see the familiar Golden Arches calling out to me. I spent three of my twenty dollars and I filled myself with the first solid meal I've had in days. With a stomach full of cheap meat patties and fries, I left the safety of the restaurant and wandered out into the unknown.

I walked around the gum and cigarette littered streets, passed bodegas, hair-cutting franchises, and pay-day loans. I ran possible scenarios in my head: I don't have enough money to take the bus back. But what's back home, anyway? Zeke who abandoned me, my mother who kicked me out, and Charel who I hadn't talked to in about a year. It would make more sense to stay put for now. But staying put still left me with seventeen dollars and no place to sleep.

I was considering hitting up an old woman at a bus stop when my eye caught something down the street. I got closer and saw a chubby, pock-marked teen boy attempting to place a credit card skimmer on an ATM.

I slide up next to him and whisper, "What are you doing?"

He stood back and threw his hands in the air like I'm a cop and repeated in a frantic voice, "I wasn't doing anything. I wasn't doing anything."

"Relax," I said. "There's no one around but you, me, and the old lady."

He looked around the empty street as if he didn't believe me.

"If you want to stay in the skimmer game, you first got to learn how to get in and out fast," I told him as I grabbed the device from his hand and slid it into place for him.

"And second of all," I looked into his eyes wide with confusion, "you've got to work on your startle response."

He still didn't say anything, but he let his hands drop a little.

"When someone notices you doing shit, there should be none of this—" I threw my hands in the air and imitated him. "But there should be more of this—" I crossed my arms, widened my stance and looked him in the eye to say. "What are you talking about?"

"Uhh, thanks," he said, letting out an exhale. He gave the empty street one more nervous glance and tried to book it.

I ran after him and pulled on his sleeve, "Wait now, I didn't tell you all that for free."

He stopped. Already panting, he asked, "What do you want?"

"I want a place to stay for the night and I want in," I tell him.

"In?" he asked.

"In on the business."

CHAPTER 35
TAYLOR CALLAHAN

May 1, 2012
3 Years, 5 Months, 3 Days Before The Switch

I went back to the boy's home. He told me his name was Max. He smuggled me up to his attic bedroom in his parents' home without them noticing. I was glad I didn't have to spend a night on the streets.

I spread out on his black dog-fur-covered futon on the other side of the room from his gray twin-sized bed. In between them, he had two large computer screens up against the wall and a rather large desk for the small space.

After Max said goodnight to his parents, he came up and looked around the room not knowing what to do with me. Before he could speak, the phone in his pocket let out a faint ringtone that I recognized as the *Legends of Zelda* theme.

He answered the phone and spoke in Russian while frantically looking back at me every few seconds.

He hung up and in ten minutes there were footsteps coming up the stairs. A man with a shaved yet still obviously balding head stomped up the stairs in an all-black outfit including military boots. Behind him was a tall teen boy older than Max. He had brownish red hair and a face pinched in like a pug's.

The man yelled something in Russian at Max with a hateful look then he turned and grabbed me by the neck and pulled me to my feet.

"What do you think you are doing trying to get in on my fucking business?" he barked.

I stared into his dull brown eyes petrified.

"Speak, bitch." He gave me a shake.

I blinked away my fear and spoke. "Clearly, you need my help. Your boy, here, didn't know what he was doing. About to get his ass busted if he lingered any longer."

The man relaxed his grip.

I continued, "I can tell you've got *fresh* talent on your hands. But really if you want to play the game, you can't send in amateurs."

The man stepped back giving me more space, I read this as a sign of respect.

"And you're a professional? A homeless teenage girl." He asked. I could now clearly detect an accent.

"I'm not homeless, I'm in-between opportunities." I responded.

"How old are you?" he asked.

"Seventeen," I answered

He laughed. "Seventeen-year-old vagrant who talks like a businessman and knows how to skim."

"Skim, deal, knock-over, cheat, lie, hide from the cops. Would you like to see my resume?" I smiled.

He let out a laugh again. "You, you amuse me, not a lot of people amuse me. How exactly did you learn all this?"

"I won't name names. But that's basically what I've been doing for the last two years with a variety of associates," I told him.

"And what happened?" The man asked.

"The DEA found our supplier. I bolted." At least, my story was partly true.

"I see. Well, I do count myself lucky to have someone who is willing to help me out with my new business venture. Certainly, you've got more backbone than these two." He said, tossing a shameful look at the two boys. "But I can't risk a woman on my payroll."

"And why's that?" I asked, squinting at him.

"I don't want my boys to get too attached. Or worse. I don't know how you can defend yourself." He came closer to me.

"What do you do if some man wants to have his way with you?" he asked, and he shoved me against the wall with his hands over my neck.

I brought my left arm around and across his arms with enough force to make his elbows buckle and let go of me. I swiftly brought my foot into contact with his balls and he fell to the ground. I flipped out my blade, grabbed his forehead that was dripping with sweat and pulled his head up. I placed my knife under his throat and asked, "Give me one good reason not to kill you."

Through a muffled and slightly shaky voice he said, "You're hired."

CHAPTER 36
TAYLOR CALLAHAN

May 2, 2012
3 Years, 5 Months, 2 Days Before The Switch

In the morning, after Max's parents left for work, the man came back. This time he didn't stomp in with anger seething behind his eyes. Instead, he glided in like a performer taking the stage.

"I believe we haven't been properly introduced," he began. "I'm Saul, Max's uncle. This one here is my son, Ivan." He smacked the back of the tall boy's head,

Ivan gave me a slight wave and a smirk. He was clearly embarrassed by his father but tried to hide it by seeming nonchalant.

I nodded and said my name.

"Nice to meet you, Taylor," said Saul. "If you're truly interested in joining our efforts, I need to explain to you what is going on. My nephew is the tech genius of our little operation. We feed him information from the skimmers and other documents we collect and he compiles them. After verifying that these details do in fact belong to real people and have actual value, we sell them to the highest bidder."

"So, it's just the three of you? What about Max's parents?" I asked them, my arms crossed over my chest, almost like a hard-boiled detective looking for any crack in their scheme.

"My brother and his wife know nothing about this which is why I've got to get you out here." Saul circled me like a vulture. "But to answer your first question, no, it's not just the three of us. We're only a small part of a larger group who has guys like us across the country. The big boss provides us with resources, distribution, and insider information on law enforcement, so we know where to operate with the lowest risk of arrest. For all of this, he cuts us in for a percent of the business. I was trying to keep this operation running light but," Saul walked over to his nephew and smacked him on the back of the head like he did to Ivan a moment ago, "since Max over there lacks discretion, and my son doesn't have the same enthusiasm that you do, I believe bringing you into our fold would be mutually beneficial."

"I agree," I told him. "When do we start?"

"Now." He took me by the back of the arm and rushed me out of Max's house.

Saul took me back to their home, a three-bedroom apartment located in the middle of a noisy street. The place was dark as it didn't come with overhead lighting, and they only bothered to put in one lamp. The kitchen was white and bare, with a pine table in the middle of it. Everything in the apartment looked stark and unused.

There was a big black leather couch that faced a TV on a low stand surrounded by DVDs and VHS tapes with the titles of movies printed on white strips of paper, clearly pirated.

"You can sleep on the couch till we can afford a third bed," said Saul.

I nodded.

Saul began again, "Or you can share the bed with Ivan. I'm sure he'd love the company." He threw a wink at his son.

"Dad," Ivan huffed, his fair skin glowing pink.

"What? I'm just a father trying to help his son out." He turned to me. "He doesn't seem to have much luck with the ladies."

The cellphone on his belt clip vibrated. He hurried off into another room to take it.

Ivan was burning red and he couldn't look me in the eye.

"Hey, it's okay," I said to him, "I know parents can be a pain in the ass sometimes."

He let out a sigh and some of his embarrassment went out with it.

"Listen, I'm not trying to sleep with you, just in case that's what my dad is making you think," he said, looking at his feet.

"Good, cause I ain't interested," I replied.

There was no time to discuss Ivan's love life or lack thereof. Saul got off the phone with a perturbed facial expression. He opened a gym bag full of skimmers and he made it clear that it was our task to run around the general area in Saul's ten-year-old Mercedes dropping them at several locations.

CHAPTER 37
TAYLOR CALLAHAN

June 8, 2012
3 Years, 3 Months, 26 Days Before The Switch

Saul's scams lasted for weeks, and I did most of the dirty work. When Saul had us dumpster dive for important documents outside of banks and hospitals looking for personal information, I was the one who did all the climbing and sorting while Ivan was the look-out. When Saul had us dress up like waiters and swipe credit cards and dollar bills off restaurant tables in Manhattan, I did all the talking. I'd entertain the customers with a smiling face and apron tied around my waist, explaining their server just went on break and I'd be happy to take the bill for them. Ivan would wait at the back door for me to drop unsuspecting patrons' money into his hands.

These schemes were high risk and weren't always easy to pull off. Plus, Saul often spent far more than what we were bringing in. It soon got to the point where Saul made Ivan get a job at a coffee shop, so he could bring in extra coin. I would have been put to work too if I hadn't left any form of government identification at my mother's house. Sadly, Saul took most of Ivan's wages, leaving us so little that we barely could survive off the food we could afford. This meant we had cereal, toast, and cans of tuna (which I loathe) for almost every meal.

To make more money that Saul couldn't get his hands on, I started robbing people's homes. I had done it a few times with Zeke. We normally would break in and steal from someone who owed us money. Now, I was reluctant to start again. But I was getting desperate. I spent most of the time awake hungry and Ivan, who clearly needed more calories than me at his height, started to look pale and sick from lack of food.

Enough was enough, I thought. If Saul wasn't going to provide for us, I would. But first, I had to find the right victim.

Ivan told me about a woman who came in every morning with a shitty attitude and demanded her usual latte while complaining about how this neighborhood wasn't good enough to put in a damn Starbucks. Perfect, I thought.

I came by the place the next morning to get a visual of this woman. I took a seat in a wooden chair at the table closest to the register, so Ivan could give me a sign when she arrived. Within fifteen minutes, Ivan eyed a short woman in her forties and gave me a nod. That was her.

"Large vanilla latte. I want it hot this time. Not warm. Not cold. Not room temperature. Piping hot, understand?" she barked at Ivan.

"Right away, ma'am," he replied and started on her drink.

She punched a few buttons on her BlackBerry and took a call. "Hi, Amanda. I wanted to go over plans for tonight one more time. Rick and I will be out until eleven tonight. Understand that I want extremely limited TV time for the two of them and please don't give them anything extra after dinner even if they beg."

Crap, she has kids. How can I steal from her place when a babysitter and children will be home?

The woman continued barking into her phone. "Pumpkin is overweight so be sure to take him on an extra walk after he has his dinner. Put on Beethoven for Missy while you're out with Pumpkin so she doesn't whine too loudly."

They're dogs, not kids.

"You've got the address right, this time? It's the Elliot Towers in case you get lost like last time. See you at 6:30 tonight and don't be late," she said and then hung up the phone.

Ivan gave me a raised eyebrow look indicating he was sure glad he wasn't Amanda right now. He handed the woman her drink and he rang her up with her AMEX card. She left without further acknowledging him.

When Ivan had a free moment, he rushed over to me. "Her name is Lizette Fitch. Well, more like Lizette Bitch, if you ask me but how are you going to get her?"

"She's going out tonight, I'll figure something out."

•   •   •

This neighborhood we lived in was mostly shit but there were a few beacons of the upper-middle class that shone out from the general worn-down streets. Aggressive business types made their way to the train that would take them to their corporate city jobs which seemed to involve a lot of phone calls, email-checking, and wearing the same business pin-striped wardrobe. They returned home in the evenings to blue glass high rises that had orchids in the lobby and at least two doormen on duty to keep the trash, like me, out.

One of these buildings was the Elliot Towers.

A few minutes before 6:30 that evening, I made my way into the lobby. Thankfully I was wearing my newest jeans and least depressing hoodie so I didn't look too out of place. I looked around confused as if the very concept of an elevator in a building was too much for my little brain.

"Can we help you, sweetie?" said one of the velvet-wearing doormen.

"I'm here for Ms. Fitch. I'm the new dog sitter."

He smiled and nodded.

"Glad they're finally getting a night out," said the other.

I took out my phone and began scrolling through the menu, making it look like I was reading something carefully.

"The only trouble is I can't remember the apartment number. I seem to have deleted that email and my mom is gonna kill me if I mess up this job."

"No worries, sweetie. It's 1214."

I gave him a giant smile. "Thanks, so much."

I headed for the elevator and headed to the twelfth floor. Then, I hid in the stairwell and stomped up and down between several floors until I finally saw a couple leaving for a night on the town. A man in a pale gray suit and a woman in a black dress with a turquoise shawl emerged from their apartment.

"You know how delicate that fabric is," Lizette barked at her husband.

"I forgot. I'm sorry. I thought I could just move your clothes to the dryer so I could use the washing machine. I didn't know your favorite dress was in there," the hen-pecked man replied.

"After all these years, you would think to…" Lizette ranted on as they rushed out of their apartment and into the elevator still deep in their fight. They let the door slam behind them and neither of them turned around to lock it. The only question was if those doors are self-locking or if they just forgot.

As soon as the elevator doors shut, I wiggled the nob. To my luck, the doors weren't self-locking, and the Fitches did indeed forget to lock it.

Now I know how this is supposed to go. How amateur, typical, simple criminals knock over houses. They trash the place, looking for anything hidden anywhere. But I see several flaws in that.

First, as soon as the owner comes home, they know the place has been robbed. They'll call the police and soon the police are hot on your trail.

Second, if they come home in the middle of it, they know someone might still be there and you're fucked because you're too busy throwing shit around to know you've been caught.

Third, it's easy to get caught if you're carrying tons of stuff with you and dressed in all black with a ski mask. It's just too obvious and too careless for me.

I went in and was greeted by two yapping yorkie terriers. I rushed over to the kitchen and reached into a bag of dog biscuits. I took a handful and tossed them across the rooms. The dogs left my side and rushed after their treats. While they feasted, I headed straight for the bedroom. The woman had a whole vanity covered in make-up and jewelry. I slipped a pearl necklace and two big rings into my pockets. I found their birth certificates and passports hidden in a box at the top of the closet. Too easy.

In the fridge, I discovered a box of truffles and I helped myself to several of them, imagining the returning couple accusing each other of being a fat ass for eating half the box. I skimmed a few pieces of mail off a pile of envelopes, only taking the ones marked "Important" and made my way out of the stairwell and into the alley behind the building. I was out and down the street before a teen girl with red pigtails was entering the lobby. I assumed she was the real dog walker and wouldn't be any the wiser. To this day, I'm not sure how long it took the Fitches to notice what went missing from their home.

One of the guys who ran the Bodega under our apartment was part of an identity theft ring. I knew I could sell these documents to him for a pretty penny. But there was no time for that now. Ivan and I hadn't eaten well for weeks. So, after spending fifteen minutes at a pawnshop, I walked away with 500 dollars for the stolen jewelry.

With Saul out of the house, I ordered Chinese food and had a huge buffet of noodles, beef, chicken, fried rice, and eggrolls spread out on the table.

Ivan walked in the door and his eyes lit up for the first time since I met him.

"You did it!" he said. "I can't believe you pulled that off."

"I sure did. Don't ask me the details but I wasn't going to let that bitch treat you that way and get away with it. So dig in and enjoy." I handed him a pair of wooden chopsticks.

He smiled at me, the first genuine expression on his face I'd seen since I met him. The ice was finally melting, and the real Ivan was coming out.

CHAPTER 38
TAYLOR CALLAHAN

July 14, 2012
3 Years, 2 Months, 20 Days Before The Switch

It was a burning hot day. Our little air conditioner that dripped water on people's heads in the street below was barely improving the temperature in our apartment. Ivan was still indifferent to me at this point even if he was thankful for my help. When he wasn't at work, he hid in his bedroom and played a load of first-person shooter video games while I watched one of Saul's bootlegged DVDs in the living room. And today was no different.

We were in our standard routine of ignoring each other when Saul busted through the front door. "Alright, you loafers, I'm going to need you out of here until tomorrow morning."

Ivan's game let out a big explosion followed by rapid firing. Saul pushed the door open to Ivan's room and yelled, "Listen when your father's speaking."

He came into the living room where Saul continued, "I was telling the girl that I need both of you out of the apartment until tomorrow morning. I have a lady friend coming over for a date and I don't need any kids around."

"What? You can't just kick us out like that," Ivan protested.

Saul grabbed him by the back of the neck, "You're over eighteen now and the girl is not even my child so yes, I can kick you both out anytime I like." He tossed Ivan to the side and added, "Don't you forget that."

We left the apartment and split up in different directions down the hot asphalt streets. I circled the block several times, keeping my pace fast to make it look like I had somewhere to be. This way the cops wouldn't think I was a working girl, and muggers would have to work to catch up to me.

After I walked the same four-block radius several times, I went off in a different direction, not knowing where it would lead. A few minutes later, I got to an area where dive bars with Rainbow flags lined the streets. The men who I passed on the street gave me the "You don't belong here, honey" look.

I saw two women with chopped short hair enter one bar three doors down. I figured I could at least hang out inside for a few hours, maybe get a few drinks for free. I was about to enter when I noticed Ivan leaning against the wall. A tall black man stood in front of him, one arm pressing against the bricks near Ivan's head. The man wore all leather and had five piercings in one ear.

They chatted for a minute before the man leaned down and kissed Ivan. He handed him a piece of paper and left.

I slid up to Ivan who jumped back upon seeing me.

He turned around and hid his face against the wall. "You fucking bitch, you're going to get me killed," he yelled at me.

"What are you talking about?" I asked.

"Because you're a crazy stalker psycho bitch. You couldn't just mind your own business. It's bad enough that we have to live together and work together. But no. You had to follow me. Now, you're gonna tell my dad and he's gonna kill me. He hates fags."

"I'm not gonna tell anybody." I said lifting the arm that was shielding his face. I wanted him to see it in my eyes that I was being sincere.

"Why?" he asked.

I smiled. "Cause I don't have a problem with it and I'm not about to let you get your ass kicked because your dad is a bigoted dick hole."

He smiled back, and I saw his whole body relax.

"Does this place card?" I asked him.

He shook his head no.

I grabbed him by the hand and said, "Good. How about we get in there and flirt ourselves into some free drinks?"

CHAPTER 39
TAYLOR CALLAHAN

December 5, 2012
2 Years, 9 Months, 29 Days Before The Switch
It had been over six months since Zeke abandoned me, but the wounds still felt fresh. I'd see his face everywhere.

When I was walking down the street, bound to pick up two large pizzas for Ivan and me to devour, suddenly I'd see Zeke's tall frame coming down the sidewalk in my direction. He'd get closer and closer until he was an arm's length away from me and his face would transform back into a stranger's.

Several times when Saul, Ivan, and I would be in the car on our way to one of his schemes, I'd look out the window to see a man in the car next to us and he would look back at me with the cold dark eyes of Zeke. It only lasted for a few seconds then the fog would lift, and Zeke's face would disintegrate and return to the stranger's original features.

It haunted me most of my days. Sometimes it made me want to turn the other way and run. Other times, it made me want to go after him and drive brass knuckles into the side of his face. I knew he would laugh at me if he saw me living with two Russian criminals, ripping information off people's credit cards.

Good money had been pouring in from the credit card business, but the issue was that it was inconsistent and so was Saul. One week he would surprise Ivan and me with a nice dinner out, usually Red Lobster. I can still smell the cheddar biscuits being placed on the table as Saul ushered us with over-the-top hand gestures to order whatever we wanted. Other times, he would have blown through what we had on his girlfriends and Ivan and I would share a bag of microwave popcorn for dinner.

• • •

On this particular day, Saul came home and ran with all his might into the kitchen table, toppling it over. He picked up each one of the four chairs and threw them across the room. One almost hit Ivan in the face.

"What the fuck, Dad?" said Ivan as he got to his feet.

"Don't you say "What the fuck" to your father. Show a little respect to the man who is keeping a roof over your head. Do you have any idea what just happened?" Saul yelled.

"No, obviously not," replied Ivan. We both turned around and kneeled on the cushions of the couch, using the back of it as some type of protection, like a trench between us and him.

"Those motherfuckers think our cut is too big. So, the big boss isn't going to pay us anything until I agree to a lower payout."

"Shit, what are we going to do?" I asked.

"I don't know. I don't know." Saul stomped around the room, attempting to pull hair out of his head even though there was barely any hair left to grab.

I asked Saul, "How much do we have left?"

"Practically nothing. I just paid the rent so I'm almost dry," he said as he cupped his face in his hands.

Ivan and I looked at each other knowing that "rent" also included gambling and buying gifts for his random girlfriends.

"This is ridiculous. What are we gonna do?" Saul asked.

"Then let's just agree to a smaller price and be done with it," Ivan suggested. I knew he wanted no part of this scheme to begin with.

Saul threw his hands up in the air. "The rate they wanted would land us in poverty. It wouldn't even be worth it."

"Everybody, relax. I'm sure we can think of something," I told them.

"There is nothing we can do. Nothing. We're screwed, we're finished!" Saul yelled.

I took a deep breath, annoyed by Saul's bad attitude. "Look, they can't keep operating if they don't have any cards."

He shrugged his shoulders. "So?"

"So, let's go take our scanners back," I began. "They are ours, right? We can do what we want with them and the big guys in charge can't do shit without any new credit information coming in. So, let's wait till after midnight, drive around and pull as many scanners off the machines as possible."

Saul clapped his hands together and a grin stretched across his face. "That's going to get their nuts in a twist. Brilliant! I knew there had to be a reason why I kept you around."

"Thanks, man." I rolled my eyes.

"Midnight is almost thirteen hours away, what are we going to do till then?" Ivan asked, clearly nervous about our plan.

"We can find something to do to kill the time," I said.

"Something cheap," said Saul.

"Let's go walk around the mall. That's free."

"Good, I'm supposed to meet Yasmin tonight and I need my last fifty dollars for that."

Ivan and I both rolled our eyes, swung on our coats, and we were out the door.

•   •   •

The warm and stiff temperature-controlled air hit the frosted tips of our noses and fingers as soon as we entered the mall. Every pillar, banister, and entrance were decorated with wreaths, ornaments and big red bows. "It's The Most Wonderful Time of The Year" was playing but Ivan's mood was not elevated by the Christmas spirit around us.

"What kind of father is he?" Ivan snorted. "He'd rather spend his last fifty bucks playing *rich daddy* to some chick than make sure his son is fed."

I shrugged.

"Oh, don't give me that," he scoffed.

"Give you what?" I asked.

"That   *I-don't-know-who-my-real-dad-is-so-you-should-feel-lucky* look."

"I may not know who my dad is, but I still think dads should feed their kids first. I'm on your side, don't worry. I'll help get him out of this mess as always." I gave Ivan a side squeeze.

We walked by a Cinnabon and the smell of sugary glaze sliding over a fresh hot cinnamon swirl made both of our stomachs roar.

"When's the last time you ate?" he asked me.

"When we polished off that box of Cheerios this morning," I answered.

We both dug through our pockets and found what amounted to seventy cents.

"Great," Ivan said. "Let's take our minds off food and go in here." He dragged me by the sleeve into the most fancy-pants department store in the mall.

"Ugh, this place is so boring," I moaned.

"Dude, relax, let's just browse okay? Let's pretend we're prep school kids with a big trust fund."

Ivan darted across the aisle into the Men's section. He threw on a gray tweed coat with brown elbow patches and wrapped a checkered bowtie sloppily around his neck.

In a British accent, Ivan said, "I hear this Polo season is going to be top notch this year. Top. Notch. But most unfortunately, Bonnie and I will have to miss it because we are summering in Spain."

We both fell over laughing and grabbed on to the racks of clothing to hold ourselves up.

I noticed a pencil-thin man behind the cashier counter gave us a sharp look.

"Come on, my turn." I told Ivan as I helped him get his bow tie off.

We darted off into the Women's section. Ivan called after me, "I'm going to make you look like the next first lady of the United States," as he dashed out of my view into the pantsuit section.

I thumbed through the rack of blouses in front of me imagining the accountants, schoolteachers, and paralegals wearing them in their offices on a Friday morning and nudging their co-workers and playfully shouting "TGIF" at each other.

To my left, a young salesgirl at the cash register was trying as hard as she could not to get into an argument with the customer at the counter.

"I don't understand why you won't give me a refund. I have the receipt," a tall woman with tightly curled white-blonde hair yelled at her.

The clerk cleared her throat and said, "I'm sorry ma'am, but you bought these shoes at a forty percent mark down, and we don't offer refunds or exchanges with sale items."

The customer let out a dramatic sigh, reached into her shopping bag and pulled out a pair of brown pants. "What about these? I'd like to return them too, and I've bought them at full price."

"I can take those back. I just need the credit card that was used to make the purchase and I can refund the amount back on the card," she said.

"At least you can do *something*," the customer replied. She swiped the card then set it down underneath the credit card terminal.

"Alright, you've been refunded for 108 dollars," said the cashier as she handed the woman a receipt.

"Good. I've just got to figure out what to do with these shoes now." The customer threw the shoe box into her shopping bag and marched away leaving her credit card behind.

The cashier rubbed her forehead and stepped away from the register as no one else was in line.

As soon as she was busy folding cardigans at the other end of the department, I made my way to the check out.

With my left hand, I flipped through the assorted gift cards that were on display while my right hand slipped the woman's credit card into my jacket pocket.

"Can I help you?" The cashier was making her way from her cardigans to the check out. *Shit, she thinks I'm trying to purchase something.*

Before I could explain myself, she was behind the register and ready for action.

"Sorry, I was just looking at the gift cards. Grandma's birthday is next week, and I have no idea what to get her."

I thought I was a better liar than this.

Just then Ivan sprinted across the Women's department, holding a black and white houndstooth skirt and blazer with a string of pearls draped over the hanger. "Taylor, look, isn't it perfect?"

I called back, "I don't know if Grandma will like it. Let's look some more."

I threw a smile at the cashier and quickly rushed Ivan out of her line of sight.

"Grandma?" His brow scrunched up.

"I'll explain later. Just dump that shit and let's get out of here."

Ivan hung up the snobby outfit on the rack closest to us and we rushed out of the store.

"What do you want? Prime rib? Lobster? Tiramisu? It's on me," I pulled the credit card out of my pocket, "Well, it's actually on Mrs. Priscilla J. Whitaker."

"How the fuck did you get that?" Ivan whispered.

"When I see an opportunity, I strike," I told him.

"Like a snake," he added.

"Seriously, what do you want to eat?"

"Panda Express will do."

"Fine by me."

•   •   •

After our bellies were full of Chinese food, I knew I should have stopped there. I should have left the card in the women's room or another store to make it look like Pricilla's just forgot it. All we really did need was a good meal, but I couldn't help myself.

I decided to treat myself to a day at the mall before I ditched it. I didn't want to pretend like I was rich—well not rich—just not dirt poor for once.

I bought myself a pair of shiny black Doc Martens. I got Ivan a maroon-colored hoodie at a skate shop that cost ninety bucks for some reason. I was pulling every black, grey, and dark blue clothing item off the shelf and making it my own.

I walked up to the boy around my age who was behind the cash register at a clothing store. I dumped a pile of new jeans and shirts on the counter. As he asked for my card, it happened again. The boy's soft features grew darker and more chiseled. His face changed to Zeke's and I froze. The boy must have processed the payment, but I was in a fog. I didn't snap out of it until a voice called out behind me, "Taylor Callahan, please come with me."

CHAPTER 40
TAYLOR CALLAHAN

December 5, 2012
2 Years, 9 Months, 29 Days Before The Switch

I turned around. A woman in a business suit flashed her police badge at me. My blood turned to ice. I saw Ivan was about three yards behind me, staring with his mouth open. The cop didn't seem to know he was with me. As the woman pulled me away, I gave Ivan a slight nod to let him know I would be okay and that he shouldn't try to interfere.

She escorted me out of the mall where two uniformed cops stood waiting to see if I would put up a fight, but I didn't.

She read me my rights and dropped me off at the station to sit in a tiny interrogation room for almost an hour before she graced me with her presence.

I was angry at her for catching me and at myself for getting caught.

I knew I shouldn't talk but felt this desire to set the record straight and keep any attention off Saul and Ivan if the cops even knew about them.

"Listen, I'm sorry, I know what I did was wrong, but I never had a chance to buy anything nice when I was growing up," I told her.

She took a sip from her coffee cup and thumbed through some papers in front of me before she said, "I'm not here to listen to your sob story, Ms. Callahan. Yes, you are here for possible counts of fraud and identity theft which I am prepared to bring you to trial for. But we are after a much bigger fish, Ezekiel Warren-Hernandez."

My heart raced. "What about him?"

"We believe he could lead us to a very large shipment of cocaine that seems to be slipping past border control. We have sources that say you used to have a relationship with him. We would appreciate it if you tell us everything you know about him."

"Appreciate?" I asked.

She nodded. "Yes, so much so that we'll forget about your little shopping spree."

"Okay, well, I can't tell you where it comes from. I don't know that. I know that there is one guy in charge, he would just call him *the boss*. But I don't know his actual name or location."

She crossed her arms. "I wouldn't start by telling us what you *don't* know."

I took a breath and held back my desire to beat this woman senseless, in handcuffs or not. "Okay, fine. In AC, they keep the coke at a warehouse on thirteenth street and Ocean."

"AC?" she asked.

"Yeah, Atlantic City. I'm surprised you don't know that. Aren't you from New Jersey?" I asked her.

She didn't acknowledge my comment and said, "Continue, Ms. Callahan."

"So, in Atlantic City as well, the pot is at some grow house on Elm. I don't know the house number. It's a one story, light yellow, with three beat-up cars in the driveway. He also keeps a lot of it at his house on Maplewood. I don't know if he still lives there but if he does, you can easily bust him there," I said. "And when I get to his address and it turns out he is still living there, where can I find it?" she asked.

"Look under his couch, in the pull-out mattress. That's where he keeps his supply. If you can't find him there, we used to eat at this diner, the Redstone. It's just down the street. He might be there. He also hits up the 7-Eleven at the end of his street once a day for beer around six in the evening. Millers and Heineken, mostly."

"So, the grow house on Elm, the Warehouse on Ocean, and a house on Maplewood. That's it?"

I was getting annoyed with her. "That's all I know. I know he used to sell pills like prescriptions sometimes and party drugs, but he never took me with him to pick it up. Same with heroin. He didn't deal with a lot of it when I was with him, so I never saw where it came from."

She asked, "Is he armed?"

"He has a Glock. Sometimes it's with him or in the car. When he brings home a big supply and is organizing it, he keeps it in the house. He usually has a knife strapped to his ankle too, like the one you guys took from me when I got here. I can't say he is always armed but there's a good chance he is."

The corners of the detective's mouth turned up slightly like she was hiding a smile. "Thank you for your cooperation. We will have to wait until tomorrow to get a warrant from a judge. Until then, I'll see to it that you have a place to spend the night."

"Spend the night? I thought we had a deal?" I shouted.

She started straightening her papers into a neat pile on the table and scooped them into one arm. "We do. We'll drop the charges if your information turns out to be valid."

"It's been months, I don't know if the supplier is still there," I protested.

"Regardless, we must check it out. We'll let you know." She left the room.

CHAPTER 41
TAYLOR CALLAHAN

December 6, 2012
2 Years, 9 Months, 28 Days Before The Switch
A policeman led me out of the room and down a hall.

"Hey, don't I get a phone call?" I asked him.

He nodded and took me to a phone and dropped a quarter in.

I dialed Ivan's cell.

"Hello?" he answered.

"Hey. It's me," I said, clutching the phone.

"What happened? Are you okay?" he asked, his voice shaking from nervousness.

I told him, "Yeah I'm fine. I'm at the police station. I'm going to be spending the night here, but they might let me off."

"How?" he asked.

"It has to do with Zeke. And if everything pans out, I'm free to go tomorrow. If you don't hear from me by tomorrow night, come look here."

He took a breath, "Okay."

I knew that I'd be out of time soon. "I've got to go. See you soon."

"Taylor?" he asked.

"Yeah?" I replied.

"Promise?" he asked.

"Promise what?"

"That I will see you soon."

I smiled. "Of course." I hung up the phone and the officer led me to a small cell with three out of four walls being concrete, the other iron bars. There was a small cot on the left with a metal sink and a toilet at the other end.

Sleep faded in and out as I heard tiny drops of water fall from the sink. There were people in the cells around me. I heard them talking to one another, but I forced myself to ignore what they were saying.

Finally, the sun shone through the window that was at the top of the hallway.

A different officer from the day before gave me a tray of mushy oatmeal for breakfast. A few hours later, he turned up with a dry sandwich made of crumpled lettuce and some form of meat I don't want to know more about.

Just as he took my empty tray away, the detective woman held the door open to my cell. "Taylor Callahan, you're free to go."

Before I could leave, they had me sign a stack of paperwork in a tiny yellow room.

The detective said, "Thank you for helping us with our investigation."

I knew this meant the intel I gave was not only true but useful. Zeke hadn't moved, neither did his supply, and he was going down.

As I left the police station, a man in a gray jumpsuit was climbing a ladder in the lobby. He pulled down a water-stained ceiling tile and replaced it with a clean one.

In a flash, I remembered Zeke standing on a tiny purple chair and pushing a ceiling tile up with one strong arm. He tossed a kilo of coke up there and a few baggies of pills. There was faded alphabet wallpaper that wrapped around the top part of the room. It was the old abandoned elementary school where we had first met at my sweet sixteen. I turned on my heels and was about to march back into the police station to inform that woman that there was another place to look. But I stopped myself.

She already had enough information to release me. What good would this do? Plus, she doesn't need money that would come from selling those drugs. I do. Saul and Ivan do. I bet there's fifty grand worth of shit sitting there and it's going to be mine for the taking.

CHAPTER 42
TAYLOR CALLAHAN

December 6, 2012
2 Years, 9 Months, 28 Days Before The Switch

On foot, I rushed across town, dodging cars and cat-calling homeless men until I stomped up the stairs to our apartment.

Ivan came running out of his room and grabbed me. "Holy shit, Taylor. What happened to you?"

"I'm fine. I made a deal and I'm off the hook," I told him.

"What? How?" he asked.

"They wanted Zeke. They said if I give them what I know about him, they'd let me go. I just had to wait overnight so they could check out my story," I said as I walked over to the kitchen and grabbed a bowl of Apple Jax. I needed to get that prison food taste out of my mouth.

Ivan scratched his head. "That's some spy-level shit."

"Hell yes, it is," I said in between bites.

"That asshole got what was coming to him." Ivan beamed.

"Is your dad here?" I asked.

"No, he stayed over at Yasmin's last night after we finished pulling off most of the skimmers. Hasn't been back yet," he told me.

"So, you didn't tell him?" I asked him.

"Are you kidding? He would have a cow," Ivan exclaimed.

"Good. Want a way to make a few grand?" I asked him.

"Um...yeah but how?" He threw me a skeptical look.

"Let's just say I didn't tell the cops every single location Zeke used to hide his drugs in." I swallowed another heaping spoonful of the cereal.

"Are you saying we're gonna take his supply?" he asked.

"Why not? He's busted. Sold down the river. Down for the count. He can't use it. The cops don't need any more evidence. So, let's make a profit for ourselves." I nudged him with my elbow.

"How much is there?" he asked.

I shrugged. "I don't know for sure. But it's got to be at least a kilo."

"Of coke?" Ivan's eyes bulged out of his head, making his pug-face look even more puggish.

I held back a laugh. "Yeah."

He looked away from me. "I didn't realize how serious you guys were."

"Still am serious. Now let's get down to Atlantic City before the cops get to it." I picked up his coat off the back of a kitchen chair and handed it to him.

"Wait. How? Dad's got the car," he asked.

I told him, "Call your dad. Say you need the car. We'll walk to Yasmin's and pick it up. She can give him a lift home. If he gives you any shit, tell him to tell Yasmin, his son needs it and he has to be a good father."

Ivan did as I said, and Saul was waiting outside of Yasmin's duplex in her fuzzy teal robe with the keys in hand. "This better be for a good reason."

"Trust me, it is," I told him.

He tossed Ivan the keys and said, "Be careful in the backseat. Lost a condom there last night."

"Dad! That's so gross," moaned Ivan.

"What? It happens." He threw up his hands in the air and went back inside.

Ivan got behind the wheel of Saul's ancient Mercedes. It smelled of cigarette smoke and Old Spice.

"God, I'm dying for a smoke," I announced.

"I thought you quit," Ivan smirked, knowing my various attempts to quit only lasted a month at best.

"Yeah, yeah, yeah. After a night in jail, I deserve it." I rummage through the glovebox finding half a pack of American Spirits under a pile of receipts.

I rolled down the window and took a puff.

Ivan sped down the Garden State Parkway.

"You've got to drive more carefully on the way back. We don't want to attract any attention," I told him.

．　　　．　　　．

We made excellent time and arrived in Atlantic City in just over two hours.

"So, this is your hometown?" Ivan asked.

"Yes, it is. Raised, not born. I was born in Union. My parents came down here when I was four," I said.

"Do you miss it?" he asked.

"Hell no, are you crazy?" I laughed.

"Like Jersey City is the height of luxurious living?" he replied.

"I don't need luxurious living. I just need..." I trailed off.

"Need what?" Ivan asked.

"I don't know. I feel like I don't have the words for it. Just a life, away from drama and doing dumb shit for money. Where I can just be myself and don't have to feel like someone's coming after me all the time," I said.

"I don't think stealing your ex-boyfriend's drugs is a way to do that," Ivan said.

I told him, "I know, but it's the only option we've got. I don't see Saul out there hustling to feed us."

He sighed, "That's the truth. Now where the Hell is this place?"

"Keep going, five blocks from here take a left."

We passed rows of tiny houses, some with laundry lines hanging between them. Others had chicken wire over their upstairs windows with dirty hay dripping in between the wooden slats.

Ivan took a turn and the houses disappeared behind us. We came across a big empty pit filled with broken bottles and potato chip wrappers to our right and an abandoned apartment building to our left.

"Keep going," I told Ivan.

After we passed the pit, we came up on the three buildings that used to be a school. In front of the building's driveway was a metal chain but it had been pulled down and now lay across the asphalt.

A sun-bleached "No Trespassing" sign dropped off the chain link fence as we drove by.

We parked as far away from the street as possible. Before we got out, we looked around. I didn't see any movement in the buildings and not a soul was around. There was a burnt-out car in the parking lot, but it looked like someone gave up on it a long time ago.

"Which building is it?" Ivan asked.

"The left one. It's in a kindergarten room. It has small colorful chairs and the ABCs on the wall," I said.

Ivan nodded, "Let's go for it."

We rushed out of the car and I led him to a big metal door which was kept partly open with a cinder block.

We squeezed through the opening, not wanting the door to squeak as we opened it. We stared down a long hallway that led to many classrooms. It was dark except for the cracks of sunlight that came through the holes in the ceiling and broken windows.

It was in worse shape since I last saw it: giant holes in the drywall, trees bursting through windows, water damage making the place smell of rotting wood.

We were five doors down before Ivan whispered, "Is it this one?"

I poked my head in and saw overturned short round tables next to cracked and scattered tiny colored chairs. The faint ABCs wallpaper could still be seen.

"Yeah, this is it," I said.

In the corner, to the right of the door, there was one purple chair pushed up against the corner looking remarkably serene among the rest of the mess.

I told Ivan, "Get that chair and start lifting up ceiling tiles."

Ivan, who was just about the same height as Zeke, stood on the chair and started opening the ceiling. The first tile landed on him, giving him a face full of dust. The second and third were completely empty.

He pushed up on the fourth tile, bracing for more dust to fall on him but instead he saw a white packet.

He reached in and pulled out a kilo. He rooted around more and pulled out a freezer bag filled with dime bags of little square-shaped blue and white pills.

He handed them to me, and I stuffed them into his backpack.

Just as we were about to close the ceiling title, I heard two male voices coming down the hall.

I noticed a connecting door to the next classroom. I grabbed Ivan by the wrist and slipped through the wooden door.

We stayed silent with our hands over our mouths to suppress the sounds of our breath. I heard them speak again.

"Nah, man, I'm telling you. It's in here," said the first man at a confident volume.

"You better be right, or the boss is gonna kill you," said the other.

"He can't afford to lose another one of us." The first man laughed.

I recognized the sound of the first guy's voice. It's Manny. He must have come to collect what Zeke left behind.

They got closer and I could tell they were now in the room behind us.

The other man asked Manny, "Why are you talking so loud? Someone else probably is in here. You saw that Mercedes."

Shit. He knows we're here.

Ivan's eyes bugging out of his head in fear.

Manny continued at the same volume as before, "That car is old as shit. Someone probably just left it here a long time ago."

I motioned at Ivan to follow me.

We carefully stepped around a row of fallen chairs then over a pile of broken beer bottles.

I looked out the open door to the room we're in. The front door we came in from is at the other end of the hall. There was no way we could make it down there without getting caught. I turned to my right and saw there was another exit right next to us.

We took a few light steps out into the hall then darted out of the building.

Ivan's boot crushed a piece of glass on the concrete stairs leading down steps.

I heard Manny call out, "Did you hear that?"

Ivan and I rushed around the opposite side of the building, ducking our heads under the windows as best we could.

We made it to the car and just as I was about to get into the passenger side, I saw Manny and his friend staring at me from the front door of the building.

"Taylor!" he screamed.

I got into the car and Ivan took off, his tires burning as he sped down the driveway.

•   •   •

In a few blocks, we merged back onto the freeway and I saw no sign of anyone following us.

"We got away with it," I cheered.

"Yes, we did, but you didn't." Ivan was fixated on the road.

"What do you mean?" I asked him.

"I assume that guy knows Zeke, right?"

"Yeah, they work together," I told him.

"He's gonna tell him that you stole from him and he might come after you." Ivan said.

"But he'll be in jail," I said.

"But not forever."

We drove the rest of the way home in silence and came home to find Saul sitting at our kitchen table with a pile of skimmers in front of him and a grin on his face. "We did what you said, Taylor. I finished taking back the rest of the skimmers and now we're getting an even bigger cut."

"That's great, I told you that you should always listen to me," I said.

"Now what did you two need my car for today? Was it to help Ivan pick up chicks? I have a feeling that Taylor is a good wing woman." He let out a laugh.

"No, it was for something more serious. A big help to the household," I told him.

"What kind of help?" he asked.

"Five figures worth of help."

"Let me see."

I took the drugs out of Ivan's backpack and tossed them on the table.

Saul placed his hands on his head and cackled with a mix of laughter and tears.

He stood up and hugged me. "You know I never wanted a daughter. But now I have one and you have made me so proud. Ivan, learn something from her, will you?"

CHAPTER 43
TAYLOR CALLAHAN

January 2, 2013
2 Years, 9 Months, 2 Days Before The Switch

With our new influx of cash, Saul had us move out of his little apartment into a house with a garage and three bedrooms. We rolled up to a new roomy pad in a nice neighborhood with a U-Haul truck driven by Saul and Ivan behind the wheel of the old Mercedes. Both vehicles were filled with poorly-packed brown boxes with bootlegged DVDs and worn-out clothing poking out.

As we started to unload the truck, an old couple in matching royal blue pant suits approached Saul.

"Welcome to the neighborhood," beamed the old woman.

Saul nodded, "Thanks."

"It's so nice to see a family move in," said her husband.

The couple looked at me and then at Ivan.

"Where is your wife?" the old woman asked.

"She is sadly no longer with us. She passed shortly after my youngest was born due to complications. So, I've raised these two all by myself."

"Heavens, that is so sweet," the woman cooed.

The old man looked at Ivan and said, "You're lucky to have such a good man as your father."

Ivan smiled, holding back a laugh. "I sure am."

As Saul continued chatting with the neighbors, Ivan and I carried boxes into the house. After the seventh trip, we sat down in the empty living room to catch our breath.

"So, do you wanna know what really happened with my mom?" he asked me.

I nodded. I was curious.

Ivan began, "She ran off with some big Wall Street guy when I was in middle school. Dad never took it well, so he's been trying but mostly failing to get rich. It's his way to show her what she is missing. But as you know, he's not so good with holding on to cash for long periods of time."

"Sounds about right," I said, with a laugh.

"Do you ever think of your brother?" Ivan asked me.

"Yeah, but my mom would flip her shit if she ever saw me again. Plus, I don't know if they still live in the same house anymore. Nadine tends to get evicted," I told him.

"I still see my mom once in a while but don't tell my dad," Ivan confessed.

"Of course, I won't." I would never betray Ivan's secrets, any of them. "So, you think I should try to find my brother?"

"Yeah, I mean it can't hurt to try and if you can't find him or he doesn't want to see you then at least you can say you tried instead of intentionally disappearing from his life forever," he said.

•   •   •

A few days later, we drove two hours southwest to my old house. Nothing had changed. The vile green duplex with the bars on the window was still standing as if no time had passed.

I walked through the rusting gate made of chain link and stomped the familiar path of chipped cement to my old house. I peered in the front window. The curtain had been drawn away from the window in between vertical blinds. I saw the same lumpy blue couch, the coffee-ring-stained table, buttloads of Neil's video games, all new stacked around the TV.

"What are you doing?" a voice called out behind me.

I turned around to see a boy with dirty blonde hair that sprung out in spirals from his head. Poor kid, looks like Mom's hair snuck up on him as puberty approached. I'm lucky to have dodged that genetic bullet.

"Neil?" I asked with a smile.

"Taylor? You came back." He rushed up the path and gave me a big hug. "What happened? Why did you leave and where did you go?"

"Mom didn't tell you?" I replied.

"She changes her story so many times I don't know what's real. Wanna come in? She won't be home for another two hours," he told me.

He unlocked the door and we went inside.

Neil sat on the mushy blue sofa and I sat next to him. "So, Mom has said some pretty terrible stuff about you and after a while I realized she had to be lying."

I felt anger rise in my cheeks. "What did she say?"

He sighed, "That you're a crack whore or a heroin junkie. Then she told me you were planning on selling me into child slavery for drug money and a hundred versions of the same thing."

Tears filled up my eyes. Imagine little chubby-faced eight-year-old Neil being told I was going to sell him. How evil could she be?

"I can't believe she would say that. I did not ever try to or plan to sell you," I said with my voice shaking.

"I figured that you didn't," he replied.

"And I never sold myself either." I looked away from him for a minute, so I could dry my eyes with my sleeve. "Look, I'm not gonna lie to you. I'm no saint. I don't think anyone from this neighborhood is. But anyway yes, I did deal drugs and that's why Nadine kicked me out. And honestly I'm not exactly on the up and up right now but I'm not a monster and I would have never left you on purpose."

He nodded.

"Why did you start?" he asked.

I replied, "Start?"

"Start dealing?" he answered.

"I met a boy. I know it's stupid, but I was sixteen years old and all hormones. I would have done anything to make him happy. And he wanted me to deal so that's what I did. I'm not proud but—" I trailed off, feeling embarrassed.

"And did you use?" he asked.

"Not really," I answered. "I never tried the serious stuff. I did a little weed and coke, but I never shot up or anything. I don't really like the feeling of being high anyway, I prefer some vodka and a smoke from time to time but, that's not the point. I'm not a druggie whore like Mom said."

He took a deep breath, "How are we supposed to make anything of ourselves? We've got no money and no one to really look after us. School is filled with teachers who don't care and kids who want to get in fights. I want to be someone. I want you to be someone."

I smiled. "Wow. You're really mature beyond your years."

"What I'm trying to say is that I get it. I'm not happy you left but I understand. How is everything where you are now?" he asked.

"I live with friends in a house in Jersey City. Things are good most of the time. I still have to hustle for a living and can't even get a job because I don't even have my freaking birth certificate to get a real ID," I said.

"I think I know where Mom keeps them. I can get it for you," Neil offered.

"You'd do that?" I asked, feeling my heart melt.

He got off the couch. "Of course, it isn't hers anyway."

He ushered me into my mom's bedroom. Her lavender sheets are tangled in the corner of an unmade bed. Stacks of boxes were overflowing as a tower of paperwork looming over her tiny desk in the corner.

Neil started unstacking boxes. "I think they're in the bottom one. She went into this box when she had to go to the DMV a few months ago, so I figure it has to have important information."

We shuffled papers around in the bottom box. It seems she kept everything, old bills and receipts from the 1990s and earlier. The whole room began to smell of dust.

We found it. A certificate that had "Taylor Elizabeth Callahan" written on it with Nadine Callahan and Andrew Callahan as my parents.

"Do you need anything else?" asked Neil, "Money? Mom's jewelry?"

I salivated at the thought. I wanted her money and her valuables so I could stick it to her one last time. But I shouldn't because I didn't need to. Ivan, Saul, and I had gotten better at what we did. We hadn't been strapped for cash in a long time. I should have left it, but I couldn't resist.

"Oh, stop it," I said. "This is enough, but it would be great to get her back for throwing me out all those years ago."

"Nothing stopping you. I won't say a word." Neil smiled with a mischievous shine to his eyes. For a second, I thought I could see Drew's features in his face. Maybe he was one of our fathers after all.

Neil handed me a heart-shaped box with Mom's jewelry in it. Inside was a tangled gold chain running through several rings with big shiny stones on them. To the side a few gaudy pearl earrings were hidden behind a rhinestone-laced leopard print bracelet. I knew I wouldn't get a lot for these at a pawn shop, but I took them anyway.

I dumped the box into my bag and opened my mouth to say my goodbyes to my brother when I found him arms deep under the mattress, ready to flip it.

"What are you doing?" I asked him.

He pushed the mattress off its frame. "This is where Mom keeps the money," he grunted, clearly wearing himself out.

Hundreds of green dollar bills spilled onto the floor. I opened my bag with my left hand, the one Nadine broke when she threw me out. It hadn't healed properly and every now and again it ached, and it ached like Hell at that moment.

She deserved this. I scooped up the cash by the fist-full and dumped it into my bag.

"Yeah!" cheered Neil. He tossed a wad of cash into my bag. "I think she has some more in the cookie jar in the kitchen, let me go and get it."

I couldn't believe how awesome my little brother turned out to be. Nadine didn't ruin him after all.

I heard a bang, the sound of the front door slamming shut on its metal frame. I froze knowing that it only meant one thing.

"What in the Hell are you doing with that cookie jar?" I heard Nadine screech.

Neil muttered a few "ums" and "uhs" before she said, "Whatever, you mush mouth, just put it back. I just got fired, the last thing I need is any shit from you."

She turned the corner and she saw me leaning over her bed with both my hands full of her money.

"You little tramp," she screamed at me. She took her bag off her shoulder and started slapping my face.

The first blow cut my lip, the second almost knocked me to the floor. By the third, I was able to curl up into a ball, hiding my face in my arms as she rained blows on my back.

"You're robbing me, you little whore. Didn't I throw you out once before? It's like I can't get rid of you," she yelled as she grew tired of hitting me with her handbag.

I looked up to see her fishing her cellphone out of her bag. "Hello, 911? I'm being robbed."

I jumped to my feet. "No, Mom. I'm sorry, you can have it all back." I start dumping the cash out of my bag.

"She is right here, robbing me. She has my cash, she has my jewelry, send help quick." Nadine continued to give the operator her information.

If it had been any other house, I would've ran out of there. But I knew the police station is two blocks south and I wouldn't be able to get far.

Two police cars parked outside.

There was no escaping this one.

CHAPTER 44
TAYLOR CALLAHAN

November 1, 2013
1 Year, 10 Months, 6 Days Before The Switch

I found myself celebrating my nineteenth birthday inside a correctional facility for women. Though there wasn't much to celebrate. Everything in that place was dull. The buildings were these large oatmeal-colored rectangles and everything inside was the same lifeless color. The bars on my cell were a faded white, our prison uniforms were shapeless tan scrubs that made us look like the world's saddest medical team. The food was beige, the walls were beige, the floors and ceilings were beige.

The dullness of the place seeped into me and made me just as sad. I thought that this level of confinement would bring out the worst in me. I pictured myself secretly digging a hole out of my prison cell or finding ways to blackmail the guards into doing what I wanted. I thought that the most "criminal" of places would turn me into some sort of super criminal, but it didn't. I caved in on myself like a deflated basketball. I had no desire to run around, hustle, finagle, or cheat my way out of this. I barely had the desire to leave my bed in the morning and I wouldn't have if the guards didn't make us.

Everything felt dense, heavy, and blurry. My memory turned to mush and the several months I had spent in this facility blurred together. The food wasn't disgusting like I first thought, it was tasteless. The manual labor of janitorial duty wasn't hard, it was boring. This feeling made me recoil from all human contact. I didn't make friends and I ate by myself. My cellmate and I barely spoke.

A riot broke out once. I heard the women screaming down the hall. I saw guards with helmets and shields running past my cell and I remember thinking that I wouldn't have cared if these bitches killed me in their pointless riot. It would beat the Hell out of three more birthdays in this place.

But on this day, a guard appeared in my cell. He took me to this tiny office with a Hispanic woman in black blazer sitting on the other side of the desk.

The woman smiled, "Hello Ms. Callahan, I'm Nancy Martinez."

I nodded.

She said, "I've been reviewing your file and you have one of the best behavior records I've ever seen."

I told her, "I just like to keep to myself."

"That's really good. It looks like we can get you released early for good behavior," she said.

"Really?" I asked her. "I haven't even completed a year yet.

"There is an initiative to not waste taxpayer dollars on keeping inmates in prison if they pose no real threat to society. You're a young, non-violent first-time offender who has been on excellent behavior. So you fit the bill. We have a release date for you, November 25th."

She has me sign a few forms all the while I'm jumping for joy on the inside. The fog lifted and was replaced by a jumping bean of nervousness inside of me.

CHAPTER 45
TAYLOR CALLAHAN

November 25, 2013
1 Year, 10 Months, 9 Days Before The Switch

I spent the last twenty-four days burying my anxiety into anything I could get my hands on. I sped through my normal routine of mopping the halls and volunteered to help the girls on the bathroom crew even if the mess was disgusting.

It wasn't until I was about to sleep my last night on a prison cot did I realize how screwed I was. Of course, I wanted out of there, but I didn't have anywhere to go. I put Ivan's address on my release papers saying that he was my cousin, but in reality, I hadn't spoken to him since the day of my arrest during my one phone call. I knew once he saw the cops coming outside Nadine's house he sped off and I couldn't blame him. He told me over the phone that he would convince Saul to help me out, but I never heard from either of them again.

But it didn't matter where I was going, I couldn't stay there.

I was buzzed through a heavy metal door where an officer handed my clothes and belongings back from the day I was arrested. I threw on my ripped jeans, AC/DC shirt and faded hoodie. I walked on the sidewalks narrowed by patches of recently plowed snow. My breath formed little clouds in front of me as I walked. It was too cold for what I was wearing, and my bones began to ache from the cold.

There was nothing around the prison, just old warehouses and industrial parks. I had no idea where I was going to go or where I was going to find shelter. Just as I was about to give up and spend the night in an abandoned building, I saw the yellow neon glow of my favorite fast-food place.

I rush in, the heat warming my body. I only had forty dollars in my wallet, but it was worth spending the six dollars on a quarter pounder with cheese, a large order of fries and a milkshake.

As I ate, I pitied myself. I was back where I had started five years ago, when Zeke first got rid of me. I'm alone in a strange town, no family or friends to turn to, and no money to my name. I put down the lopsided bun with a chunk of meat hanging out. My appetite disappeared. I hung my head in my hands and cried. I worked so hard to pick myself off the street. And once again Nadine wrecked my life and the men I cared about abandoned me. I knew that Ivan wasn't my boyfriend, but I honestly expected more out of him than Zeke. I took a deep breath and forced more food into my face, knowing I wasn't sure when the next meal would come.

Once the food hit my blood stream, I felt a surge of energy I hadn't felt since before prison. It made me feel pathetic for feeling sorry for myself. It was not my fault I was in prison, it was Nadine's. She threw me out in the first place, and she didn't have to call the cops on me. Fuck her. I'm a survivor and I would be rolling in dough right now if it wasn't for that bitch.

I got up and asked the women behind the counter where the nearest bus station was. It was five miles away and I walked the whole way with a fire burning inside me and intention in each step. I walked under freeways, over bridges, past bodegas with catcalling men. Nothing was going to distract me.

I spent the rest of my money on a bus to Manhattan. I sat down next to an unwashed hippie who had one backpack at his feet and another strapped to the front of his chest. I get comfortable on the strangely crusty, possibly bed bug ridden seat and sit through the mind-numbingly slow traffic into the city.

We pulled into the Port Authority and the hippie jumped up and dashed out the front as soon as we made a full stop. I laughed at his sudden eagerness. I got up and stretched my legs before I noticed that he left his other backpack on the floor. I looked at the window and he was nowhere to be found. I unzipped it to find nothing but body odor-soaked clothes. I forced myself to wade through the whole thing until

I found a handful of change, about three dollars' worth. At least it was something.

I rushed across the crowded bus terminal until I found a pay phone. I dialed Ivan's number. With my fingers crossed, I heard it ring and ring and ring. No answer. No voicemail. Nothing.

I was truly on my own now.

CHAPTER 46
TAYLOR CALLAHAN

November 27, 2013
1 Year, 10 Months, 7 Days Before The Switch

I found myself sitting on the cold chewing-gum-coated concrete. The air smelled like cigarettes even though no one was smoking. My back muscles stiffened against the rough brick of the building I was sitting up against. My hip bones ached from poking into the concrete. My body wanted to shiver but I forced every muscle to hold tight.

With a pen from the hippie's backpack and a piece of cardboard I had torn off a box that was shoved into a trashcan, I had made a sign: "Please help, I'm pregnant and have nowhere to go. Anything helps. God Bless."

I leaned back and held up my sign. I had shoved the hippie's backpack under my sweatshirt making it look like I'm about five months pregnant. I hoped it would bolster some sympathy from passersby.

My spot was a few blocks from the bus station on a street that was busy enough for people to see me but not so busy that the police would be hanging around. Some might think that the big tourist spots like Times Square or Grand Central are the best place to panhandle. But I was not willing to risk going back to the slammer.

Most of the pedestrians ignored me. The locals with their big puffy coats hurried along while yapping into their cell phones wouldn't give me a first glance, let alone a second. Most of the chubby Midwestern tourists would shoot me a pitiful look but never speak to me. It wasn't until a family of both tall and wide Minnesotans all wearing the same purple shirt that read "I heart NY" on the front under their coats approached me.

The matriarch of the family with big 1980s strawberry blonde hair came over.

"Oh good heavens, darling. Are you alright?" She bent over and put her hands on her knees like she was leaning over to talk to an adorable pet.

I nodded, "I'm fine or I'll be fine once I can get a hot meal. I'm very hungry."

"Of course, you are! You're eating for two," cooed a shorter woman to her left.

"We've got to hurry. We have got tickets to see *Wicked* but I want to help you first." The woman took out her wallet from her fanny pack and tossed a few ones my way.

"Come on, we can all spare a few extra dollars." The second woman glared at the eight other relatives around her. A few of the older men let out a huff and handed over some cash.

"Thank you, my God. Thank you." I stared up at them with a blazing smile.

"You're welcome now, go feed yourself and that baby."

For a moment, I had forgotten about my fake little miracle growing inside of me.

"Yes, of course. Thank you so much for your kindness," I shouted as they started to walk away.

The family wandered down the street and I began to count my money. A full twenty-three dollars.

I stayed at my spot until the sun began to set. In that time, I got another twenty dollars from passing strangers, mostly tourists or anyone new to the city.

I made my way to the nearby K-Mart. My ass cheeks and knees ached from sitting so long on the ground. The store was filled with all the things I wanted: a new pair of sneakers and thick socks to keep out the cold, knitted white sweaters and red mittens, a new wallet that smells of leather, a purse for a grown woman, not a backpack under my shirt.

I shook my head. I didn't have the time to focus on my have-nots. I made my way to the clearance section and found a well-padded greenish gray jacket that goes all the way down to my shins. It was on sale for thirty-eight dollars, and I was left with five after I purchased it.

I spent the next few hours in a KFC using up my money on fatty chicken. I sat in the warm, grease-scented place until the men behind the counter started to give me unwelcoming looks. With nowhere to go, I forced myself to leave the restaurant and face the cold.

After peering behind rows of apartment buildings and store fronts, I found a small empty alleyway. I curled up under some boxes meant for recycling and tried to fall asleep. I was alone except for a man who came out to toss a white bag of trash in the dumpster. He either didn't notice me or didn't care. I managed to get a few hours of sleep in the cold of the night.

I woke as the sun slowly crept up in the winter sky. My joints throbbed from sleeping on a hard surface all night in the cold. It took me several minutes to pull myself up from my sleeping spot.

I circled back to my old spot from the day before. I took out my little sign and attempted to make sad eye contact with everyone I saw. A few of them gave in to my occasional pleas and dropped loose change or a crumpled bills in the cup I left out.

This day was colder than the day before and I felt my body struggle to keep warm. I wanted to get up and move so I could heat up, but I didn't want to miss any potential donations, so I forced myself to stay put.

My fingertips began to burn from the cold and eventually went numb. The world around me grew foggy then faded to black.

CHAPTER 47
TAYLOR CALLAHAN

November 28, 2013
1 Year, 10 Months, 6 Days Before The Switch
I awoke from a deep sleep in an alleyway behind a fancy restaurant. Old eggs and leftover meat rotted in the dumpster next to me. I had just made my way through the third bruised apple the restaurant had thrown away for no good reason when I realized today was Thanksgiving. Now, I never had much of a holiday tradition with Nadine usually working and Saul not giving a shit about an American holiday, but I at least had a roof over my head.

I forced myself to shake off my despair. I wasn't going to survive much longer. I needed a place to sleep indoors. Maybe I could find a cheap motel somewhere. I set up my little camp a few doors away, in front of a jewelry store that is closed for Thanksgiving hoping people would give generously during the holiday.

My plan started to work and almost everyone was taking pity on me. People dropped five-dollar bills in my cap and wished me well. Even a college girl with her blonde hair tucked under a beanie bought me a slice of pizza.

The sky grew dark, and I was just about to start packing up to find a shelter or maybe a hotel room I could afford with my plunder when a husband and wife with two little kids and an adult son walked by me.

The woman with a thick Russian accent said to her husband, "Can you imagine being pregnant and homeless? What a mess!"

Their older son peered around them and locked eyes with me. It was Ivan.

"Taylor," he called out and squatted down at my eye level. "Are you alright? What happened?" he asked, staring at my belly.

"It's a long story, really," I told him. He scooped me up in a giant hug.

"Do you know this girl?" asked the man. He spoke with an American accent and had his brown-black hair perfectly moused and combed into place.

"Yeah, I do. We were best friends." He looked up at them. "Can she join us?"

Both parents looked at each other. I could tell they were trying to find the most politically correct way to tell me to fuck off.

After they neglected to answer him, Ivan shouted, "It's Thanksgiving!"

"Daddy, it's Thanksgiving, we have to help," a little girl with wispy brown hair shot out from behind the man.

"Dad, we have to," said a little boy on the other side of his parents. "Mrs. Clayton at church told us we have to."

"Alright, fine," the man huffed before he turned the charm — fake charm — on me.

By this time, Ivan's pulled me off the ground.

"What is your name?" asked the man.

"Taylor Callahan," I said.

"Hi, Taylor. I'm Bill, Ivan's stepdad. We would love it if you had Thanksgiving dinner with us." He gave me a small pat on the shoulder then tried to discreetly wipe his hand on his overcoat.

I smiled at him, trying to control my shaking from the cold and hunger pains. "Thank you so much. You don't know how grateful I am."

"This is my mom, Matilda," said Ivan. Matilda looked me up and down, gave me a smile and a nod.

The two kids rushed up to me, but Bill held them back. Ivan let out a nervous laugh and said, "This is Bill, Jr., and Christina, my brother and sister. They're twins."

I gave the kids a wave.

Inside the restaurant, I'm overwhelmed by the smells of gravy and pumpkin pie. The dark wood furniture shines from polishing and the white tablecloths look too pristine and expensive for someone like me.

They all stared at me in awkward silence. I blurted out, "I'm not normally like this. I mean, I've never lived on the streets before. I've had a bit of hard luck."

"What happened?" asked Bill.

I swallowed hard, "I got released early from being incarcerated, you know, for good behavior. Don't worry, I'm not dangerous or anything."

"How are you pregnant if you've just gotten out of jail. Oh, dear Lord, did the guards—?" his mother asked, shushing her voice.

"Oh no, I'm not actually pregnant. It's a backpack." I lifted up my shirt real fast to flash my Jansport at them.

Both parents let out a sigh of relief.

"It helps you raise more money," I admitted.

"Were you okay in there, did anyone hurt you?" Ivan asked, leaning over and rubbing my back. He's much more affectionate than he used to be.

"I was fine. No one bothered me. I just kept my head down, stayed out of trouble. Didn't have friends, didn't make enemies," I told him.

"How long have you been on the street?" he continued.

"Only three days. Not too bad," I replied.

Bill perked up. "Well, that's long enough."

"What did you do to go to jail?" asked Bill, Jr.

"Honey, don't ask those things," scolded Matilda.

"No, it's okay. I won't lie to you. I'm trying not to do that anymore. I was caught robbing a house, my mother's house. I know that sounds terrible and I know I shouldn't have done it. You see she kicked me out when I was sixteen years old, and I went back for some of my stuff. Anyway, my little brother was happy to see me and wanted to help me out, so he gave me some money my mother had hidden around the house, but she came home and called the cops on me," I said.

"That's terrible," Matilda stared at me slack-jawed.

"To be honest," began Ivan, "it was my fault. I got the idea in my head that she should see her brother because she missed him and had no idea how he was doing this whole time."

I felt tears rising in my eyes, but I forced them back. "It's not your fault."

I reached over and gave him a side hug. "It was kinda worth it to know Neil was okay. The way Ivan talked about how important it was for him to still see you, his mother, even though his dad didn't want him to, made me want to see my brother again."

"Oh, Ivan," his mother grabbed his head and kissed it. "You are such a good boy."

The waiters brought out the food from the pre-selected menu. Our plates were filled with juicy turkey meat and a mountain range of mashed potatoes, both covered with the right amount of gravy. We had sides of green bean casserole and freshly steamed broccoli. To end the night, we each got a thick piece of pumpkin pie with a scoop of ice cream. Nothing in my life has ever tasted so good.

As the waiters cleared our plates, my heart sank at the thought of the next night's meal of fast food or even food from the trash.

"Thank you so much for sharing this meal with me," I told the family.

"It was our pleasure," said Bill as he handed the waiter his credit card.

"Can we let Taylor stay with us?" Ivan asked. "Just for a little while."

"Son, that's a lot to ask. I mean sure we can give her some money, find her a nice motel but we can't—" Bill was interrupted by his stepson slamming his water glass down.

"You don't understand what Taylor means to me. Taylor kept my secret from that man for so long. She protected me, she took care of me. I can't let her spend her nights on the street or bouncing from motel to motel," shouted Ivan.

"Alright, she can stay. Not forever, just a little while till she is on her feet," said Matilda.

Ivan wiped a tear from his eye.

"What happened to Saul?" I asked.

Ivan grimaced, "I'll tell you later, when the kids aren't around."

CHAPTER 48
TAYLOR CALLAHAN

November 28, 2013

1 Year, 10 Months, 6 Days Before The Switch

After surviving an uncomfortable car ride with Ivan's family, we arrived in front of a picture-perfect colonial house in the New Jersey suburbs.

From the dark garage, the family ushered me into the house where they threw on the lights. The living room contained nothing but two couches and piles and piles of boxes. In the kitchen to the left, pots and pans were thrown about the countertops.

"We just moved," explained Matilda, "that's why we had dinner in the city, so I didn't have to cook in the middle of this mess."

"Good idea," I said to her.

"Follow me, please," she said as she marched up the stairs.

She pointed to a room right off the top of the stairs.

"This is the guest room," Matilda began. "I'll find you some sheets and a blanket. You can use the bathroom down the hall."

I knew that meant I smelled like a bum and she wanted me to shower. I took the hint and hurried off into the bathroom.

Feeling the steaming water cleanse my skin was probably the best thing I've ever felt. I scrubbed the oil from my hair, the dirt from under my fingernails, and washed away my memories of the street. I opened the bathroom door to find a folded pair of Matlida's sweatpants and one of Ivan's big shirts.

Ivan was waiting for me in the guest room.

I entered the room, rubbing my hair with a towel and asked, "So, what happened? How did you end up with your mom instead?"

He took a deep breath. "I started seeing this guy, Andre, around the time you left. I had kept everything real quiet, and Saul didn't suspect a thing. Then one day, Andre, who was about to graduate from college, wanted me to come with him to pick out a new outfit for graduation. So, we went to the mall. He was trying on clothes. We're having a good time, laughing and just being ourselves. He grabs me and kisses me. And when I let go I turn around and see my dad—Saul, looking right at me with rage bubbling in his veins. He screamed at me, called me horrible names and lunged at me. Andre and a store manager had to fight him off me. When he was leaving, he told me I wasn't allowed back in our house."

"Jesus, what a douche. I'm so sorry." I sat down next to him on the bed. I felt anger flush my face red, but I wasn't mad at Saul, I was mad at me for not being there for him.

Ivan leaned in. "It's not your fault. You kept my secret long enough. It was bound to get out."

I began, "And are Matilda and Bill alright with—"

He nodded. "Yeah, they're fine with it. I mean, I don't think Bill is too crazy about having a step-son in the first place, but we get along for the most part. You really did win them over with that *Ivan's love for his mom inspired me to find my brother* bit."

I laughed. "It wasn't a bit. It's what really happened."

He elbowed me and said, "I know, I'm just giving you a hard time."

"I think I've had a hard-enough time. I've been homeless and been to prison." I jabbed back.

"Shit, you're right. I'm an asshole, I'm used to us being the same, you know, like we were before."

"Well, we've both been kicked out of our houses by our parents. They can't take that away from us," I laughed.

"Who would ever want to?" He wrapped his arm around me and pulled me in. "It's great to have you back."

I placed my arm around him and squeezed him closer. It really *was* great to have him back but my mind filled with questions: How long could I stay here? What am I going to do with myself? Will I always be like this, or can I ever get my life back to the straight and narrow? Questions that will have to wait to be answered.

CHAPTER 49
TAYLOR CALLAHAN

March 11, 2014
1 Year, 6 Months, 23 Days Before The Switch

After living with Ivan's new family for a while, we fell into a comfortable routine. I'd get up early with Matilda to help her make breakfast for the whole family. I'd pour steaming hot oatmeal made with organic milk into six bowls. I'd cut up a few bananas and place them on top of each bowl and drizzle syrup on to each one.

As I would glaze my bowl with extra maple syrup, Ivan's mom would slap my hands and say, "All that sugar is no good for you."

I'd pick out the children's outfits for the day and help them tie their shoes when they finished dressing. Matilda would pack their backpacks and shuttle them off to school. When she returned, I'd help her with the mountain of laundry the family would accumulate over the week or assist her as she bought food for the family.

My favorite part of living with them was playing with Christina. She was such a unique little girl. On weekends, she was allowed to wear whatever she wanted. So, she'd come downstairs in a pink, white and orange striped dress with red glitter shoes from her Dorothy costume left over from Halloween. She also never wanted to wear a coat even when it was cold outside. She'd sometimes put on a fashion show just for me. I'd watch her prance around her pale pink room in outfits made from tutus over patterned pajama bottoms and her brother's sweaters.

Ivan got a job at the local juice bar to help support the family even though there was no need. Apparently, Bill went on and on about kids these days needing to learn how to have a *work-ethic* to the point that Ivan broke down and took the first job he could find.

Matilda and her new husband were never mean to me, but I couldn't help but feel a little unwanted.

They couldn't be upset about letting Ivan live with them. After all, he was Matilda's son but I was just the down-on-her-luck friend of Ivan.

Even though I was helping them out in every way that I could, I knew Ivan's step-father was not happy to have me there. He wasn't too thrilled about Ivan hanging around but he couldn't kick his wife's son out of the house without feeling the wrath of Matilda. But with me, I wasn't family and I had a record. He wanted me gone.

His feelings were especially clear on this particular day when Christina rushed up to him and Matilda as they were sipping cocktails at their bar cart in the dining room. She had a picture in hand. Her drawing showed two stick figures: one was clearly Christina in her signature tutu and sparkly shoes. The other was an image of a taller girl with wavy yellow hair in what looked like jeans and a dark shirt. It was clearly a picture of me.

"Ms. Moore told us all to draw a picture of someone special in our life. I told her Taylor is special because she helps me get dressed when my mom is busy. I told her I love having her live with us and I'm so glad she doesn't have to live on the street anymore."

"Did you really say that?" asked her father.

"Yes, I just told you," she said in that child-who-is-excited-but-frustrated-with-an-adult tone of voice.

"You shouldn't go around telling people that," he told her with a frown contorting his face.

She put her hands to her hips. "Why? Don't you like Taylor?"

I could feel the blood rush to my cheeks as I watched their conversation.

"Yes, I do. But we can't go around telling people she was homeless," he insisted.

"Why not? You told me we're always supposed to help poor people." Christina put her hands on her hips waiting for an explanation from her father.

Matilda turned around and mouthed, "I'm so sorry," to me.

"Yes, but it's not something we're supposed to talk about. Why don't you start your homework and I'll help in a few minutes?" he told his daughter.

Christina sulked away to her room.

"Sorry you had to hear that," said Matilda to me.

"No worries, I know I'm not rich," I said.

"It's funny that you have been living here and I actually don't know where you were born or where your family is," Bill said, circling me like a shark.

"Union, New Jersey. But my parents moved me out to Atlantic City where my dad was a blackjack dealer and my mom was a waitress," I told him.

"Are they still in Atlantic City?" he asked.

"My mother and brother are," I answered.

He came in closer to me and I could smell his aftershave. "Isn't she worried about you? I'm sure she must miss you."

"She's the one who put me in jail," I stated.

"Oh, right." He took a step back. "And your dad? What about him?"

"Well, the man who raised me turned out to not be my biological father. So, he probably doesn't care where I am, and my real father doesn't know I exist," I explained.

"I see. Any other family, friends, boyfriends?"

"I have no idea where my grandparents are. My mom has a brother, but I haven't seen him since I was little. I had a boyfriend who I used to live with, but he abandoned me in a motel a few years ago and all my friends know him, so it wouldn't be safe for me to go back to my old neighborhood."

"You really don't have anywhere else to go, do you?" he asked. There was a sense of defeat in his voice.

I asked him point blank, "Do you want me to leave?"

"It's not that I don't like helping you out. It's just I don't want people thinking we're taking in random girls."

Matilda stepped in. "She isn't random. She is my son's best friend. She helped him and kept Saul from hurting him. We owe her a place to stay."

I told them, "I'm sorry. I don't want to overstay my welcome. I just don't know where else to go. I didn't finish high school and I have a record. The chances of me finding a good job are slim."

Matilda continued, "It's not like she is just coasting by here. She is helping me with the chores and the kids every day. She cooks, she cleans, she watches the kids when we need to go out. A babysitter or housekeeper would cost a lot more than just giving her a place to stay and some food to eat."

"I know. I know. You just have to keep the future in mind. You and Ivan can't live here forever. I mean you both are legally adults. You have to get your life on track. How about we help you finish your degree? You can go to the community college and study for the GED. That's got to help," he suggested.

I shrugged. "I don't know if I'm smart enough."

"Of course, you are!" said Matilda. "It's too late for you to start school this semester but I bet there is a summer course you can start."

The next day, I signed up for a spot in the summer GED course. But I never got the chance to start it.

CHAPTER 50
TAYLOR CALLAHAN

April 4, 2014
1 Year, 6 Months Before The Switch

Bill stomped into the house two hours earlier than normal and slammed his briefcase down on the marble countertop in the kitchen. The bang radiated through the whole house.

"What is it, honey?" asked Matilda.

"I just got laid off!" he screamed.

I was on the other side of the kitchen island, placing clean dishes from the dishwasher into the cupboard. He was leaning over the counter with his hands holding his hair in clumps. I tried not to look at him.

She patted his shoulders. "I'm sorry, my darling. But everything will be fine. I'm sure you can find another job in no time."

"I don't think it is going to be that easy. There are industry-wide cuts," he grunted.

I let a plate slip and it landed on top of the stack with a loud clanking. Thankfully, it didn't break.

"Taylor!" he shouted.

"Yes?" I replied.

"Can you please give me and my wife some privacy. The last thing I want to look at is another mouth I have to feed."

I left the rest of the clean dishes in the dishwasher, grabbed my coat and headed out the door.

I didn't have access to any of their cars, so I went on foot to Ivan's work.

I walked in and there was only one person being checked out by Ivan in the store. The other employee was cleaning out a series of blenders that were caked with pale pink goo.

After the customer left, I went to Ivan and said, "We need to talk, now."

Ivan sighed, "Can't you see I'm working. We can talk at home."

"Lady troubles?" laughed the other juice bar employee.

"Ignore Emilio," said Ivan. "What is so important?"

"Your step-dad lost his job and is freaking out at home," I told him.

"Oh shit." Ivan took off his gloves and rubbed his forehead.

"Yeah, you know what this means right?" I asked him as I forced my way behind the counter.

"What?" he asked.

I groaned, "My God, you are blind sometimes. They're gonna kick us out. He said he didn't think he was going to find another good job again and he was panicking. He's practically pulling his hair out."

"Fucking shit, man, this is the worst," he began. "I can't afford an apartment with just this job."

"Have you thought about my side-hustle bro?" asked Emilio.

"I told you I'm sticking straight," Ivan shouted at him.

Emilio said with a laugh, "I thought you were gay."

"Straight as in not messing with illegal shit, you idiot," Ivan huffed.

"Wait, have you gotten a business offer and you didn't take it?" I asked.

"I thought after your little stay with Uncle Sam, you would want to avoid that life again," Ivan explained while drumming his fingers on the counter.

Frustrated, I said. "Not if it means money."

"Stay with Uncle Sam? What does that mean?" asked Emilio with a crooked smile.

"Don't play stupid," said Ivan.

"I'm not." He said as he walked over and threw his arm around me. "I just can't imagine such a sweet thing being locked in a big scary jail," he continued in a baby voice.

I pulled my knife out of my boot. "If you call me *sweet thing* again, I'm going to start cutting things off you."

He put his hands up and said, "Relax, girl. It's fine. What were you in for?"

"Armed robbery," I answered.

"Holy shit!" Emilio took a few steps back.

"You must be one lame-ass dealer if you're impressed with that." Ivan gave me a knowing smile.

Emilio said, "I'm just starting out. How bad can it be? People want some shit and I bring it to them. It's like being a pizza delivery boy that the government doesn't like."

I laughed. "How bad can it be? Let's see. There was the time a bachelor party tried to stiff me on my payout, so I threw a champagne bottle at the groom to get them to pay up. Some crazy busboy accused me and my partner of shorting him, and he started chasing us around the kitchen of a busy restaurant with a butcher knife. Oh, and there was one time I had to steal a pimp's gun and held it to his head."

"Okay, I get it." Emilio threw his hands in the air in a mock surrender.

"Yeah and that's not even the stuff I did with Ivan. We had the Russian mob threaten us, we had his crazy-ass dad drive us around looking for shit to steal."

"Ah the good old days," joked Ivan.

"For a gay dude and a white chick, you guys are street as fuck," Emilio gaped.

I smiled and rolled my eyes. "Thanks."

"So, you want in?" Emilio asked.

"Fuck yeah. You got the connections?"

"Yeah, but it's kind of a drive. I usually handle the party boys at the Shore."

"Easy. We'll have your business booming in no time," I told him.

After two months of running back and forth from inland New Jersey to the boardwalks of the shore, we had enough money to put a deposit down on an apartment. And that is where I stayed until I became Jamie MacKenzie.

Part 3

CHAPTER 51
TAYLOR CALLAHAN

November 2, 2015
30 Days After The Switch

I had survived the last two weeks by staying at home and recovering from my injuries. Joan didn't seem to question me anymore and we went about our lives. But the cabin fever of never being able to leave this house was getting to me, hence my search for my grave on my birthday yesterday.

After I searched for myself online, I drifted into an unrestful sleep littered with nightmares. I saw Jamie's dead body, bloated and buried deep in the earth. She came to life and scratched at her wooden coffin. She dug faster and faster until she forced herself up above the earth at Green Oak Cemetery. I felt her next to me. She smelt of rot and damp soil.

She said nothing, but I could hear her thoughts asking me, "Why didn't you let my family bury me? Why didn't you let them mourn me? They will never be able to miss me. The real me. I hope it's worth it. I hope it's worth it."

I opened my eyes, and she was gone. I glanced at the clock, it's two in the morning. I told myself it was just a nightmare, but it felt too real. With fear still pumping in my blood, I needed to get out of bed. My ankle slightly throbbed in its boot. My burnt skin was slowly turning pink underneath the bandages.

I thrusted the heavy duvet off my body and reached for one of my crutches. I touched the tip of it and it fell over and slammed the wall. I turned to look at Faith, but she wasn't woken up by the noise.

The house was warm and oppressive. I went to the sink for a glass of water. As I sat at the kitchen counter, facing the hallway, I saw something I'd never noticed before. There were three doors on the left side of the hallway. The first door was Jamie and Faith's bedroom and the second was the bathroom. The third door hasn't been opened since I got here.

I limped down the hall and carefully twisted the doorknob. The smell of dust hit me, and I held back the urge to sneeze. With the door closed behind me, I turned on the light. In front of me, I saw a queen - sized bed with a blue and pink quilt laid over it.

They had an extra bedroom this whole time.

On the bureau, a lid-less can of hairspray was rusting at the mouth. The closet door was open, displaying long billowy dresses of various patterns hung up. I thumbed through them and found a pair of God-awful overalls with pink flower patches ironed on to them. I couldn't imagine a time when these clothes were ever in style.

I noticed a picture on the nightstand. I leaned closer and saw that it is Jamie and Faith as young children with Aunt Wendy, her dark blonde hair brushed and teased out on all sides like it was in the photos of her in the scrapbooks. She had an arm around each of them as they sat together on a big white porch swing. Wendy was even wearing the same ugly flower-covered overalls that hung in the closet behind me. I let out a small giggle at her poor taste in fashion.

"Something funny?" a voice asked.

Joan was standing in the doorway with her arms crossed and her eyes narrowed in on me like they are a pair of crosshairs.

I almost jumped out of my skin. "Nothing. I was just thinking about Aunt Wendy."

Joan looked unamused. "I thought we all agreed to leave this room alone to pay homage to her."

"I don't think she would mind. I was just reminiscing on the good times we had together," I explained.

"From now on, leave this room alone like we agreed. It's late. Get to bed." She turned off the light and left me in the dark.

These people are hiding something. I just don't know what.

CHAPTER 52
TAYLOR CALLAHAN

November 14, 2015
42 days After The Switch

I was in the backseat of the MacKenzies' green Yukon, staring out the window. It's almost night outside. The triangle outlines of pine trees stood pitch black against the fading blue sky.

I didn't like these moments when everyone was quiet and the world outside was dark. All I could do was sit and think. And when I sit and think I begin to baste myself with self-doubt like a Thanksgiving turkey. I wanted to get up and run. I wanted to go and do something, anything that would take my mind off the insanity that was my life. But no. I was trapped here with my thoughts.

Should I have switched places? Did I take this too far? Do they know who I really am? What won't I do to keep a gig going? Am I a bad person?

•   •   •

Yesterday, I thought everything would get back to normal. Well, as normal as they could be given my weird situation. But my hands had healed, and I got my boot taken off at the doctors. I came home to find Joan taking a homemade lasagna out of the oven.

"One of your favorites." She smiled. "I thought you deserved a treat after surviving all those weeks with your burnt hands and your poor hurt foot."

"Thanks, Mom," I beamed, glad this meal didn't contain canned fish.

We gathered at the table and bowed our heads in prayer.

Phil began, "Dear Lord, thank you for the bounty you've put on our table. For my wife and her capable hands that made this blessed food. And for my daughters, Jamie and Faith, who continue to serve your Will to the fullest even when the task seems hard or when this worldly life tempts them away from the righteous path. Amen."

"Dig in everybody." Joan dipped a knife into the lasagna.

In the middle of my third bite of the delicious meal, Joan said, "Guess what day it is tomorrow, girls?"

"Saturday," I said, imitating Jamie's excited inflection.

"Yes, but it's hunting day!" she exclaimed. Both Joan and Phil looked absolutely thrilled, but Faith stared down at her food.

"Really?" I asked.

"Yes of course. We've been waiting till you got that boot off to go," said Phil. "We couldn't very well have you out there in the woods with dangerous game on crutches, now could we?"

Joan said, "I bet you've been missing it."

"Yes, I have," I said with a fake smile.

"Well, I've already got the trunk packed," said Phil, nudging Faith with his elbow, "be ready to go by five in the morning."

•   •   •

I woke up today with Faith dropping a hunting outfit on top of me.

"Wake up," she said, giving me a cold glare.

"What's your problem?" I asked her.

"You know I hate this." She crossed her arms over her chest and leaned against her bed.

Pretending to know anything about hunting, I said, "I know it's gross, but you'll get used to it."

She shook her head.

"You might have fun this time," I told her while getting out of bed and taking my pajamas off.

She shook her head again.

I pulled on a new pair of panties and an undershirt before I layered myself in heavy camo pants and a matching coat.

I said to Faith, "Don't be such a stick in the mud."

"I understood the first time, but I don't know why we keep doing it. They never did anything to us," she said.

I let out a sigh. I wasn't in the mood to get into an argument about the ethics of hunting with a whiny teenager. "Just get dressed, will ya?"

I saw Joan and Phil in the kitchen ready to go. Joan poured me a bowl of fruity cereal and I scarfed it down.

We drove two hours south with the scenery getting more wooded and the roads getting narrower as we continued on.

Phil turned the car on to a gravel road and drove deep into the woods. Tree branches grazed the windows and rocks picked up and hit the side of the car making little pinging sounds.

We got to a clearing and parked on the patchy brown grass. I got a sense of Deja-Vu. The trees, the clearing, and the dead grass all look familiar to me. As I tried to recognize this place, Joan interrupted my concentration.

"Before we start, Jamie needs to practice. It's been a while for her," said Joan.

Phil handed me one of the rifles. Joan walked about to the edge of the clearing and placed a few empty Coke cans that were laying down in the car on to a fallen tree.

As soon as she got back to the group, Phil told me to fire.

I aimed for the Coke can in the middle but the bullet flew by it. I fired again, and the same thing happened. I was rustier than I thought.

"I guess you lost your touch, Jamie," joked Phil.

I don't know why but that angered me. I lifted the rifle again. With four sharp blasts, I knocked down every last can.

"Well, I think she's ready now," Joan laughed.

I took a few steps forward thinking we're heading into the woods to hunt deer.

"Jamie, where are you going? We haven't released him yet," said Joan.

Released? I turned back around to see Phil opening the hatch of the SUV and pulling back the cover. There was a man locked in a cage with a bag over his head.

CHAPTER 53
TAYLOR CALLAHAN

November 14, 2015
42 Days After The Switch

As I looked at the man, my eyes widened and my heart pounded so hard in my chest I thought it would burst.

Phil spun the numbers on the lock on the cage to the correct combination. With a clunk, it opened.

"Wakey-wakey," Phil said to the man, clutching him by his collar and throwing him out onto the ground.

Joan grabbed the man and propped him up on his knees. She pulled the bag off his head and ripped duct tape from his mouth.

"Help!" he screamed.

My skin almost jumped off my bones.

"You can keep screaming all you want but no one is gonna hear you," Phil told him.

He looked about thirty-five years old. He had a messy beard and hair to match. He wore a stained t-shirt and a pair of worn-out cargo pants.

"Why are you doing this?" he asked the two of them. His eyes shifted to his left and noticed Faith and me staring at him. He looked around confused, not understanding why he was here.

"Are you Michael Francis Millwood?" Joan asked him.

He nodded.

"And did you or did you not break into the house of Ms. Xavier, rape her, kill her dog, and rob her house?"

"Yes, I did, and I served time for it," he said, almost proud.

Joan continued, "You served six months instead of the minimum of ten years because why?"

He answered, "I was never read my rights. I got a re-trial and they let me go."

"How convenient. You see I know for a fact that police officers almost never forget to read someone their rights so were you telling the truth," Joan asked him, circling him.

"Yes," he said.

Phil draws his weapon. "Listen, chances are you aren't getting out of here alive so don't you want to do the right thing and die with a clean conscience so then maybe, just maybe, God can forgive you."

"Alright," his voice quaked, "I lied. I didn't want to go down the hill for ten years. My lawyer was able to discredit the arresting officer's testimony, so the jury had enough reasonable doubt to let me go. It's not right but I did what I had to do."

Joan nodded.

Phil rushed up to the man and grabbed him.

"This is how this works. We give you a two-minute head start into those woods and if you can make your way out of here before either we kill you or mother nature kills you then you get to keep your life. And if you tell anyone about this or mess up and commit another crime, we will come for you and put a bullet in you for sure," said Joan as she undid his handcuffs.

Phil thrusted him forward yelling, "You have two minutes, go." But the man fell onto his back from Phil's push.

He stared back at us, shaking. He could barely able to pull himself to his knees.

"Look, he's too scared to run," said Joan.

"A sinner who does not want to protect his own life? That's a first," said Phil with a chuckle.

Joan looked at me and said, "This is an easy one, Jamie. Why don't you do the honors?"

The family gaped at me for a second until I realized what they were asking me to do. I swallowed hard and swung the rifle off my shoulder and pointed it at him.

I stood in the proper stance, feet apart, legs solid. I looked at him, half thanking and half cursing Drew for teaching me how to shoot and at that moment, I felt Jamie with me, and it was as if all the bad that was in me and all that bad that was in her joined together to make one person. It was that person that fired the gun.

His chest caved in and erupted with blood. The muscles in his arms and legs that were keeping him upright collapsed causing him to fall on his back.

The three of us crowded around him, staring into his up-turned eyes. Joan checked his pulse. He was no longer alive.

Phil pulled out a plastic trap out of the trunk and rolled the man on to it.

"Why are you two just standing there? You know what we have to do," said Phil to Faith and me.

I picked up the feet of the dead man and walked deeper into the woods. Joan and Phil were holding the top of him. He was heavy, over 180 pounds of dead weight. Faith, as the look out, walked several yards ahead of us and left a marking in red chalk on the trees as she passed so we know the coast is clear.

The ground turned to mud under my feet as I realized that they must bury the bodies of their hunting victims where the ground was soft.

CHAPTER 54
JOAN MACKENZIE

November 15, 2015
42 Days After The Switch

Dear Lord,

I had that dream last night again.
The one where I see Tommy.
At first there are flashes of us.
Me, Wendy and Tommy riding our bikes around the neighborhood on a fresh spring day.
Tommy blowing out seven blue candles on a vanilla frosted cake.
Dad teaching Tommy how to throw a ball in the backyard while me and Wendy drew on the concrete patio with pink and orange chalk.
I can still smell the dry powdery chalk being rubbed against hard pavement.
Then, I'm in my room. I know it's late because it's almost pitch black and Wendy is fast asleep in her bed next to me.
I feel a weight and it's Tommy pressing down on my feet at the end of the bed.
He's glowing white and his eyes look hollow but there is no doubt in my mind that he is my brother. He whispers, "You've got to help me."
He holds his hands up to his neck grasping it like a brace for a second before he releases.
His head swings to the left side, twisting his neck down and around.
His skin grays and his eyes grow dark.
It is a full minute before I realize that Tommy's dead. I rush over to Wendy and shake her, so she can see what has happened.

By the time I woke her up, Tommy was gone.

Wendy told me to go back to bed, that I was having a nightmare and that Tommy was safe at camp miles away.

But in the morning, we weren't greeted with Mom's loving smile and fluffy pancakes like most Saturday mornings.

Instead Mom and Dad held each other at the kitchen table.

Mom's eyes were red, pouring out tears across her face.

Someone had just called to tell us that Tommy died yesterday evening.

He broke his neck while swinging from a rope into a lake.

I know it is wrong for me to believe in ghosts or the supernatural.

I know that when a soul is called from this life, it's you, O Lord, who decides that soul's fate.

But I can't help what I saw.

And I fear that it is happening again.

This time it's happening longer.

This girl talks like Jamie, dresses like Jamie but I just know it isn't my Jamie.

Is this an omen, a sign that my real daughter is in danger?

I know I'm just being silly and weak. This can't be true. It has to be my real Jamie but maybe she has sinned greatly, and it has changed her.

Please Lord, give me the wisdom and the strength to deal with this in the right way.

Amen.

Tonight, we gathered around the TV and watched the News. To my surprise, the News lady with tan skin and puffy blonde hair announced something about Jamie's friends' case.

No one at work mentioned that they spoke to the press. I had thought that we were going to keep this development out of the media for the sake of the grieving families. It was the respectful thing to do.

In her emotionless voice the woman said, "There has been an update in the case of two local teenagers who were killed last month during what appeared to be a drug deal gone wrong. Police have Ezekiel Warren-Hernandez in custody tonight after he avoided their efforts to find him for three weeks. The thirty-year-old man had recently been released from prison on drug charges and vowed revenge on his ex-girlfriend who was killed in addition to the teenaged girls. A trial date has not yet been set but police hope that we can soon find answers and closure for the families of the victims."

I looked over at Jamie and expected to see her bawling her eyes out of the thought of such a dirty criminal taking the lives of her best friends. But instead of tears, I saw a smile. The type of smile that looked like she was pleased—like she had gotten away with something and was proud of it. She doesn't seem overjoyed that her friends' killer was found. She doesn't seem relieved that a dangerous man was off the streets. No, she was happy about something I knew nothing about.

That wasn't like her. I was afraid she was hiding something. Maybe she was more responsible for setting up the drug deal than I thought. Maybe she was the one who went to Derek to ask for the drugs. Maybe she was there and escaped everything. She didn't want to be part of the blame, so she pretended she wasn't there at all. Maybe she wasn't my daughter at all.

CHAPTER 55
TAYLOR CALLAHAN

November 21, 2015
49 Days After The Switch

We drove towards The Pine Barrens once again. This time I am fully aware of what *hunting* means to this family. I tried to keep my mind from picturing some unlucky bastard who got picked off the street by these two wackos and has been tied up in a cage for God knows how long.

I forced myself to get into my Jamie mindset. I thought to myself: *He deserves it. He was a bad man and there is no saving him so the best thing we can do is erase him from the Earth.*

It wasn't easy for me. I know that there wasn't much but dumb luck, if you even want to call it luck, that landed me in the back seat versus in the cage in the trunk. They could have attacked me while I was out trying to make a deal. They could have read my file and saw I barely served any time for the crime I committed and decided they needed to bring me their idea of justice. And Bam! I would be dead in the woods too.

I kept looking behind me as if my conscience or what little was left of it kept pointing me in the direction of the trunk. But it wasn't just the kidnapped criminal in the back of the car that was bothering me. Every time I looked behind me, the clouds grew darker. Now, there was a full-blown storm nipping at our heels.

"You worried about the weather, kiddo?" asked Phil from the front seat.

I snapped my head forward. "Maybe a little."

"It'll be fine. Gives us a better advantage," he said with a chuckle.

How much more of an advantage do we need? He's the one tied up in a fucking cage.

The storm was chasing us with its thick clouds blocking the light, forcing Phil to turn on the headlights. Soon, we're getting pelted with large drops of water that sound like bullets from a machine gun pounding the metal of our car.

Phil flicked the windshield wipers on to their highest setting but it was no use. The world was a wet blur outside our windows.

Faith shifted in her seat. "Why don't we pull over and wait it out?"

"Not with the type of cargo we're carrying," Phil snorted.

Lightning broke through the sky. Thunder crashed and it made my ears ring. Phil sped up. He took us from a cautious fifty-five miles per hour to seventy. I can tell he is getting nervous. His face tightened, and he turned his Country music off.

The roads curved and Phil slipped in between two lanes. The car behind us in the right lane blasted the horn. Phil put up a hand in an apologetic wave and returned to his previous lane.

A Honda Civic merged in front of us and Phil hit the brakes. The car behind us slammed into our bumper. My heart jumped. The seat belt dug into my waist as I swung forward. A second later, I was thrown back into my seat as our car collided with the bumper of the Honda Civic ahead of us.

The MacKenzie family gaped at each other with eyes wide and faces drained of blood. But my mind was flooded with horrible images. I saw myself serving twenty-five years for being an accessory to murder. Growing old in a jail cell, forgetting what freedom felt like.

I worked too hard to change my identity only to have this "straight and narrow" family land me in prison. I would have been better off if I had just stayed as Taylor. Even if I got caught, dealing would get me way less time.

"Everybody okay?" asked Joan.

Faith and I nodded.

"It can't be that bad. The airbags didn't even go off." Phil was breathing fast and looking around the SUV in a panic.

Joan snapped at him. "We need to get out and see if the other people are okay."

"Car's running just fine. Let's just go," he protested.

"We aren't fleeing the scene of an accident, Phil," Joan barked.

"Even with what's..." his voice trailed off as he gestured towards the trunk.

"Yes, even with what's in our trunk. No one's gonna look in there. Just act like you've got nothing to hide."

Phil began sweating heavily. He wiped his brow and screamed, "Joan, we've got to go."

"Relax, we'll be fine. You're useless under pressure. No wonder you never made Sergeant." She opened her door and stepped out onto the pavement.

Faith and I followed her. I pulled up my camouflage hoodie and the rain ricocheted off the waterproof material.

In the gray Nissan behind us, a young black woman was on the phone probably calling her insurance company. The man in the front passenger seat stepped out. He was about six foot two and towered over the three of us.

"You guys okay?" he asked us.

"Yes, everyone is fine. What about you?"

"We're okay, thanks, just a little shaken up. It's impossible to see in this storm."

I glanced at the trunk of our car. The Nissan's nose was planted firmly in our rear end pinning the hatch of the door inward. Only someone with a very large pair of pliers could get that thing to open.

From around the side of the Honda, a skinny old woman with long messy hair and big bifocals came rushing towards us.

"Hey, what is wrong with you idiots?" she screamed at us.

"Listen lady, let's not get nasty. No one wanted this to happen," said the man.

"What do you know? You should have been driving more responsibly," she scolded us.

Phil finally got out of the car and made his way over to the hollering woman.

"And you had to run into me, didn't you? You absolute moron." She threw her hands up in the air.

Anxious to get out of there, Phil said, "Calm down, let's just exchange information and be on our way."

"No way in Hell," she answered. "I want the police. I'm calling the cops. There was criminal negligence on both of your parts. They should lock you up."

The group let out a collective moan.

She pulled a flip phone out of her oversized tote bag and began to dial.

Joan moved in closer to her and pulled out her badge from her back pocket. "When you get them on the line, be sure to give them my badge number."

The woman's face darkened, and she slammed her phone shut.

"That's how you want to play it. Fine." The woman scratched her insurance information onto a receipt she found in her bag and threw it at Phil. "Pay up or I'll see you in court." With a screech of the tires, she drove off.

Phil gave his information to the couple in the Nissan and they drove away. We returned to the Yukon and Phil stepped on the gas. I knew we were heading towards our spot in the woods regardless of what just happened.

CHAPTER 56
TAYLOR CALLAHAN

November 21, 2015
49 Days After The Switch

We drove the rest of the way in silence. The rain still poured, and Phil drove slower than a senior citizen. As far as I could tell, the accident didn't wake our sleeping cargo because I didn't hear anything stirring in the back.

We turned off the main road and went down our usual gravel trail to get to the clearing. Phil rested his head against the steering wheel. His cheeks were flushed and beads of sweat rolled down his neck.

"That was close," he called out.

"Oh no, it wasn't." Joan dismissed him with a wave. "Even if they called the cops, they wouldn't check us out. Not with my badge."

"You don't know that, Joan." Phil picked his head up and gave her a grim look. "They may have wanted to help us out by trying to get the trunk open for us. Last time I checked, having a kidnapped man in our trunk outweighs your badge."

Joan let out a sigh. "If you're so worried about it, why don't we just get this over with?"

He nodded and they both exited the vehicle.

From the backseat, Faith and I watched them attempt to pry open the dented hatch, but it wouldn't move.

Joan popped her head in the backseat. "On to Plan B, girls." She signaled for us to come out of the car.

Both of them pull down the seats in the back, revealing another man in the metal cage, completely unconscious.

Phil thrusted his full body into the backseat and reached into the truck. He moved the cage over in a counterclockwise rotation. Just when the little door was in sight, the man woke up. He banged his head on the low roof. "Where am I?"

Phil said, "Easy now, I'm working on getting you out."

"Thank you," the man called out, his voice dripping in desperation.

Phil popped off the lock and the door swung open. "Okay, just follow the sound of my voice. With a hood on his head, the man belly crawled headfirst towards the opening of the door. When he was half-way out, Phil grabbed him by the shoulders and heaved him out onto the ground.

"Oh my God, thank you," the man called out again. "You wouldn't believe what happened to me. These two people with ski masks come up to me while I'm taking a smoke break and the next thing I know, I'm in handcuffs, blindfolded and in a cage."

"We know," Joan said.

The man asked, "How? Did you catch the guys who did it?"

Even my cold heart was shaken by this guy's sad belief that we rescued him when in reality his nightmare had just begun.

Joan tore the blindfold off. "Are you Matthew Christopher Kauffman?"

The man shook his head.

"Get his wallet," said Joan as Phil retrieved his photo ID from the man's back pocket.

"Driver's licenses don't lie," Joan sneered.

"I don't understand what's happening here. Do you guys need money? I don't have a lot. And why are these girls here? Did you kidnap them too?" Matthew asked.

Joan threw back her head and laughed. "This one is quite the Chatty Cathy."

The man stared at her and went silent. He had a canned-cheese colored beard that barely grew in around his jawline. His hair on his head was just as thin, allowing you to see the shiny curve of his scalp underneath. His face was scarred with deep, wide pockmarks.

"So, we've established that you're Matthew Christopher Kauffman. That you can't deny. Now, can you confirm whether or not you and your buddies hit up a construction site for metal to sell for drugs and ended up shooting two security guards on duty?"

The man looked down and nodded his head in agreement.

"I can't hear you," Phil yelled at him.

"Yes, I did," he admitted.

"And how many years did you serve for murder?" Joan continued.

"Three in juvenile hall. One in minimum security," he replied.

"Four years for murder, how did you pull that off?"

"I was only sixteen at the time. I wasn't tried as an adult. At twenty, I aged out, so I served one year somewhere different."

"Now as much as I love the law and want to uphold it, it seems silly to me that a sixteen-year-old killing someone would be treated differently than an eighteen-year-old killing someone. It's not like you can't understand that murder is wrong before your eighteenth birthday. Those men you killed left widows behind with children, bills, and mortgages. One of them lost their house and the other had to drain her kid's college fund to pay for the medical bills and funeral expenses. That isn't fair. They are still living with the consequences to this day while you get to wander around scot-free. Not fair at all," Joan said.

She went into the truck and grabbed her rifle. "This is how this works. We give you a two-minute start and we are going to hunt you like the pathetic animal that you are. If you're still alive, which I highly doubt, by nightfall, you can keep your life. But if you say a word of this to anyone, there will be a bullet with your name on it, for sure."

The man's eyes widened as Phil unlocked his handcuffs.

Phil glanced at his watch. "Your two minutes start...now!"

The man took off into a sprint into the woods.

One hundred and twenty long seconds passed, and we descended upon the woods. Joan took Faith with her, and I partnered with Phil.

My eyes scanned every rock, every bush, and every tree for the man. Phil and I took careful steps. I could barely hear the crunch of leaves as we prowled through the forest.

We moved deeper into the pines. Their height blocked out most of the light. Their needles scratched my skin and sent a dusty evergreen smell into my nose. I felt a tickle burning in my nose, a sneeze that needed to be released.

I froze. Holding the bridge of my nose, I tried to force the sensation away but it was too late. A huge "ah-choo" echoed through the woods causing birds to flee from their nests in the tree next to me.

Out of the corner of my eye, a figure flinched. In between the twisted branches of a low bush, a man was crouching down, attempting not to be seen.

I took a few steps forward and he panicked. He stood up, looked me square in the eye and took off down a narrow corridor of trees.

I went off after him. Phil's footsteps crushed against the ground behind me, but he couldn't keep up.

I stopped out of breath in the middle of a deeply wooded area. The man wasn't in front of me, and Phil wasn't behind me to lead me back to safety.

"Fuck," I sighed, out of breath.

I racked my brain for possible ways out of this situation. *What if I can't get out? What if I die out here?*

I saw movement in the tree to my left and two squirrels came rushing out just as the man leapt out from the underbrush and pushed me to the floor.

He grabbed me and shook me. "What the fuck is wrong with your sicko family?"

"I don't know," I told him.

"Taking two young girls on a murdering spree is not much better than what I did, for fuck's sake," he screamed,

My mouth felt paralyzed and I couldn't answer him. I couldn't exactly say, "I'm not really their daughter, I'm just playing her to escape my real life."

"I bet you can't even kill. Look at you, so young and innocent, with your pretty blonde hair." He stroked the top of my head. "I bet you can't even do it. You poor little thing."

"I'm a killer," I warned him.

He chuckled. "I doubt that."

"I'm a killer," I said louder. "I shot a man in the chest at close range. His body ripped open, and blood flooded out everywhere. Then I left him in a hole in the earth, a hole not too far from where you are."

I hadn't noticed that my hands had moved to his throat, and I was slowly squeezing it tighter and tighter till that pock-marked face of his glowed red like a tomato just about to be pulled from the vine.

I pushed hard on his chest and climbed on top of him. His undernourished and drug-abused body reminded me of the guys at MAGIC's house. He, too, crumpled like a tin can. He kicked and wiggled his legs around. His hands tried to pry my arms away but we're in a deadlock and no one can throw me off. I squeezed his greasy neck harder.

"I'm a killer. I'm a killer," I told him.

He stopped moving. His body went limp and his eyes rolled back. A few more seconds went by before I released my grip.

"Do you believe me now?" I asked his lifeless body.

Joan, Phil, and Faith busted through the tree branches behind me. Phil and Faith looked horrified at what I'd done.

Joan clapped her hands together and cheered, "Look at my baby girl! She got him with just her bare hands." She came over to me and hugged me saying, "I'm so proud of you."

CHAPTER 57
TAYLOR CALLAHAN

November 21, 2015
49 Days After The Switch
When we got the body to the grave site, Phil looked at me and said, "Boy! I knew you liked hunting, but I didn't know how much until today."

I plunged a shovel with a splintering handle down into the wet earth. I wasn't in the mood for any compliments that this psychopathic family could give me. I never thought I'd cross the line this far.

I am doing what I need to do to survive here but how much longer will that be my excuse?

When the four of us finished digging the grave, we collapsed down into the ground that surrounds the pit. Phil wiped his nose with a handkerchief, Joan sipped from a bottle of water, and Faith sat on the ground, tearing up. Her poor little nose bubbled with snot and her eyes were reddening from the tears.

"What's wrong, sweetie?" asked Joan.

Faith shook her head.

"Come on, tell me." Joan got to her feet.

"I don't want to do this anymore," Faith said between quick hiccupping breaths.

Joan's boots stomped through the mud around the grave getting closer to Faith. "How many times do I have to remind you that we are doing God's work?"

Faith leaned away from her as if she was bracing herself against strong wind.

Joan took in a deep angered breath. She started shaking her right index finger at Faith while leaning over her. "The Justice System is flawed, Faith. It's created by humans and we are flawed, damaged creatures who don't deserve God's love. We try to maintain order and justice among ourselves, but the law is getting more tainted."

"These secular politicians are pushing Christ out of the law. They're purposefully ignoring God's will because they don't want to offend anyone. And even when us cops try our hardest and get the bad guys, stupid laws let them walk or get them out without serving barely any time. That's when we are called by Our Creator to set things right. To right the wrongs that other humans have done. That is what this is. Do you need me to remind you of what happened to Aunt Wendy?"

Faith curled up into a ball in the dirt and sobbed even harder.

"Hon," said Phil. "You can lecture her all you want on the drive home, but we got to get a move on here."

Joan nodded and released Faith from her death glare. The three of us dropped the body in the pit while Faith remained curled up on the ground as if she was trying to survive a bear attack.

We worked around her, shoveling pile after pile of wet ground over the man until his body disappeared.

As we finished, Faith pulled herself to her feet and I helped slap the dirt off her clothes.

We all heaved our exhausted bodies in the car.

As soon as Phil started the engine, Joan turned around to face Faith in the backseat. "I know that this isn't your thing, Faith but can't you try to see the good we are doing? I don't know why you aren't more like your sister. She is so brave and enthusiastic about this." Joan threw a dismissive hand gesture at her and turned around to face the front again.

Tears rolled down Faith's cheeks once again.

In a calmer voice, Joan said, "I think you need a reminder of what can happen when people like us don't step in."

"No, Mom, I don't need to hear the story again," cried Faith.

"Clearly you do," Phil snapped at her. "I'm sick of your belly-aching. Now listen and maybe you'll remember why this is our calling from The Lord."

"Ten years ago," began Joan, "your Aunt Wendy mustered up the courage to leave that cheating alcoholic scumbag of a husband. But she had been a housewife for the past six years and couldn't find any other job but to be a night clerk at a Motel off Route 22. I hated the idea of my baby sister sitting up all night as drunks and whores filed past her each and every shift. It made my stomach churn, but she told me she was going to be just fine."

"I remember that day, she came by around four in the afternoon and I cooked her an early dinner before her shift started. She wore a hand-me-down wool sweater from our mom and a black pencil skirt. She was beaming, so proud of herself for making it on her own. I believe she called herself Mary Tyler Moore, but I bet you girls are too young to know that show. Anyway, I remember she let Jamie sit on her lap and you, Faith, sat on mine. We laughed about old times. This one when these mean girls at school started a nasty rumor about her. It was so bad I won't even tell you girls, but I got them back by getting my friends to egg all their cars. Not my finest moment, but it was worth it at the time. So, we have a laugh, finish our meal, and she leaves to go off to work.

"Around three in the morning, I get a call telling me Aunt Wendy is dead. She was shot at close range several times while sitting at her desk with the phone off the hook. Her wool sweater now soaked red, and her blood coated the walls in her office. At first, we all thought it was Hal, her soon to be ex-husband. He had a mean temper, and I knew he could commit such a heated crime like this. But his alibi checked out. He was celebrating his best buddy's birthday at some bar. Seven people vouched for him, and his credit cards showed he paid for a round right around the time of her death.

"But Jerry, one of the janitors on staff at the motel, was the only employee that raised suspicions. He was seen entering the building around one in the morning and he wasn't on schedule to work that night. He claimed he forgot his iPod in the supply closet. Jerry was a haggard-looking thirty-five-year-old man, his hair already graying and his teeth already yellowing. It turns out he had a pretty serious meth habit. It was obvious he would need drug money and would think Aunt Wendy was an easy target and she would let him take whatever he wanted from the motel safe. But my brave sister put up a fight against her attacker and was about to call the police before she was shot.

"Everyone seemed to know it was Jerry but there was not enough evidence to put him away. He left no DNA, they never found a weapon, and he got some neighbor friend of his to say that Jerry was with him all night after he got his device from work. We had waited through months of trial only to be disappointed. But I wasn't about to let that sucker get away on a technicality. I wanted to hurt him, to make that man fear for his life the way my sister did. So, your dad and I found him leaving a donut shop one rainy morning and we grabbed him. We drove all night to this spot we have here, and I told him just who we were, and he began to look nauseous. I informed him that he had no choice but to run for his life in the woods and we were going to hunt him down like the lying fox he is.

"He took off in the forest. Because of the rain, he left tracks in the mud. It wasn't long before we found him attempting to climb a tree. One quick shot was all he needed. After we laid the last shovel-full of dirt over him, the rain dried up, the sky lit up with the most glorious blue and a rainbow shot around the sky. I knew that meant God was pleased with my work. I could feel his spirit within me, encouraging me to purify the world of such sinners. That's why, Faith, it is important that you do not hesitate from this work for it is the Lord's work and he commanded you to join Him." Joan finally finished her story.

Faith stopped crying and said, "I'm just worried, Mom. I'm scared."

"Scared of what?" asked Joan.

Faith whimpered, "Of getting caught. I don't want to die in prison because of this stuff. I'd rather try to help people become better than kill them for being bad. I think that's what God's work is really about."

"We won't get caught. I'm on the inside. I'll know if they are looking for these men. Trust me, no one ever does. And even if you do get caught and go to jail until you die, you will be dying for God's work, and it will be a proud death."

Faith didn't reply. The rest of the family stayed silent until we returned home.

CHAPTER 58
TAYLOR CALLAHAN

November 22, 2015
50 Days After The Switch

That morning Joan stomped out of her bedroom with a frown stamped on her face. I could tell she was still pissed at Faith.

"Normally, I'm happy on Sundays. I thought we'd attend the later service, so I'd have time to make everyone a big breakfast of pancakes and bacon but I'm just not in the mood," she announced.

She prepared the coffee machine and slammed her finger on the power button. She turned around sharply and was about to open her mouth to start in on Faith again, but I interrupted with, "I think it's best for the two of us to have some sister time. How about we grab something for breakfast?"

Relief spread across Faith's face. "I would love to go."

Joan let out a sigh, "Fine. Maybe you can talk some sense into your sister."

In fresh jeans and T-shirts, we grabbed our coats and headed off in the Hyundai. I even picked a location that is an extra fifteen-minute drive from the house so I could have time away from the looney bin that was now my household.

We ordered greasy-covered hash browns and breakfast sandwiches in the drive-thru and parked the car.

We enjoyed our food in silence for a few minutes before I said, "Mom is really in a mood today."

"Yeah, she is," agreed Faith. "I can't stand it when she is mad at me. I don't want to disappoint her, but I just don't like what we do. Are you mad at me for saying that?"

"No, of course not," I said in between bites of hash brown.

Faith wrinkled her forehead and frowned. "But you seem so into it."

I shrugged. "Yeah, but that doesn't mean you have to be."

"Why can't Mom understand that?"

"Clearly what happened to Aunt Wendy changed her. It's one of those things that happen and afterwards you can never be the same. It's a kind of feeling like you remember the person you were before it happened, but it doesn't feel like you anymore. And the people around you might not see it or might not get it but you're not the same and you're capable of doing things you never thought you could do."

Faith let out a small laugh. "How do you know about all this? You're only sixteen."

"Yeah, almost three whole years older than you. I, like, know more things," I told her.

We plough through the rest of the fast food.

"OMG that was amazing," sighed Faith. "You've got some ketchup on your face."

Faith pulled a napkin out of the bag and rubbed it against my right cheek.

"What just happened?" Faith said, staring at my face.

"What?" I asked.

"Your freckle just came off," she said as she stared at me.

I closed my eyes as I felt fear pumping through my veins and pounding in my head.

"It's always been like that. It's never been real, something I do for fashion," I blurted out.

"You've got it as long as I can remember. It's even in your baby pictures. How could it just come off like that?" she asked.

I turned on the ignition and slammed the car into reverse. I pulled out of the parking space without even looking behind me. "I'll tell you. I just want to get on the road first."

I turned out of the burger place and punched the gas.

"Jamie, why are you driving so fast? Tell me what's going on?" Panic stretched her big brown eyes open.

"I'm not your sister!" I screamed. The pain of keeping this secret fluttered away as I uttered the words.

"What?" she screamed back.

"I'm Taylor Callahan. I'm the dealer who was with Ali and Courtney the night they died. I just so happen to look exactly like your sister," I confessed.

"This isn't funny, Jamie, please stop," Faith begged.

"I'm not joking. It's true. I met Jamie, Ali, and Courtney that night. That douche Derek from their school put them in contact with me. I met them at the pier to give them what they ordered. Zeke was my ex-boyfriend, and he did want to kill me, only he didn't succeed at it. I dropped my phone and was on the ground when he showed up. He saw Jamie and thought she was me so he open-fired on them. And since my life has been basically a giant shit basket, I wanted to start over. I wanted to go back to my high school years and do it right this time. So, I switched clothes and IDs with your sister. I'm sorry, I never meant for you to find out."

Faith heaved over. "My sister is dead!" She wailed high-pitched sobs.

I was driving with no destination in mind, blasting through yellow lights at the last second. I couldn't slow down. I wouldn't slow down. I was going to crash the car and let my secret die with us.

A concrete wall stared at me from three traffic lights ahead. I stepped on the gas and got the car up to sixty miles per hour. I plowed through the first two lights. The wall was calling to me with its cracks and graffiti curse words becoming clearer by the second.

I heard Faith let out a sob and my heart melted. I threw the steering wheel as far right as it could go and merged onto the highway.

CHAPTER 59
TAYLOR CALLAHAN

November 22, 2015
50 Days After The Switch

"Where are you taking me?" she screamed.

"Nowhere. I'm just driving. I don't know what else to do. Look, I'm not going to hurt you, okay? If I wanted to hurt you I could have, easily, over the last few months, but I didn't," I told her.

"That's so comforting. Well, if you're such a bad person, why not? Why not kill me? You already lied to me and my family, you put my sister in danger, and you didn't even give us the chance to bury her." Faith wiped her eyes with her sweatshirt.

"I'm sorry, I've never wanted to cause anyone any grief. Second of all, she put herself in danger by meeting me. And last of all, I don't want to hurt you because you're my sister," I said.

"What? No, you're not!" she yelled.

"Yes," I began, "I know that, I'm not your sister but you're mine. I never had this. I never had a family, or at least, not a normal one. I've never been close to anyone like this but you guys even though you do some serious fucked up shit in your family. I mean *serious* fucked up shit. I've never had a family that wanted me or a place where I belong. I wouldn't want to hurt anyone who gave that to me even if it was all just a lie."

"I don't care. I want to see her." Faith's voice was stern, and her jaw was clenched.

"She's dead, like I said."

"No, her grave."

"Technically, my grave?"

"Yes, that's the one."

"Okay, whatever you want. Get your phone out and turn on the GPS for directions to Green Oak Cemetery."

We drove in dead silence for twenty uncomfortable minutes before we arrived. White headstones littered the green rolling hills for miles out in front of us. We walked along the dirt paths down to where the freshest graves are.

We searched through several rows of flat concrete headstones until we spotted my name.

"There she is," I told Faith as she dropped to her knees in tears again.

I sat next to her on the ground, the dead November grass crunched underneath us.

"Why did you have to do this?" Faith moaned.

"I really am sorry, but I had no choice. I couldn't be Taylor Callahan anymore," I said.

"What about your life was so bad that you had to come and take over Jamie's? We have our own problems too as you know. Why did you have to take her from us?" she sobbed.

"Have you ever had to beg on the streets?" I asked her.

"No." She looped a strand of loose hair behind her ear and turned away from me.

"Has your mother ever literally thrown you out into the cold? Has your boyfriend ever manipulated you into doing crimes for him and then abandoned you in a town you've never been in with no money or a way to get home? Have you ever had to spend a year in jail because your own mother called the cops on you?" I looked directly at my grave as I spoke. I didn't want to look at her. I felt like she was judging me like she had the power to decide whether I am good or bad.

"No, nothing like that has happened to me." The tone of her voice was free from anger, and she seemed almost embarrassed.

"I'm not saying I should've done what I did. There is a whole Hell of a lot of shit I should have never done but I did it to survive."

"No, you didn't," said Faith with a laugh.

"What are you talking about? You don't know me, the real me. You don't know what happened to me. Half of this shit happened before you were even in grade school."

"I know. I mean, you have done other things like begging and dealing to survive but you didn't take Jamie's identity to survive."

"What are you saying?" I asked with my voice shaking with irritation and fear. *Is she trying to call me a liar? Is she going to let my secret out?*

"You took her identity because you are seeking salvation," she started. "You could have run away from Zeke. You could have found a million illegal ways to make money and get out of town after the shooting but no, you chose to live a better life. You said it yourself, you wanted to do it right this time. You wanted to change and for the most part you have. I mean I had no idea you weren't my sister."

Shit, this girl is one insightful fourteen-year-old.

"Yeah, I guess," I replied.

"I'm right. I have to be right."

"What does it matter?

"That means bad people can change and that Mom is wrong. They have been playing with my head this whole time, saying it's God's will for us to cleanse the Earth of sinners by hunting them. Instead of killing, we can help them see the light again."

"Exactly. I'm not beyond improving," I said, half-believing it.

She replied with an almost smug tone. "I know, that's what proves I'm right."

I took a deep breath and said, "So, are you going to tell your parents the truth about me because I need to know if I should just take off now?"

"No, I'm not. I don't want you to go now."

"Really? Just a few minutes ago you looked like you wanted to kill me."

"Well, I was mad and I still am. Anyone would be, but I like that you're trying to become a better person. Besides, I don't want to lose my sister twice." She leaned in and nudged me.

I smiled. The MacKenzies might be religious vigilante freaks but maybe I belonged there with Faith. Maybe we were supposed to find each other and help each other out.

CHAPTER 60
JOAN MACKENZIE

November 22, 2015
50 Days After The Switch

It had been over an hour since the girls went away on their little fast food run and they hadn't returned. I grabbed my phone and called Jamie. No answer. She was probably driving and didn't want to pick up. I tried Faith and she didn't answer either.

I pulled out my laptop from my work bag. It made a thump as it landed its hard-plastic shell down on the dining room table. I logged in to our cellular provider's account. The beauty of paying for parental controls is that you can check the location of your kids are at all times.

A map of the United States appeared and then it zoomed in closer, first the state, then the county. Two red pins dropped down on the map and located my girls at Green Oak Cemetery.

What in the heck are they doing there? That was just some graveyard that we use to bury the bodies of criminals whose families can't afford to or don't want to. Just like with Taylor Callahan. Wait. That's where she is buried. *Are my daughters visiting the grave of the woman responsible for their friends' death?*

I couldn't deny my suspicions anymore. An array of pictures shot through my head. I saw the image of Jamie coming home and setting off the alarm that night. I saw Jamie's busted ankle and burnt fingertips. I saw Taylor Callahan's mugshot and her disfigured dead body. Something clicked, it was as if a switch turned on inside of me like I was a machine that suddenly sprung to life. Jamie was really Taylor and that dead girl was really my daughter.

I buried my face in my hands and started screaming loud primal wails.

Phil came running out from the backyard, rifle in hand. "What's happening? Is everything okay?"

"I don't think that girl is our daughter," I yelled.

Phil swung his rifle back on his shoulder. "Now that is a mean thing to say about Faith. She is just fragile."

"Not Faith. Jamie. I think Jamie is that Taylor girl," I said.

He sighed, "Not this again. You talked about how she seemed different weeks ago. She is perfectly fine now."

"Then why are Faith and *Jamie* visiting Taylor's grave?" I pointed at the screen to show him the GPS location.

"That's weird," he said, leaning over to look at the laptop.

"Weird?" I began with rage burning behind my eyes, "A criminal has been pretending to be our daughter for months and that's all you can say?"

He patted me on my shoulders. "Now honey, let's not get ahead of ourselves. Let's go find them at the cemetery and ask them what's up."

"If that's what it will take to convince you, fine, let's go."

• • •

Phil and I sped down the highway, darting in and out of lanes. The GPS said it would take us thirty-two minutes to get there and we did it in twenty.

We pulled up to the parking lot, but Jamie's Hyundai was nowhere to be found. My phone rang. It was Faith.

"Hey, Mom, sorry we missed your calls. We're almost home now," she said in a sweet voice.

"Where did you girls go?" I asked.

"We got some breakfast sandwiches and then we went for a drive," she said.

I had no time for their games. "Faith Wendy MacKenzie. Why were you and Jamie at the Green Oak Cemetery?"

"The Green-what Cemetery?" she asked.

"Don't play stupid, Faith. I can see where you two went from our AT&T account. Why were you there?" I yelled as Phil leaned over to me and told me to calm down.

"You know, GPS isn't always 100 percent accurate. It can get you close to a location, but it can be off by several yards. We weren't in the cemetery. We were next to it," she explained.

"You were next to it?" I growled.

"Yeah, we went for a drive, but we hit traffic and I remember looking over and seeing a big graveyard. That must have been it. We were stuck there for a few minutes. There was an accident ahead of us. That's why it took us so long to get home."

"Oh, I see. So, you didn't make a stop there to visit anyone's grave?"

"No, Mom, that's creepy. Why would we do that?" she asked.

"I'll see you girls soon." I hung up the phone.

"What did they say?" asked Phil.

"They were stuck in traffic right next to the cemetery." I looked over across the rows of tombstones and saw cars on the highway whizzing by.

Phil laughed. "Of course, that's why they were here. You know that GPS stuff ain't always right."

"I know," I grumbled.

We returned to the car and we pulled out of our parking spot at the cemetery. Phil turned to me and said, "Stop worrying yourself about all these weird theories. Our kids are our kids. End of story."

I told him I would stop it with my "crazy" theories but I know I won't. I had to get to the bottom of this.

I decided that I'd ask Jamie, or whoever that is, to join Phil and me as we search for potential hunting material. At work, I often look through the files of a few men I think should be wiped off the face of the Earth, you know, real leeches of society. But there's a catch this time and the real Jamie wouldn't fall for it.

CHAPTER 61
TAYLOR CALLAHAN

November 27, 2015
55 Days After The Switch

It was Friday night. Black Friday night, to be exact. The three of us left Faith at home and got into Joan's Yukon and headed down the parkway.

She began, "Alright Jamie, I've got three lucky gentlemen to choose from tonight. The first one is—"

Phil interrupted her, "Say, how come we never look for any girl-criminals? You know girls can commit crimes too. It's not just us men."

She looked over at me and said, "I'm sure that day will come." She cleared her throat and started again, "Our first is Damien Jensen, a known animal abuser. He recently spent six months in Juvie for setting a cat on fire. He lives at 55 Glenview Road."

Phil took the next exit and headed off in search of the dangerous Damien.

We pulled up to a house with dark gray siding and old leaves covering the driveway. Newspaper was taped over the windows of the first floor, and it looked like no one had been in there for weeks, if not months.

"I don't think anyone lives here," I said.

"Oh, trust me, he does. I scouted him out myself." Joan didn't take her eyes off the front door.

Fifteen minutes went by and no one has said a word. Joan held out a map of New Jersey in front of her, a prop to make it look like we were just people sitting on a side road trying to figure out where they are. It doesn't help that most people navigate by GPS nowadays, but Joan seemed to think it was a good ruse anyway.

"I doubt he's going to be home anytime soon. I don't want to waste time on him," said Phil.

"Now, I told you this is going to take patience, now be patient," Joan said.

"Fine," he huffed.

An hour passed by slowly as I stared out the window at Damien's house. Nothing has changed, not even a breeze rustled the leaves on the ground. I knew he wasn't at home.

Then, a maroon pick-up truck came barreling down the street, swung into the driveway and parked.

"Is that him?" Joan asked, still pretending to study her map.

"Think so," Phil glanced at the house.

"When he gets out, get ready to make our move. We want to get him before he gets in the house," she said, not looking up.

The driver's side door opened and a skinny guy in his twenties hopped out of the truck. He had a beanie covering his head with black hair poking out from it.

Joan was just about to get out of the car and head towards him when I saw the passenger side door of his truck open. A short, fat man with a buzzed head and a Green Lantern sweatshirt got out and made his way to Damien's house.

"Wait, Mom. Don't. He's not alone," I whispered.

Joan stepped back inside.

"I hate when that happens, we were so close." She shook her head in frustration.

"That's okay, we've got more on the list," said Phil.

"Alright the second one is Mark Schuster, an eighteen-year-old who started a forest fire when he was fifteen years old and still participates in arson to this day."

"Oh boring." Phil laughed.

"Arson is a serious crime," she snapped.

"Fine, fine. What's next?" he asked.

"Oh Jamie, I think you'll like this one." Joan turned towards me and gave me a sharp smile, her green eyes blazing with joy. "You know that drug dealer who got your friends killed? Her brother is not exactly a great person either. Neil Callahan. Fifteen. He was just released from Juvie last year for assault. Neil is known to have a violent temper and gets into fights with just about anyone. He was arrested a total of ten times trespassing and disturbing the peace. A teacher even reported that he threatened to blow the school up though he had no real plans for going through with it. Like his sister, he is also scum of the Earth and needs to be purged."

I couldn't believe these people are going after my baby brother. *Neil, violent?* He was such a sweet kid growing up and the last time I saw him, he risked everything to help me out. There is no way he would blow up a school or beat someone up. That's just not my brother, it can't be.

Before I could respond, the car was already heading towards my old address.

"So, does he sound like a good catch, Jamie?" asked Joan, with a look of excitement on her face.

"Yeah, he seems like a real problem child," I forced myself to say.

"Problem child is putting it lightly." She laughed.

"Well, he is still a teen, maybe he'll straighten out," I said.

"Guys like him don't change. They can't. It's best if we just do everyone a favor and take them out, so they can't hurt anyone ever again."

"You're right," I nodded while biting the insides of my cheeks.

We rolled through the highway and exited into my old neighborhood. The casinos where Drew and my mom made their living loomed over streets filled with trash and broken bottles and the small wooden houses on the verge of collapse.

My neighborhood had barely changed, the duplexes were still guarded by chain link fences with plastic bags and weeds tangled in their metal. The 7-Eleven where I used to get chips and candy bars with Chanel on Fridays was still there, the wall behind the dumpster covered in new layers of graffiti.

As we turned down my old street, my heart ached, and I felt acid rise in my stomach and burn me from the inside out. *How can I stop them from hunting Neil?*

The street was full of cars parked curbside. Phil slid the car into an open spot across the street from my old house. I knew Neil would never see a stranger's SUV parked outside his house as anything out of the ordinary.

I stared at my old house and wondered how something that never changes continues to break your heart. Even the landlord still hasn't done away with that horrible green color, but I guess with a tenant like Nadine, there is no point in going the extra mile.

Speak of the devil. Nadine with her yellow-turning-gray hair stepped out of the house. She was wearing one of her signature black-lacy outfits while puffing on a cigarette. She took two more drags as she marched down the path and crushed the butt under her boot. She got into a brown Buick with a rusting dent on the passenger side door and sped away.

"That was his mom, which means she won't be around when he gets home," Joan said.

Forty-five minutes later, Neil made his way down the street.

Phil and Joan perked up like excited school children at the site of him. Joan ducked behind her old-school map in an attempt to cover herself up. I wanted to point out how appearing lost in this kind of neighborhood only made you a target, but I couldn't let her know that I know that.

Neil was almost a foot taller than the last time I saw him and had his curly hair shaved to the scalp. He was wearing a baggy blue sweatshirt and black jeans that sagged at the back revealing his plaid boxers.

"Who is this kid?" I whispered to myself.

Joan heard me and responded, "I know, right? Let's go now." Phil grabbed the handcuffs he keeps stashed in the side console and Joan dabbed a small vial of liquid onto a white towel and shoves it into her pocket.

Phil said to me, "We'll be right back, don't move."

Joan and Phil made their way towards him. Phil called out to him, but I couldn't hear what he said. Neil froze in his tracks. I looked back and forth between their faces, trying to understand what was going on. I felt powerless to help him, I wanted to get up and scream, "Let my brother go!" but I knew I can't do that without them killing us both.

Neil started to back up against the fence by our house with his hands up in self-defense. The two of them were talking to him and facing away from me.

I rolled the window down as slowly and silently as I could.

Neil made eye contact with me and his face went white. He knew I was supposed to be six feet under.

"Run for your life," I mouthed at him and he took off into a sprint down the street.

I pulled on the button to roll my window back up but it was too late. They saw me.

"Jamie, you scared him away," shouted Phil as they got back in the car.

"Why in God's Holy Name did you just roll down your window?" asked Joan, her face pulsing red.

"I wanted to get a better look, I couldn't hear what you were telling him, and I was curious." That was the best defense I could muster.

Phil started the engine and let out a mad sigh. "I'm disappointed in you, girl, I really am."

"I expect this kind of dumb thinking from your sister but not from you. It's almost like you're not even the same person as you always are," said Joan.

I told them, "Look, I'm sorry. I was just trying to learn."

"Maybe we were wrong, you aren't mature enough for this yet," said Phil.

"He was probably going to be our last kill of the season. Soon the ground will be too hard to bury anyone. We lost a few precious weeks due to your injuries in the first place. And now, because of you, we might have to wait until spring to do anymore. That boy is free to do as he pleases when he is a serious danger to society. I don't think our good Lord would be happy with that." Joan slammed her body back into the seat and crossed her arms.

"I'm so sorry, Mom," I told her.

"You better pray for forgiveness tonight," she barked at me.

"Yes, I will."

"And every night for a month," Phil added.

"Yes of course."

I never thought I'd be asked to pray for forgiveness for not killing my own brother.

CHAPTER 62
JOAN MACKENZIE

November 28, 2015
56 Days Post Switch

Dear Lord,

Thank you so much for answering my prayers.

I know I don't deserve to know the wisdom of Your ways, but I praise thee and thank thee for shining a light on the truth.

My daughter is not possessed nor is she some paranormal being.

My daughter's rotting in a government grave while a wolf in sheep's clothing is living in my house.

Oh, dear Lord, I am so sorry for whatever I did to deserve this.

I must have not listened to you.

I must have not worked hard enough to do your Will and rid the world of sinners.

I would do it every day if I could.

I do not know why you took my daughter away and gave me a hooligan instead.

But I know it must be to teach me a lesson but what could that lesson be?

I guess I wasn't vigilant enough. I was not wary enough of the sin in my own house.

I didn't know that Jamie's friends had strayed so far.

Maybe I shouldn't have let them have friends outside of church, but I thought that would make me such a cruel mother.

I should have known better and protected my daughters from Satan's ways.

And then now, I've lived with such a horrid sinner for months, treating her with love like she is a daughter.

It disgusts me.

It makes my stomach turn.

But maybe this was Your intention all along.

Maybe, the sinner you wanted purged from this world the most was this Taylor Callahan.

That is why you have sacrificed my daughter.

So, I can remove this horrid girl from the Earth.

I will follow your will, oh Lord, I promise.

But I need my husband's help and he doesn't believe any of this.

I need proof to show him that I'm not paranoid.

Please dear Lord, give me something, a scrap of proof I can show my husband, so we can carry out Your Divine Plan.

Amen.

I got up from kneeling at the base of my bed and proceeded to dress myself in my uniform. It was early and no one else was up as I left the house for the police station.

As I sat down at my desk, Detective Fisher said he needed me. There was another witness in the murders that killed Jamie's friends. A drug store clerk who might have seen something that day.

Ever since the old, wrinkly Detective Weber was caught offering reduced sentences for sexual favors, a female officer must be present during all questioning of female witnesses or suspects. Detective Fisher looked past my personal ties to the case, so he didn't have to go through the hassle of calling in another female officer from a different precinct.

We entered the room.

"Hello, Ms. Norman. How are you today?" asked Fisher.

A chubby middle-aged woman sat in front of us. She was intensely focused on pulling the zipper of her sweatshirt up and down its tracks.

"Ms. Norman?" he asked.

She stared at her zipper.

"Ms. Norman?" he repeated and snapped his fingers over her face.

She finally looked up.

"Would you like anything? A glass of water?" he asked, attempting to sound courteous.

She shook her head no.

"I'm Detective Fisher and this is my colleague, Officer MacKenzie. Now what is it that you would like to tell us?" he continued.

"I'm not sure what I saw or if it's important." She had a voice that was both childish and hoarse like a chain-smoking Muppet.

The detective softened his voice and said, "That's okay, anything you can tell us might help."

"Well, I was working at Easy Drug Pharmacy a few weeks back in October. And I remember this girl and guy came in. And I didn't like the way they looked," she said.

"Why is that?" asked Fisher.

"The girl, her hair looked all messy. It was darkish blonde, dirty and tangled with beads!"

"Beads?" he asked.

She sat forward in her chair, almost leaning over the table. "Yeah, she had beads in her hair and she looked messy, almost like a hobo but not all the way."

Fisher ignored her strange posture. "Could you tell us what the man with her looked like?"

"He was tall and thin. Had a mushy-looking face. He wore a black sweater with a hood. I didn't like him, didn't trust him," she said, shaking her head in a dramatic way.

Fisher pressed on. "Okay, did this guy or girl do anything?"

"Yeah, they bought blonde hair dye, teeth whitening stuff, and make-up," she told him.

"Did they do anything else other than buy those items?"

She started to rock herself slowly. "Yes, she asked for the bathroom key, and I gave it to her and they were in there for a long time! I know because I was watching the clock, but I couldn't go and check on them because I had other customers to check out. When I had a chance, I knocked on the door. I was so scared, I thought they might be doing drugs or making love." She whispered the last sentence and hid her face with her hands.

He asked, "And were they?"

"No, they weren't. The girl had dyed her hair and whitened her teeth. She looked younger and prettier now. She was very rude and told me they weren't doing anything wrong. Then pushed past me and left the store." Her face flushed with anger.

"Ms. Norman, why did you feel this was important?"

"Because the girl, the messy one, looks like the girl that was killed. Taylor. I saw her picture on the News."

"I see. It has been almost two months since Taylor and the other two young women were killed. Why didn't you tell us this earlier when we were looking for the killer?"

"I couldn't. I was busy." She stopped rocking and she looked away from us like a child being defiant.

"Look, Ms. Norman, we know that you were in a psychiatric hospital for the last month. You don't need to hide anything from us."

"Fine, that's where I was. You see, my head got run over by my daddy's truck when I was a little girl. Sometimes I'm fine but other times I can't think or concentrate and then I get mad and I can't stop being mad and then I get in trouble."

"I see, Ms. Norman. We thank you for telling us what you know." He stood up and ushered her out the door.

"Oh man," he sighed. "You really never stop having to deal with the crazies in this line of work."

I replied, "Ms. Norman's mind is not as sharp as the rest of ours, but she could be telling the truth."

He took a swig of his coffee and wiped the brown residue from his mouth with his sleeve. "Who cares if Taylor lightened her hair before she was killed. She was probably changing her appearance to hide from Zeke. Besides that, there is no proof it was her. They paid in cash. Plus, there are hundreds of ratty girls that look like Taylor out there. Mrs. Norman is just another paranoid nut."

I'll be the judge of that.

•   •   •

On my way back from a call, I stopped at the Easy Drug where Ms. Norman said she worked. I asked to speak with the manager.

An Indian man who was graying at the temples came out to meet me and showed me to his office in the back of the store.

His office was covered with piles of papers and had pictures of his family pinned up on the wall.

He shook my hand and told me his name is Mr. Mehta.

"Well, Mr. Mehta, I want to ask you about a former employee. Did you hire Ms. Cathy Norman through a Supported Employment Program?" I asked.

"Yes, that is true, but she was only here a short time from May of this year until October," he told me.

"Why did she leave?" I continued.

"She couldn't continue employment here because she had gotten into an altercation with her neighbor which led to her being hospitalized. I'm hoping she hasn't repeated the same mistakes. Is that why you are here?" He was nervous. His brow was beginning to sweat and pool in his eyebrows.

I told him, "No, she hasn't. I want to know if I can see the security footage from the night of October third."

"We don't hold security footage that long. If nothing happens, we reuse the tape within a week," he explained.

I stood up. "Thank you for your time, Mr. Mehta. That's all I need to know."

•　　•　　•

I returned to the station. Fisher met me at the door and pulled me into his office.

"I just got a call from a very nervous sounding Indian man named Arjun Mehta. He says a female officer just came to his store asking about Cathy Norman and security footage. He said that he found footage from October fourth, not October third, and wanted to know if we would like to look at it instead. Funny, since we don't have a record of any officer being dispatched to his store."

I got up from my chair and stood over him. "I know it was not right, but I had to know."

"Know what? Listen, I know those girls were friends with your daughter but why do you care what some weird lady says? Some girl, possibly Taylor, dyed her hair. So what? Zeke is still the killer."

"I know that," I said between my teeth, "It's just I have this theory."

"What theory?"

I closed my eyes and said it out loud: "I think Taylor is at my house."

"What?"

"I think Taylor made herself look like Jamie with the hair dye, the teeth whitening, the make-up, then got Jamie killed and took over her life."

Fisher let out a big belly laugh. "That is insane, I mean, really MacKenzie? I know Callahan had a reputation, but she still got busted for robbing her mom. That doesn't sound like a criminal mastermind to me. There is no way she could have pulled off something like that. You've got to get your head checked, Joan."

Asshole. I knew I shouldn't swear, not even in my thoughts because God is listening but come on, he had to laugh at me? It's just my luck that the only person who might believe my theory about Jamie being Taylor is mentally incompetent. *Does that mean I'm mentally incompetent too?* No, I'm not giving in to him. I'm not letting Fisher make me think I'm crazy.

As he bowed his head in laughter, I grabbed the file for Cathy Norman off the cabinet by his door and slipped away. If her statement didn't convince Fisher, it still might convince Phil.

CHAPTER 63
TAYLOR CALLAHAN

December 5, 2015
63 Days After The Switch

For early December, it was warm. I stood out by the Yukon and took a deep breath of fresh air that didn't even fog up when I exhaled. A morning like this would be perfect for a smoke but my desire for cigarettes has simmered down over the last few weeks. I barely missed it.

The sun wouldn't be up for at least an hour. I was dressed in my hunting camo and ready for action. I'd surrendered to the bizarreness of this life. I wasn't going to fight it anymore. I had Faith on my side, and we were going to ride out this crazy family together.

I rubbed my smooth, pink fingertips across my palm. I was thankful that both my missing fingerprints and my new sister were hiding my identity. I'd made so many sacrifices for this life, a life that is so much better than the one I was born into. These hunting trips into the woods were just another sacrifice I had to make for my new identity.

I leaned against the trunk and tried not to think of the drugged stranger in the dog cage. If I had to shoot the guy, I didn't want to acknowledge his presence before it needed to be done.

Faith ran out the door, dressed in hunting clothes but with tears running down her face.

"What is it?" I asked her.

"I had a dream last night," she stopped mid-sentence to let out a cry, "that Jamie came back from the grave and hovered over me in my bed."

"Shh, it's okay." I pulled her into my chest partly to comfort her, partly to muffle her cries.

She continued, "And her face was all decayed and bugs were crawling in and out of her nose and ears. Her eyes were white and empty. And she asked me, "Why didn't you bury me? Why didn't you mourn me?" And she started to crawl out of the ground and—"

I hugged her harder and said, "Oh, it was just a nightmare. I've had a lot of those myself. But I promise, everything is fine."

But tears kept pouring down her cheeks and she almost shouted, "But I miss my sister."

I held her and let her sob into my chest.

Joan came out of the doorway. "What is going on over there? You're going to attract attention."

"No one is up yet, it's fine," I told Joan. "Faith had a nightmare."

She ran her hand over Faith's head. "Sweetie, it's alright."

Faith ignored her mother and kept crying. Joan pulled her off me and forced Faith to hug her.

Faith pushed her away and went back to clinging to me.

"This is ridiculous," said Joan, "she always preferred to have her mother's comfort."

"I guess people change," I said.

Joan had Hellfire in her eyes. "I guess they do. And sometimes more than you think."

Phil came out of the house and locked the front door. On hunting days, he was usually peppy but today his face looked grim like he just ate something bad.

"Get your sis—Faith in the car and let's go," he said to me.

I opened the door for Faith and let her climb in. When we were all buckled up, Phil pulled out of the driveway and sped away towards the highway.

As he merged onto the parkway, I could hear the engine hiss as he pushed on the accelerator.

I leaned over and saw that he's going almost eighty miles per hour.

"Dad, don't you think you're going a little too fast?" I asked him.

"You don't get to tell me how fast I can drive," he snapped at me.

"Sorry," I said and rolled my eyes.

"Dad," Faith called out. Her voice was still thick with mucus from her crying spell. "I'm scared. I don't want us to get into another accident."

"We'll be fine," he dismissed her.

After the first hour of the drive, I was getting sick and tired of the heavy energy. Phil was sulking, and Joan was sitting all grumpy in the passenger seat. I knew talking about their next kill would cheer them up.

"So, who do we have in the trunk this time?" I asked them.

Neither answered me.

"Is it a pervert, a rapist, a dealer, or an animal abuser?" I continued.

"You'll see when we get there," said Joan.

"I don't want to go on these trips anymore," whined Faith.

"Yes, I know," said Joan.

"When can we stop doing this?" she huffed and said, "I know, I know, I know. When the Earth is pure and there are no more sinners to clean off this beautiful planet that was gifted to us from God."

"No, actually, I think this might be our last time," Joan said.

"Really?" Faith grinned.

"I think it's all for the best."

So, that's why Phil was in a bad mood. He loved this sick version of hunting and now he couldn't do it anymore. *Maybe, this won't be so bad going forward.* These weirdos are coming to their senses and stopping their Christian vigilante ways.

The car went silent again and my mind began to wonder.

I started daydreaming about the future. I imagined myself applying for colleges next semester. I thought I'd try to get into some low-tier school that's across the country. Maybe somewhere in the woods of Montana but I was kind of sick of the woods after all of this. Maybe I should escape to sunny Florida, though I was afraid they would want to come visit me too often. I would run away to a foreign country but I'm sure they would find that to be some sort of betrayal to America. Maybe a big city like Chicago where I could lose myself in the crowd and escape from both of my pasts.

I was getting ahead of myself. I didn't have to decide anything right now. For the first time, I felt like my future wasn't as narrow as the barrel of a gun. I don't have to jump through hoops to survive. There might be a time where I can just be, where no one will bother me, and I can do more than merely survive.

We drove on and I recognized that we're getting close to our usual hunting spot. The sky was fading from pitch black to deep blue and a beautiful sunrise was bursting up from the horizon.

Phil pulled off the parkway and traveled down the backroads that lead to the rocky path.

The tires disrupted the gravel as we went on. The SUV rocked and weaved down the uneven road.

We got to our spot and got out.

Phil had the trunk fixed from our little accident and it looked as good as new. I headed over to the back and opened the hatch. It was empty.

"What happened? Where did you put him?" I turned around and asked them.

Joan and Phil swung their shotguns off their backs and pointed them at me.

"We aren't after a stranger this time, Taylor Callahan," Joan growled.

I stumbled back tripping over a few rocks in the grass.

How did they find out?

"You think you can walk into this family and steal my daughter's life?" Joan swiped at my cheek, smearing the fake birthmark.

I walked back further and I felt the cool shadow of the woods on my back.

"You led our daughter into danger and got her killed. Then you bring your corrupt ways into my family and sleep next to my innocent daughter. You've destroyed my family," Phil said.

Faith ran out in front of them. "No, it's okay. She told me what happened. And I forgave her. I welcomed her into my family."

"You knew?" hissed Joan.

"You don't get to welcome anyone into this family. Especially her," Phil told her.

"It wasn't her fault," Faith protested.

"Move out of the way, Faith." Phil dashed his arm across Faith's side, knocking her to the ground.

"We are going to say that there was a horrible accident. That dumb little Faith tried her hand at hunting but couldn't keep her aim and in the process, she killed her big sister."

"What? No!" shouted Faith.

"This is all my fault. Don't drag her into this," I pleaded.

"I'll make sure Faith is let off easy," said Joan. "The whole town will be in mourning over our tragedy, one innocent sister killing another by mistake. Every family in the state will be offering us our sympathies. As for you, Taylor Callahan, your two minutes start now!"

I ran deep into the forest as fast as my legs could take me. I turned back to see if they were coming. In my frantic state, I fell backwards and landed straight on my tailbone. Pain ripped through my body and I couldn't stand up.

I forced myself to crawl over twigs and twisted tree roots. Sharp rocks sliced into the skin on my hands and the cuts became thick with blood and mud. I didn't recognize this part of the woods.

I must be making progress.

There is hope. Maybe I can still get away.

Eventually the pain from the fall lessened and I rose to my feet again and sprinted further away. In the distance, the tree line was changing as if something was breaking it up.

It came into view and I screamed.

A steep gorge that was several feet deep and wide snaked its way through the forest. It went for miles in each direction and must have contained the area that was their killing fields.

There was no escape. There was never any escape.

I knew time was running out. My scream must have tipped them off because I heard footsteps crunch behind me and a shadow cast over me.

A shotgun jammed its barrel up against my head.

"Please," I begged.

There was silence. Nothing but silence.

Then a blast.

A splitting pain.

And then nothing at all.

Ever again.

EPILOGUE
TAYLOR CALLAHAN

November 25, 2015
53 Days After The Switch
10 Days Before Death

I walked up the concrete steps into an aluminum-covered diner. The place smelled like old syrup and coffee. A waitress ushered me over to a small booth with cracked plastic on the seat. I told her I was waiting on someone and that I'd just have coffee for now.

Ivan called me a few days ago, wanting to see me. I agreed, and we decided to meet at this diner about thirty miles away from the MacKenzies' house. Normally, I would tell him that I couldn't meet up because it would be too risky to be seen in public with a former friend of Taylor's. But I needed to see someone who I can trust again, someone who doesn't know me as Jamie.

I stirred the sugar in my coffee while I stared at the front door. Finally, Ivan appeared and rushed over to join me at my booth.

With his phone in hand, he turned the screen towards me and said, "Look!"

I barely glanced at it. "What?"

Ivan continued in the same excited tone, "I came across this article last week and I've been dying to show you. It says that they're up to seven other people on the planet that look exactly like each other. I've always wanted to know why you and Jamie would look so similar and this answers it. See!"

He turned his phone towards me again and I saw a picture of three tall men all with long lumberjack beards and round faces. The three men looked exactly like each other.

"They aren't related," Ivan began, "one of them is even from Germany. They ran into each other in an airport and couldn't believe they found each other. This picture of them went viral. This explains the whole thing."

"Not the whole thing," I said with a pit in my stomach.

He whispered with a smile, "So being the popular cheerleader isn't going as well, huh?"

I looked up at him.

He could read the look of dread on my face. "What is it, Taylor? What happened?"

"I don't know if I can say. I'm afraid it will get me in more trouble than I already am," I told him.

"You're scaring me. What happened? Did they find out?" he asked.

"No, but it's worse than that." I looked down at my swirling coffee. My spoon clanks the sides of the mug as I stir the brown liquid.

Ivan grabbed my hand, forcing me to stop. "What's happening to you? I've never seen you like this. What could be worse than getting caught?"

"Going to jail again, this time as Jamie," I said.

"How is that even possible?" He threw his hands into the air.

"They kill —"

"Hi," The waitress came over with a big lipstick-stained smile. "Would you like to place your orders?" she asked.

"Just coffee for me as well," said Ivan, gathering up our menus and shoving them in her hand.

She poured steaming black liquid into his mug and left with a displeased smirk.

I took a deep breath and continued, "They kill people, Ivan."

He leaned in further and asked, "What?"

"They have this weird idea that it's their job to kill the people that law enforcement can't get to like people who get a mistrial or who were too young to be fully punished. Jamie's aunt was murdered, and the guy got off. So, they went after him and killed him. But they couldn't stop there. They pick up people off the streets, people like us, and they kill them," I explained.

"Holy fuck," he sighed.

"But you see, in order to continue playing along, I had to kill people too," I confessed to him.

His eyes bulged.

"I didn't want to, but I had to keep it up or otherwise they would know I wasn't their daughter because for whatever reason Jamie was really into it and actually thought it was her moral duty to kill these people. So, they take them out to this spot in the woods, hunt them, and bury them," I told him.

"How many did you kill?" he asked, not even trying to hide the look of horror that had taken over his face.

"Two. The first one I shot in the chest. The second one I killed with my bare hands. I didn't want to, but he came after me, so I had no choice. I would have let him run away if I could," I said.

He shook his head. His skin was getting paler than its normal pasty complexion. "This isn't good, Taylor. This is terrible."

"I know, I know, but I have no other choice. I can't leave and be Taylor again, she's dead. I have to be this girl, I have to be this killer," I said as I took a sip of my coffee.

"No, run away. Come find me and we can go away somewhere new, " he pleaded. "We can fake the whole thing, get you set up with fake IDs and you can start a new life that way."

"No, I'm in too deep. I can't walk away. Plus, her mom's a cop. Every officer in the country will be looking for me. There will be billboards, milk cartons, Dateline specials," I explained.

He grabbed my hand again, "I don't want you staying there."

I pulled away, "I have to. I'm so close. I just have to be this teen girl for less than two years. I just need to pass high school and I'll be fine. I can start over. I can be somebody."

"What do you mean *somebody*? Like who?" He crosses his arms, looking pissed at me.

"You know. Someone who doesn't always have to hide. Somebody with a future," I explain.

"Being in the Manson Family 2.0 doesn't sound like much of a future to me," he smirks.

I look him straight in the eyes. "Yes, it's terrible and strange and technically Murder One but it's the one shot I've got. It matters more if you *look* like you're on the straight and narrow regardless of if that's how you really are. People will forever assume I'm a low life even if I change. This way my reputation is clear, and I'll find a way out of the Manson Family. You know I always find my way out."

"Fine," he said.

We paused and just looked at each other.

Ivan asked, "What if something happens to you? What if they hurt you or kill you?"

"They won't," I said.

"Right." He smirked, then took a sip of his coffee. "In case they do, I want dirt on them. I want to know where I can find these bodies?"

"Fine, if you must know. It's in The Pines about two hours south of the MacKenzies' house. Somewhere off Route 206. There is a clearing of dead grass down a gravel road. Jamie even painted a picture of this killing spot in her art class. I finished it and it's now hanging on the walls of her high school. She also wrote these creepy poems about it in her diary. They let the people out in the woods and hunt them. The bodies are about a mile away from the clearing, straight into the wood where the ground is soft. There are some red markings on the trees that show the way."

Ivan smiled and leaned back. "If they do anything to hurt you, those bodies are coming up one way or another."

THE END

ACKNOWLEDGEMENTS

Publication of this novel has been a long time in the making. After attempting to be content with life at a "normal" job in the years following college graduation, I finally realized I had to return to my life's passion of writing fiction. Upon the completion of this manuscript back in 2016, I pitched the concept on Twitter and was met with much support from industry professionals as well as other writers. This gave me hope that I would have a future writing the stories I want to tell. Thank you to all of the people online and in-person who gave me the courage to believe in my writing.

To Black Rose Writing, thank you for giving *Dead Ringer* with its unique twists and turns and dark ending its fair shot! Thank you, Reagan Rothe, for seeing what this novel has to offer.

I wanted to thank my mother, Dr. Mary Kelly Mohr and my grandmother, Mrs. Dorothy Mohr again for giving me the support and encouragement from a young age to pursue my creative talents and interests in the written word.

This story has had many drafts and with it, the need for beta readers and proofreaders. Thank you fellow writer, J.M. Kelly (author of *Monster on the Moors*) for giving me your insights for how I could better structure this work. To all of those who looked at this manuscript throughout its various stages of rewrites and gave me your feedback, I am truly grateful to you.

Last but certainly not least, to my husband, Aaron. Thank you for being my endless sounding board and encouraging me to continue working to see this book through to its final stages of publication.

ABOUT THE AUTHOR

V.P. Morris is an award-winning thriller and horror writer and podcast host. Her interest in criminal psychology inspired both of her novels *Dead Ringer* and *ShadowCast*. When she isn't writing or reading, she is cooking healthy meals, watching scary movies, and spending time with her husband and son.

NOTE FROM THE AUTHOR

Word-of-mouth is crucial for any author to succeed. If you enjoyed *Dead Ringer*, please leave a review online—anywhere you are able. Even if it's just a sentence or two. It would make all the difference and would be very much appreciated.

Thanks!
V.P. Morris

We hope you enjoyed reading this title from:

BLACK🌹ROSE
writing™

www.blackrosewriting.com

Subscribe to our mailing list – *The Rosevine* – and receive **FREE** books, daily deals, and stay current with news about upcoming releases and our hottest authors.
Scan the QR code below to sign up.

Already a subscriber? Please accept a sincere thank you for being a fan of Black Rose Writing authors.

View other Black Rose Writing titles at
www.blackrosewriting.com/books and use promo code
PRINT to receive a **20% discount** when purchasing.